EVERYONE IS LYING

D. E. WHITE

Storm
PUBLISHING

Ebook ISBN: 978-1-80508-213-2
Paperback ISBN: 978-1-80508-215-6

Cover design: Lisa Horton
Cover images: Trevillion, Shutterstock

Published by Storm Publishing.
For further information, visit:
www.stormpublishing.co

ALSO BY D. E. WHITE

You Know Her

PROLOGUE

Brighton, 2004

The music was low enough not to alert the neighbours, but loud enough to feel like the heartbeat of the party. Cigarette smoke hung wraith-like in the air, and the heat of the room gave Lexy's skin a soft sheen with sweat as she lined up expensive bottles of wine and spirits on the bar in front of her. Neat rows of gleaming crystal glasses were arranged next to platters of smoked salmon, caviar, and blinis.

'Come and dance!' Lana, blonde, curvy, and stunning in her flame-red dress, swayed in front of her, holding hands with another girl. Lexy caught her eye and the girl smiled slightly uncertainly, big hazel eyes darting around the room.

'I can't, babe, I need to hostess, and I've got to make sure I spend some time with Rory.' Looking across the room, Lexy made eye contact and winked at one of her favourite clients. His lips quirked upwards in response, and he ran a hand through his short grey hair, self-consciously adjusting his shirt.

'This is Mina, she's only here for the night,' Lana explained, 'We're going to dance. Love you, Lexy!' And she spun off, dragging the other girl with her, Mina's long dark hair flying, entangling with Lana's blonde extensions. They made a striking pair.

Blowing a quick kiss at her best friend in response, Lexy checked on the bar and then took a tray of drinks over to a group by the window, her high heels tapping lightly across the floor. Her bubble-gum-pink skirt was so short it showed her knickers when she bent over to set the tray down. It was that kind of party. If she was honest, she preferred just doing the dates, but when the parties had become a regular fixture, she was selected by Matthew for the hostess role.

The money was far, far more than she could earn from other part-time jobs. She needed to take care of her mum, finish her nursing degree, get a house, in that order. Money was important to Lexy, and she saved every last penny: legitimate money in the bank., cash under the bed.

She pushed her waist-length chestnut curls back behind her ears and cast a professional glance around the room. Girls, hand-selected by the clients, were mingling with the men, or in Lana's case dancing suggestively. The new girl, Mina, still didn't look totally happy. It was probably her first party, Lexy thought. She looked very young.

She twisted the bracelet on her wrist. It was the same one all the Candy Girls wore: a band of pastel-coloured sweets. It spoke of childhood, of innocence, of sugary naughtiness. It was also uncomfortable and dug into the soft skin of her wrist.

Matthew thought it was cute to have them all branded like this. Lexy suspected it was just about the power. His ego, his girls. He was coming into the room now, flanked by his friends. All powerful men with money to burn.

The atmosphere changed; tension ratcheted upward. She always noticed this sharpness, not fear exactly, but just a shift in the dynamic of the room. She quickly bent to pick up another tray of glasses. Lexy didn't want to catch anyone's eye tonight, especially Matthew's.

Her hair fell over her face, as she carefully arranged the clean glasses. When she looked up, the power cliqué had dispersed, and she breathed a soft sigh of relief. Green Day came on with 'Boulevard of Broken Dreams'. She loved this band, loved the song, knew all the lyrics. Lexy made her way back to the bar, swaying in time to the music, humming along.

ONE

It was always when she woke from the nightmare, and felt the usual overwhelming relief that it was just a dream, that she had to face something worse: the quiet morning – a blank canvas for the memories in her head. The screaming or the silence, she wasn't sure which was worse.

I could have stopped it.

As ever, after the nightmare, guilt flooded her body. Every choice she had made back then had been the wrong one. Just as, when it was over, every single choice she made had to be the right one. And it was. She was living her dream life now. If she could just offload the nightmares, unhook the claws of her past life, it would be wonderful. If she believed in ghosts, she would say the girls were haunting her.

Morning light slipped into the bedroom, sneaking under the blinds, dancing across the wooden floorboards, and she tried to relax. Secrets were exhausting.

Alexandra glanced over at her husband, still fast asleep, one well-muscled arm flung across both their pillows, his dark hair messy. Harlan had been the right choice. Not a conscious one, but when she started talking to him in the bar, she had known, felt that jolt she had never experienced before. She had not been looking for a relationship, but falling in love with Harlan, marrying him and starting a family, had lulled her into thinking that finally she had laid her ghosts to rest. Harlan represented security, and everything that was good and honest. Did she love him? She bit her lip, not liking the way her thoughts twisted and turned. If she admitted that she did, and with all her heart, it left her vulnerable.

And Alexandra had promised herself never to be vulnerable again.

From the next room, she heard the sounds of the kids beginning to stir. Sophie, now ten, three years older than her brother, Tom, always woke first, and Alexandra smiled as she heard the quick pad of bare feet on the landing, followed by the bedroom door opening and shutting.

'Urgh,' Harlan groaned, waking as both children launched themselves onto the bed, and Alexandra laughed, holding their warm, wriggling bodies close.

After a few moments Alexandra slid out of bed and opened the blinds, laughing at Harlan's exaggerated groans. Behind the blinds, on the exterior of the house, smart white shutters gave extra privacy to their bedroom windows. Alexandra knew if she flicked the catch on the shutters and opened the window, she would be able to see the city coming to life, smell the salt air of the sea.

She could even spot the sea if the day was clear, a long flat line of glittering blue in the distance. Another choice. Nobody asked questions in Brighton. The shifting population, the annual influx of tourists, the students, the colour, and the dirt. Alexandra loved it, absorbed it into her soul, and used it to complete her story.

'What's so interesting out there?' Harlan asked, moving his son, who was sitting on his chest. 'Tom, you big lump, I can't breathe.' But he was laughing, and Alexandra turned and smiled back. A family. Who would have thought she would ever have every single one of her dreams come true?

Tiny shreds of her nightmares still lingered, but as usual she pushed them ruthlessly away. 'I'll get breakfast,' she told her husband.

He grinned hopefully. 'Eggs with chilli?'

'I'm sure I can manage that.' She pulled her cashmere robe over her white silk pyjamas. She was settling back into the day, and she could feel her mind returning to the present, forced it to happen more quickly, to savour these moments of joy. And yes, she had to admit to herself, even if it made her uneasy, of love. But if you loved someone, they could be taken away.

'Ugh. I hate chilli. Please can I have cheese on mine?' Tom wailed.

'If you're cooking, Mummy, then Daddy'll read us a story!' Sophie said, beaming angelically at her father, who was rubbing sleepy eyes.

'Go and find a book then.' Harlan obligingly pushed himself up to a sitting position. 'And yes, Tom, I'm sure you can have eggs without chilli.'

Her daughter's eyes were the same colour as her own. An unusually clear grey, fringed with thick dark lashes. This shouldn't be a surprise, Alexandra thought, sneaking a quick hug as Sophie ran past to retrieve a book from the bookcase in her bedroom, but honestly, she was still shocked to find herself with children. That had never been in the game plan. Being responsible for two babies was terrifying, and when they were tiny there had been times the anxiety overwhelmed her, and she had to sit by their cots breathing deeply, trying to banish her fears.

Alexandra walked lightly downstairs to the kitchen, her feet still bare. The house was still and cool from the night, and the kitchen smelled faintly of the citrus candles she loved to keep on the windowsills. The stripped wooden floorboards, the artwork on the pale walls, the oak doors, and the designer kitchen units, lit by three large copper shades – it all said success, money, and the right choices. Her luxury townhouse comforted Alexandra every day.

As she clicked on the lights, she began her usual morning routine: coffee in his favourite mug for her husband, smaller mugs for the kids, unloading the dishwasher. The rituals were soothing, taking a good half an hour. There was a framed photograph of her mum hanging above the breakfast bar. Harlan had said he was worried it might upset her. But instead she would touch her mum's face with loving fingertips, remembering, accepting, as she studied the windswept hair, the laughing mouth, the bright eyes. Her mum was in her kitchen. It would never be enough, but it helped a little.

Afterwards she would look back and wonder how she had managed to miss it. It was lying on the large, classic, scrubbed wooden kitchen table, next to a vase of early scarlet tulips.

She paused on her way back from collecting some eggs from the larder, adjusting her grip on the box, and it caught her eye. A white envelope. Addressed to Birdie.

Her breath came in gasps and her chest was tight as she stared at the object, at the scrawled writing. She was back in her nightmare, in the heat and the smoke again, with the girls. The box of eggs tilted and one slipped out, smashing on the black slate floor. She snatched the box back upright and clutched it to her stomach, eyes wild, taking in the locked windows, the immaculate state of the rest of the kitchen, thinking of the many locks on the front door.

'*Hallo, Birdie,*' he had said, as she finished setting up the bar on that last night, '*I heard singing and I knew it was you arriving to set up.*'

'Alex? Are you okay?' Harlan, sounding concerned, called from upstairs.

She cleared her throat, ran her tongue around dry lips, put a lot of effort into her response: 'Fine, thanks. Sorry, dropped an egg. Just clumsy!'

'Okay. Do you want me to come down?' His hopeful tone suggested he wanted the chance to escape from his energetic, demanding children.

'No, no, you carry on with the stories while I cook.' Alexandra wanted to scream at him not to come down, not to see her like this. She needed to be calm. Taking deep breaths, she approached the letter as one would approach a poisonous spider. She picked it up. The envelope wasn't sealed and, shaking, she drew out a single sheet of folded paper, heart hammering so hard against her ribs it hurt.

She could hear her own voice, murmuring, 'No, no, no...' and hastily shut up.

With a huge amount of willpower she unfolded the sheet of white paper. There was no writing, but her action caused another, smaller piece of paper to flutter out from the fold. It came to rest on the table and she stared at it.

An intricate origami bird, perfect in every detail apart from one. Even before she registered the significance, she was thinking how shocking it was that such perfection, such beauty, had been ruined by one cruel act.

The paper bird lay beneath the red tulips, one white wing torn and missing.

TWO

When Harlan and the kids finally erupted down the stairs, the letter was in her pocket, breakfast was on the table, and Alexandra had control of herself.

'Looks delish!' Tom made a rush for the food, almost knocking over his orange juice.

'You okay? At least there were enough eggs left for breakfast.' Harlan gave her a kiss as he moved towards the coffee.

'Fine.' She smiled, disguising her panic by fussing over the kids and checking their school bags. She tried to make her voice light and casual as she said, 'Oh, Harlan, did you take any deliveries last night?'

'Like what?' He was checking the football scores on his phone, sharing the results with his sports-mad kids.

'Oh, just a letter or anything you needed to sign for?'

'No. Are you expecting something?'

He was still distracted, oblivious to the fact her heart was pounding, her hands shaking. Her world had just been shattered, and her nightmare was there with her in the family kitchen.

Could she risk more questions? Alexandra turned away to

check her own phone for what seemed like the hundredth time since she had found the letter. She had checked the front door was locked and the back door too, multiple times, as the eggs sizzled in the pan. 'Yes, but it'll probably come today. I... I didn't sleep that well last night actually.' Everyone ignored her, immersed in food, football, and the usual morning chaos. She couldn't bring herself to repeat her question. It was too dangerous. Had she really been hoping Harlan would leap on this statement, admitting... what? That he could explain it? But if Harlan had no knowledge of the letter being there, then how could it have happened? Who could have got into their home? It was ridiculous, but terrifying, and she would have to sort this out without involving her family.

The obvious solution must be the cleaning company, who kept a copy of the house keys. But no, she told herself as she gathered her bouncing kids together, going through the teeth-and-dressed-and-out-the-door-in-five-minutes routine she had perfected – the cleaning company was positively anal when it came to security, which was one of the reasons she chose them. They had come recommended by one of her celebrity clients, a musician who lived on Dyke Road, in one of the beautiful, heavily guarded mansions.

'Are you sure everything is okay, Alex?' As she stood poised to leave, bags in her arms, car keys in her hand, her husband stood frowning with concern at the bottom of the stairs, ready to head up for a shower.

She summoned a bright smile, 'Yes! Of course. Sorry, just work stuff on my mind. See you later. Love you.' For a split second, raw from the ominous delivery, she remembered Lana, heard her voice saying 'love you' and her former best friend's glowing, overflowing exuberance seemed to be dancing in the hallway next to her. A ghost who existed only in Alexandra's head.

'Love you.' He kissed her again and waved, already deep in his phone.

The school playground was busy, but luckily Alexandra snagged a space right outside the gate. It was ridiculous, she told herself, but she almost wanted to keep the kids with her today, safe and away from the darkness that threatened their mother. But would they be safe with her?

'Mummy, can we get out?' Sophie was rattling the door, waiting for her to turn the child locks off.

'Sorry, I was just thinking.' She took a deep breath and got out, gathering bags and a tinsel creation that was Sophie's art project. 'Have a great day. Be... Be safe. Love you!'

She hugged them each for a little too long, before they ran off, to be engulfed in the screeching crowd of children For a second, she lingered, searching the adult faces, panic clenching in her stomach.

A car hooted behind her, a man's face at the open window. 'Sorry, are you moving now?'

Another parent desperate for a space. The moment was broken, and she waved back, before forcing herself to drive away.

There was just enough time, accounting for the traffic in central Brighton, to make some enquiries. This felt better, like she wasn't quite so helpless, the shock wasn't still beating around her brain, giving her a thumping headache.

The woman who managed the cleaning team in this area was on the phone quickly and assured her there had been no security breach. She seemed genuinely concerned by her questions and Alexandra sought to reassure her. 'It was just a thought. Thank you, and I'm probably mistaken. There's bound to be a rational explanation!'

'If you have had an intruder, you need to report it to the

police,' the woman said firmly, and slightly defensively, 'I'm happy to let them know our movements yesterday, just in case, but there is no chance anyone but Marianne had your keys, and I can see them back in the cabinet right now.'

'No, it's honestly fine, but thanks for... Thanks for letting me know.' Feeling a total idiot, she ended the call, just as she pulled into the tiny car park behind the clinic. What else could she do? There were no clues on the envelope. She needed to examine the house more carefully, check for signs someone had indeed broken in. Her stomach twisted at the idea that anyone could have crept into their peaceful, safe home, with her beautiful children sleeping upstairs, and pretty much detonated a bomb in the middle of her kitchen.

She locked her car and walked quickly round the front of the building. The aesthetics clinic was already busy as she pushed the door open, but Alexandra hardly noticed. Her mind was still on the paper bird, dragging her back twenty years to 2004. To the days of caffeine-fuelled study sessions, student parties, and crazy adventures with Lana. To the days when she had dreamed of qualifying as a nurse, maybe choosing a speciality, focusing on the career she had fought so hard to achieve. Being an aesthetics practitioner was a sidestep after her degree, but an exceptionally profitable one.

The warmth, the light, the familiar smell of roses and mint in reception brought her back to the present. She hastily shoved all thoughts of her previous hopes and dreams away and tried to focus on work. Preferring to spend more time with the kids and Harlan, she always arranged to come in later on Mondays and Fridays. One of the perks of being self-employed and successful, she had always thought.

Normally she entered this building feeling a little buzz of pride at the dove-grey exterior, the pale gold window trim, and the pink and grey sign with the name written in beautifully scrolled lettering: *GLOW*. But today she pasted on a smile and walked quickly over to the reception desk, feeling her hands shaking as she pulled her mobile phone out of her pocket.

Melinda, her receptionist, smiled, her pink bob glossy and, as usual, perfectly styled. 'Morning. You look wrecked. Kids keeping you up again?'

Alexandra checked her messages again. Nothing. Not that she really expected any ghosts from the past to have her phone number, but hell, someone had her address and that was far more terrifying. Could they really be in danger? Her safe place, the place where she could shut out the world, had been invaded, and she couldn't tell the police. Couldn't even tell her husband, because there was so much else she'd have to reveal if she did, and if he knew, he'd be in danger too.

She became aware that Melinda was waiting for an answer, her expression turning from enquiring to concerned.

She tried to give a quick, reassuring smile. 'I just need a coffee. Sorry, I'll be awake in about half an hour. Yes, it was Tom... um his cold isn't quite gone, but he seems well enough for school.' *Shut up, Alexandra,* she thought, *just stop talking before you say something you'll regret.* The urge to blurt out the full story, to offload some responsibility to Melinda was terrifying. But she would never knowingly put another person at risk again. It was a promise she had kept for twenty years.

'Well, that's good that he's on the mend, and your calendar today is full, so go and start mainlining that caffeine. I also brought some doughnuts in – they're on the counter in the kitchen.' Melinda reached out and squeezed Alexandra's arm. 'You looked like you'd seen a ghost when you came in.'

A few hours ago, I did, she thought, but out loud she said, 'Thank you, you are a superstar.'

'I know.' Melinda winked at her and picked up the phone.

With her mug of coffee on her desk, Alexandra quickly arranged the tools of her trade for her first patient and checked her watch. Ten minutes. She opened her MacBook and typed the names into the search engine, always the same one first. Her mind was spinning, and fear was making her stomach churn unpleasantly. As always, her entire body was tense as she waited.

After that last, terrible night, the hasty but apparently thorough clean-up operation, and the threats running through her head as she threaded her way home through the back streets, she hadn't been in touch with anyone from the party.

The girls had scattered, and she had never seen them again. It hadn't been a thing to get too friendly with anyone else, apart from her flatmates, Jess and Lana. Lana had been her best friend since she first arrived in Brighton for her university course and having her gone had ripped a hole in Alexandra's life.

'Popcorn and movie night! Lexy, get your butt on the sofa, and Jess, you can ditch that loser boyfriend for once.'

Lana had been so full of life, so impulsive, and the warmth of her personality had filled the flat, had overflowed into every area of her life. Jess, her sister, had been more cautious, her face harder, less easy to trust, less easy to love. Both girls had grown up in care, and their bond had been so strong.

'Love you like a third sister, Lexy.'

Why now? It was always going to be about the other girls, the ones who didn't get away, about what she had witnessed, what she knew. Even the thought of the money made a wave of nausea rise from her stomach. She had taken the bribe and ran. She was a coward. But now she was a successful coward with a perfect life. Resolve made her straighten her back, gulp down the coffee, and snap her MacBook closed. Nobody was going to get near her family, or spoil things after all this time.

'Alex, your first patient is ready,' Melinda sang out via the intercom, dragging her back to reality.

Hastily, Alexandra downed the last of her coffee, pushed

her hair back behind her ears, and greeted the twenty-something girl who walked into her room.

'Morning!' Extravagant air kisses, and the overpowering smell of too much perfume made Alexandra reel back slightly.

Lana, in her favourite red dress, her body hot, sweat on her face, her perfume lingering on Lexy's skin long after they got home from a party.

'One more drink before bed! Tell me everything that happened tonight before we sleep...'

Snap out of it, Alexandra. Mostly, she enjoyed her work, but just now, through her confusion and fear, she felt a stab of annoyance piercing through her preoccupation, 'Hi, Sam. Lovely to see you.'

'Yeah.'

Alexandra looked closely at her client's face. 'Sam, you're looking a bit different. Have you had anything else done recently?' It was obvious she had paid for some cheap fillers since her last visit, presumably to supplement Alexandra's highly professional work.

'Yeah,' Sam said again, as she tossed her long dark hair extensions, and fixed her unnaturally sea-green eyes on Alexandra's face, 'I got a freebie from that place in Brick Road in Seaford. Looks great, doesn't it?' Another toss of her hair.

No, not really. But Alexandra didn't say this aloud. Squaring her shoulders, she used the alcohol gel before slipping her gloves on. 'Are you okay if I take a look?' There was an open sore on the girl's top lip, and another near her eye.

'Sure, do what you want.'

She gently palpated the girl's swollen jawline, cheeks, and sore-looking lips, paying special attention to the open wounds, which were clogged with make-up. 'Honestly, Sam, this is awful. Anything you have done with me is discussed first, and we agreed you would stay with a natural look. You're a really pretty girl.' So hard to say without seeming condescending, but

Alexandra genuinely believed what she was saying. 'You don't have to go crazy with fillers. And you have two places that may be infected. I hate to even ask, but there's a possibility the needles weren't clean when you had the fillers done.'

'It was a good place, not dirty or I wouldn't have gone in, and my social media followers think it looks amazing,' Sam countered, with as much of a frown as she could manage. Her skin now had that stretched, slightly plastic appearance, which might well look amazing in her heavily filtered photographs on TikTok, but in real life, added ten years to her face.

'I'm not sure if you should be listening to what they say. Sam, they follow you because you are unique, and you are a real person. They like seeing your lifestyle as an influencer, and a model.' She hoped this was the right thing to say, hoped she was getting through to the girl.

Lana lying next to her on the beach, comforting Lexy after a breakup, leaning over to hug her so her long hair tickled Lexy's tanned face. 'You're unique, a real person. He just wanted a stupid plastic model.'

'Whatever. I need more followers so I get more brand deals though.' For a moment a tiny flash of desperation showed behind the coloured contacts. 'I want you to do some more fillers. Like you did last time.' She indicated her cheekbones and her chin.

Alexandra's heart sank. 'I can't. It wouldn't be ethical for me to ruin your face. You are only twenty-one.' She peeled off her gloves and dropped them in the bin, before washing her hands. 'You know I don't give any treatments if I believe it would be harmful, and I honestly think you are in danger of causing some real damage here. Plus, as I mentioned, it looks like you may have an infection from the work you've had done. Was it even a proper clinic?'

'No, it was a friend of a friend. But like I said, she's good and she does it for half price.'

'I recommend you get an appointment with the GP and see if you need antibiotics to clear this up.' Alexandra indicated the same areas on her own face. 'If not, you are going to end up in the emergency department.'

Sam's cheeks flushed with anger. 'If you won't do it, I'll go somewhere else then.'

Lana, shouting at Jess for borrowing her clothes without asking when she first moved in with them. Jess pouting and saying she couldn't afford designer and how the hell could Lana? 'Lexy and I have an extra job.'

'What extra job? God, I'm so skint, and they don't have any more shifts at the bar.'

'Well, I suppose you could join us, if Matthew says it's okay? Lexy, what do you think?'

'Jess, it's not a regular job, and you would have to play by the rules.' Lexy had been doubtful. Jess was certainly beautiful enough, but she had major attitude at times.

'I'll do anything to get the kind of money you have. Anything.' Jess's mouth set in a stubborn line.

THREE

'Um... Alex? Are you okay?' Sam's voice had changed, and she was close, her hand warm on Alexandra's arm. 'You just, like, totally zoned out.'

'Sorry. You just... you reminded me of someone for a moment.'

'Do you need to sit down? You're really pale.'

'I'm okay, but thanks...' Alexandra tried to focus. 'Where were we?'

Sam shifted awkwardly from foot to foot. 'I was saying I'll find someone else to do my face if you won't. You are sure that you won't?' She peered into Alexandra's eyes doubtfully.

'I'm afraid you will have to find another practitioner.' Alexandra shrugged off her lapse of concentration as best she could. This wasn't a new conversation, but she had made her professional reputation by using her subtle 'tweakments' to enhance her clients' looks, not by creating the current craze for huge swollen Bratz doll faces.

'Well, I won't credit you in my Instagram stories anymore.' Sam's bee-stung lips were set in a pout and she ran her hands through her hair extensions in a gesture of annoyance.

'Believe it or not, Sam, my business won't crumble because you don't mention me on Instagram. I will not be responsible for wrecking your looks.' Alexandra waited in the silence that followed, mentally crossing her fingers.

But Sam tossed her hair again, picked up her Chloé bag and walked towards the door, pausing next to Alexandra's desk for a final shot. 'I can't believe you won't help me. I thought we were supposed to be friends.'

'We are friends, which is why I am giving you my professional opinion. Come on, Sam, take a look in the mirror. You need to stop comparing yourself to other people and just be you. Because you're amazing?' A little OTT, she thought, but more than keeping the business she really wanted to prevent the girl from ruining her face.

Nothing from Sam. Oh well, she had tried. Alexandra moved across the room and held the door open. Sam was watching her, open-mouthed, processing her words, clearly shocked her threats hadn't worked. But she finally marched from the room without speaking, and Alexandra felt her heart sink. She shut the door behind the girl and added comprehensive notes to Sam's patient records, before heading outside towards the reception desk.

'What's up, chicken?' Melinda finished a call and swung her chair round to Alexandra. 'I saw Sam walking out in a strop again.' Her voice was low because the waiting area beyond the glass privacy door was full of clients, most of whom had hopefully ignored Sam's exit.

'She had some extra work done.' Alexandra shook her head. 'I really hoped she might be okay after she saw that therapist, but she's thrown a tantrum because I won't contribute to wrecking her looks. I mean, honestly, did you see what she's had done?'

'Silly little girl,' Melinda agreed. 'Hopefully she grows up before she ruins her looks and health.' She peered at her boss.

'Are you sure you're okay? Helen has space after four, so I can easily shift a few clients if you want to get home earlier today?'

Alexandra smiled gratefully at her. 'I'm honestly fine, but thanks,' she laughed, hearing it ring hollow and unconvincing. 'It's just the usual chaos. Harlan's back to work this week and he's on a run of nights, so I might as well stay out of the way during the day and let him sleep.' She sighed, pushed her blonde hair out of her eyes, and reached into her pocket for her glasses case. God, she was so tired.

'Can't be easy with him doing shift work. Seems like the police are struggling to keep up with all the crime in Brighton just now, too. Must be stressful. I saw the article in the paper about the Seahawk Estate yesterday. County lines and kids as young as ten being used to courier drugs. It makes me mad.' Melinda didn't have kids herself, but she was a devoted auntie to six nieces and nephews.

Harlan had often mentioned the Seahawk Estate, which sprawled to the east of the city, and was a law unto itself. Alexandra sighed. 'I know. Me too. They need more officers down there, but I think with all the cuts there isn't enough money to pay them. It's a pretty dangerous place to be as well.'

'I wouldn't want to walk through that place in daylight, let alone at night,' Melinda agreed. She spun her swivel chair around, glancing down at the piles of paperwork neatly arranged in wooden trays and moving briskly on. 'I went through your mail for you, ditched all the catalogues, and just kept the personal stuff for you to open.'

'Oh, thanks, Mel, you are a brilliant, but I could have done that later.' Alexandra pushed her glasses up on her nose then flicked through the envelopes, hands shaking slightly. Thankfully all of them bore a proper address, and she could identify almost all the senders. No paper birds in this lot.

'Your calendar was pretty full next week too, but I've worked around the jury service.'

'Shit!' Alexandra looked up from the mail, and slapped a hand to her head, nearly dislodging her reading glasses. 'I completely forgot.' She felt herself standing, gawping like a deer caught in headlights. Normally she was super organised. Harlan often joked she was superwoman. He had no idea...

'Starts on Monday,' Melinda told her with a sharp look. 'And you get hit with a thousand-pound fine or something if you don't turn up, so stick it in your calendar.'

'A thousand pounds? You're kidding, right? Do I need to do anything for it?' Alexandra almost laughed at the irony of it. Jury service. *Her.* 'I can't believe I forgot about it. I've already sorted the kids' pick-ups and things in case it runs late though. Just today my head is not in the right space.'

'What, like homework? No.' Melinda was amused. 'I did it about five years ago. You need to keep off the socials, turn up on time, actually a bit ahead of time because the security at Hove Crown Court is a bit of a nightmare. Oh, and you can't take your phone or laptop into court with you. Take a book because I guarantee you will be bored shitless most of the time.'

'Great...' Alexandra went back into her treatment room, and rummaged in her bag, producing a slightly crumpled letter from the depths. She headed back out to reception. 'Got it! It doesn't say anything about the actual trial though.' Her heart rate increased just thinking about it, and a swirl of nausea curled upwards from her stomach to her throat.

'Well, they don't tell you. They just send you in and you get picked for whatever's going on. Maybe it'll be a murder trial? Wow, maybe it's going to be Gareth Sellers. He was in The Argus, and it's all over the socials. He's accused of murdering his girlfriend.' Melinda's heavily mascaraed eyes were wide. 'But, whatever, it'll probably be some boring burglar. How on earth did you forget about that, chicken?'

'Accountant wants to finalise book-keeping, meetings with the social media hire, kids' school stuff, Harlan wants to plan a holiday...' Alexandra ticked the items off with her fingers, furious with herself for forgetting.

She wasn't sure she was capable of deciding someone's fate in the criminal justice system, but she was just going to have to deal with it. She'd have to find a way to focus. The thought of the paper bird on her kitchen table made her shiver. The envelope containing the origami creation was another thing pushed deep into her bag.

'You've got a bit of time before your next client, so why don't you fix another coffee and have a look at the paperwork?' Melinda suggested. 'Don't stress. It isn't such a big deal, the jury service. I know so many people who've had to do it.'

'Good idea.' Alexandra was grateful of the extra time, but not because she needed another caffeine fix or so she could do her prep on the jury duty paperwork. She shut her door and snapped open her MacBook. For a moment her fingers hovered over the keyboard. With nobody to help her, nobody she could confide in, she would have to figure this out on her own.

Her hands were shaking, and her breathing was fast as her fingers flew across the keyboard, searching for answers, checking names. There were only four people who had known her as Birdie, had known about her love of crafting, of making the origami birds, of singing, and she hadn't heard from any of them since that last party. One of them was dead, her grave unmarked and forgotten.

Could it be that the bird was a sign that at least one of them was telling her they were back? *Why?* After all this time. And why not just call or email? She would have been so happy to hear from two of them. Cancel that. She would have been happy to know they weren't dead, but not one of them would fit neatly into the new life she had built for herself, with her safe little routine and her nearly new identity. Alexandra was not Lexy anymore.

She rested her head in her hands for a long moment as she

gained control of herself. As usual, her searches turned up nothing new. A few scandalous historic newspaper articles she had seen at the time – the result of one of the girls selling stories. The Candy Girls had been perfect media fodder, but it never went beyond the sex and scandal element. The girl in question had been swiftly silenced, probably paid off. She'd likely signed NDAs then simply vanished, before the stories had been killed.

She quickly searched a few other names she remembered. The names of men who were now famous, faces that appeared on her TV screen, in the financial sections of *The Times*, voices that intruded via her car radio or on podcasts. Twenty years ago, she and the other girls had mixed with an exclusive group of movers and shakers, had access to the kind of people who went on to run the country. She had never sold her secrets, instead hugging the most explosive one close to her chest.

The Candy Girls wasn't the kind of business where people kept in touch. In a funny way it comforted her to know that of all those people, only a handful might even recognise her all these years later. But the fact that one of those people was now amongst the most powerful men in the country – Thomas Blake – was terrifying.

Melinda buzzed her on the intercom and the door to her treatment room opened as she was trying to banish visions of Blake from her head. She yanked her glasses off, and stood to welcome her next client, pasting on a friendly smile, trying to distance herself from her past.

FOUR

The darkness of the spring evenings seemed to come early along the coast, and by the time Alexandra had put the kids to bed, caught up with her emails, phoned her accountant, and done all the usual things that came with running her own business, she was shattered. Harlan had gone to work at six, and the only conversation they had managed before he left was when they crossed paths in the kitchen as she gave the kids their supper, to check diaries for the coming week and liaise on childcare.

Now she texted her husband quickly:

> Hope the shift goes ok. Love you x

As she studied the screen, the little dots moved to indicate he was messaging back, and a few seconds later she smiled to see four heart emojis. It was something he often did to represent their little family, and it warmed her heart. She needed to make this okay, she really did.

Now though, here she was, alone on the ground floor of her very own townhouse. It had tall windows, chessboard tiles at the entrance, and was the kind of luxurious white period building favoured by Instagrammers. In fact, she sometimes caught them posing just outside the gate, phone extended or a photographer snapping away near the hedge. Harlan hated it, but Alexandra couldn't see the harm. Twenty years ago, she had been the person on the outside looking in, dreaming of a starry future.

Pouring a glass of white wine, she walked to the window, spying on passers-by through the shutters, grateful for the privacy, the illusion of safety. It was impossible to grasp the idea that someone else had been in her house, placed the envelope gently down on the table while they all slept upstairs, before leaving the house as quietly and unobtrusively as they had arrived. She imagined the person hugging the knowledge of her reaction when she found the letter in the morning, getting some kind of perverse enjoyment from her shock. How could it have happened? She had watched the security camera footage on her phone that morning, straining to see any sign of an intruder – but there was nothing.

It was time to find out how they had entered her home. The front door had an alarm system, so the point of entry had to be the old part of the house at the rear. There was a step down into the old kitchen, now a larder slash dumping ground. Because this part was a listed building, they hadn't yet bothered with the hassle of replacing any doors or windows. She inspected the ancient wooden door, which gave out onto the lower part of the back yard, gave it a shove. Yes, the bolts rattled loose, and to her horror, when she gave it a gentle push, it swung wide. When had they last used this door? Probably last summer when they had dinners in the garden. Had they forgotten to lock it? The old-fashioned iron key hung on a hook right next to the door.

It was the only explanation for the letter left on her kitchen table. Someone had been in her house while they were all asleep upstairs. Someone who had dodged the security cameras. Checking the app on her phone had been one of the first things she did. But the range was limited round the back, and frustrat-ingly none of the cameras pointed directly at the old back door, only at the new glass sliding doors towards the side of the house.

Alexandra walked back to the kitchen, exited into the back yard, and studied the small, narrow, walled garden area. To get into the garden you would need to climb the high wall, as the gate was still securely locked. There was an alleyway for bins behind the six properties in this terrace. She scanned the area, seeing nothing out of place until she moved to turn back to the house and her gaze slid upwards, to the left.

There, on the top of the stone wall, and on the lower branches of the flowering cherry tree. Mud and grit. She looked down and saw a mark in the ground – a clear imprint where the intruder must have landed. Her pulse quickened. Someone had got in and got out. Alexandra swung around like she was being watched, staring at the back of her house, at the other houses in the terrace.

Number eight, the house next door, was empty; the couple had moved out a few months ago and the asking rent was high enough that it hadn't been snapped up immediately, even in this sought-after area. In her panic she almost thought she glimpsed a figure watching from the blank windows. Of course not. Even if someone had come over the wall, it didn't mean they had broken into number eight, it just meant they had got into the garden.

She could hear reassuringly normal noises dancing through the salty evening air, even though her heart seemed to be thun-dering in her chest. There was jazz music playing, the droning buzz of traffic further down the road where the traffic lights separated her street from the main junction to the seafront, shouts from the playing fields to the east of their road, and the cry of gulls overhead. Normal, everything was safe and normal. Nobody was spying on her.

Unwillingly, Alexandra remembered the huge rooms with

the blackout blinds covering the windows, the half derelict house transformed into a party venue for one night only, and the tiny winking cameras set high above eye level in some of the other rooms. What if the intruder hadn't just left a letter?

Moving quickly back inside, she took another sip of wine. First, she needed something heavy to wedge the old back door for extra security. There was a chest of drawers she could move with a struggle, and she managed to push it flush against the exit, before taking the key, locking the door, and shoving the key into her pocket.

If Harlan asked about it, she could joke about feeling paranoid about how flimsy the door was, and wanting to get it sorted. He didn't need to know yet that the fear was real. She could lock the internal door to the kitchen too. It would be a pain unlocking it every time she came down to the larder, but it would be worth it. That was better, and she could double check all the windows were locked and shutters drawn.

Alexandra emptied the rest of the bottle into her wine glass on the kitchen counter, finished it and began a careful exploration of the kitchen. The room, part of the new extension on the house, was clean, minimal, and there were no ornaments or stacks of books for a camera device to be hidden behind, but even so, the safety she had felt only moments earlier fled into the shadows of darkness outside.

Now Alexandra slid the envelope and contents from her bag, laid it on the table and sat slumped, chin in her palm, considering. *Lana, Niall, and Mac.* The names could have been branded in fiery letters above the fireplace. Someone from her past knew where she was, and someone wanted her to know they knew. Of course, it wasn't just those three. Any one of them could have talked to her old clients, or Thomas, or Matthew, about her nickname, her love of origami.

Alexandra found she was struggling to think logically, her brain whirling with the horror of it all, and she grabbed the remote and flicked on the TV as a distraction. She took a sharp intake of breath as Thomas Blake appeared on screen, giving a speech to a large crowd. Caring, clever Mr Blake, who had moved further and further up the ladder in his political career. There was even talk of him being put forward as a candidate for prime minister before the next election. He could be running the country, this man who had seen her and Lana dancing in their underwear, who had sat snorting cocaine with his friends, who had made cutting remarks to those he considered beneath him, and velvet promises to those with something he wanted.

And here she was, a perfectly normal wife, mum, and businesswoman, sitting on an explosive secret that could cause the scandal of the decade. Out of everyone, Thomas had to be the one who had clambered to the top of the heap. Typical.

She could still remember the panic, the hushed voices, the night that the parties ended. Maybe this was why she had been contacted. Perhaps Thomas was eliminating all the skeletons from his closet before his ultimate career leap. It seemed to be the logical explanation. Was he capable of finding someone to track her down, to scare her? Kill her? For a long time, she had thought they might kill her like the others, but gradually as the years passed, the fear faded and she lived with the hope they had forgotten about her. For some reason she had been lucky.

Eddie clinking glasses with Jess and another girl, signalling to Lexy they wanted another bottle, whispering in her ear as she poured for them, 'Why don't you join us? Matthew always keeps you hidden away behind the bar. He's not here tonight, he'll never know you skived off to play with us...'

Her brain buzzed with questions, trying to reason, to find a credible answer. She moved restlessly to the table again, picked up the origami creation and held the delicate bird lightly in her palm. If she had been going to tell the police, she would have done it twenty years ago. Lana had always had a big mouth when she was drunk or high. Alexandra's beautiful best friend had been a loose end, and she didn't know if Lana had managed to disappear – into another identity, as she had, or out of sight – or if Lana had been dead all these years. The pain in her chest was unexpected, the grief she thought she had left behind with the graves.

A noise from upstairs made her jump, and she moved swiftly up towards the children's bedroom, pausing to listen at the door. A cute wooden sign hung on the outside: 'Sophie & Tom's Room. Keep out!' She peeked around the doorframe, nerves jangling, tears still on her cheeks.

Both children were fast asleep, breathing deeply. Tom was clutching his favourite elephant and Sophie had her cheek against her 'squishy seal' soft toy. A burst of protective love made her clench her fists as she carefully withdrew from the room. She walked down the stairs, thinking hard, brushing the tears away.

Thomas, Eddie, and Matthew had all enjoyed Lana's company. It could be anyone from the parties, any of her dates she supposed. She was settled, happy, not about to start blackmailing or causing trouble. *They must know that!* The fear brought tears back to her eyes, her throat tight and clogged with emotion. Because there was the other reason someone might come after her, and perhaps it had just taken them a long time to track her down.

'*I might know about the graves, but I didn't tell anyone.*' She stood in the shadows of her immaculate kitchen, remembering the agonising moment of choice, the sweat soaking her top, the pain in her body from the blow Matthew had dealt her, Eddie's shout of warning. The past became more vivid, dragging her back, reminding her she had been living a lie for so many years, enjoying life while the others could not.

She pressed the heels of her hands into her eyes and tried to centre herself back in the present. When she looked up, Thomas Blake was back on the TV screen, giving an interview.

He sat, tall and elegant on a bright orange sofa, his dark hair matching his dark suit as he answered questions in that cool velvet tone. The sound of his voice drew her towards him, and when he smiled at his interviewer, it was that same arrogant, sexy smirk he had worn at every party.

Guilt.

FIVE

I'm pretty sure I was never meant to live the rest of my life in a cage.

I see barred windows in my dreams, and only by looking upwards, at the sky, do I see a place without barriers and padlocks. I know I did things many people would consider wrong, but I did them because I considered them to be right. I'm a loyal person, and that's probably my downfall.

My solicitor tells me they are extremely confused (not what you want to hear from your legal team), and they also tell me I need to be seen to be sorry, that I need to explain my actions and garner some sympathy. They say this because my version of events and the solid facts and evidence coming from the prosecution do not tally. This can't be uncommon.

I stretch, linking my hands behind my head, feeling the hardness of the pillow, smelling the disinfectant, the sourness that lingers in this place.

I knew as soon as I saw the police at my door that there were two options: someone had grassed me up, or the police had finally got better at investigating and dragged up a cold case from twenty years ago. Of the two options, I'd bet money on the former.

Back in the early noughties I ran a tight team with my friends. Even though the Candy Girls was Matthew's idea, we spilt the cash, and paid everyone else well too, especially the girls. I only ever saw them at the parties, and it was the last party that ruined everything in the end. Because someone got greedy. Because we needed another dangerously explosive secret to hide like we bloody needed a shot in the head! I shake my head in frustration once again. Even with so many years passing, it still seems ridiculous that it could ever have happened.

But if you have everything, you start to get bored, to wonder what you might do to amuse yourself. Something daring, something wrong. The first time is always an accident. You tell yourself that to prevent the guilt, and maybe you start to believe it. Maybe your friends start to believe it.

The second time could have ruined everything for all of us, but instead we got away with it. There was just one problem. No matter where in the world we went, or who we became, we all knew we were bound together forever after the last party.

And so now I lie, listening to my own soft breathing, feeling the rise and fall of my chest, running over the list of everyone involved in those crazy years. Because sooner or later, I know I'll figure out which one of them is responsible. I've got a pretty good idea. They've all got something to lose, but one person needs my silence more than anyone right now.

I always knew if anyone was going to take the fall, it would be me. I have the least power and money and in our world it's always survival of the fittest. Because, let's face it, who would you believe? The man currently on trial for murder, or the man on the TV, with tens of thousands of fans, who promises you he's going to change the world?

SIX

'See you later, Alex,' Harlan murmured through a bacon sandwich and a huge blue mug of tea that said World's Best Dad on the side.

He sat at the kitchen table, his shoulders slumped in exhaustion, still in his uniform trousers and shirt, dark hair hanging over his eyes.

'I've got five minutes before I go. Tough shift?' Alexandra was ready for her day in court, carefully dressed in a smart grey suit, with full make-up: her professional no-shit look. The kids had already been wrestled out the door and into her friend's car; Alexandra was leaning heavily on her school mum friends this week as she thought there was no way she could get the kids dropped off, and still make it to court on time. As she sipped her coffee, she could see a trail of detritus along the hallway. Crumbs, a plastic water bottle, a damp swimming towel, and some crumpled artwork. Hopefully none of it was needed at school today. She must remember Tom's rugby club prizegiving on Friday and Sophie's gymnastics display on Saturday.

Her husband rubbed his hand over his face. His eyes were heavily shadowed. 'I don't think we stopped working apart from the obligatory breaks. And even then, we got interrupted by the next job, because they didn't have enough people on to cover it. I'm seriously thinking maybe we should talk about early retirement plans.'

Harlan was only eight years older than her. She smiled in sympathy and bent down to kiss his cheek. 'Don't forget you've got that security course coming up over the summer. Honestly, you don't have to keep slogging all hours for minimal pay now the clinic is doing so well. And it's not like the job's easy either.' *And you keep refusing to go for promotion*, she didn't say. It baffled her that Harlan gave his all to the job, wanted less time on the road, and yet wouldn't go for a management job, which would at least give better hours and more time with the family.

He nodded, reached up, and caught her hand, his dark blue eyes focusing on her face. 'Yeah. I'll look at the course details again.' He brightened. 'Or maybe we'll find that chest of gold in the garden when we put the new shed in.'

Alexandra laughed. 'Maybe. Love you. See you later.' She had made sure she was up early, checking the rooms for any envelopes, removing the furniture from the back door in case Harlan for some reason went into the old larder, and thought she'd gone crazy, even opening the front door to check there was nothing left on the steps outside.

'Alex?' He called her back.

'Yes?'

'Remind me at the weekend, but I've got an idea I want to run past you. It's... It's quite a step, but it might be right for us.'

His gaze was bright and intense, but despite his light tone, for a moment he looked not just shattered, but afraid.

Alexandra could feel bubbles of fear rising in her throat. 'Oh... Sure. Are you okay? Nothing you want to talk about now?' She was torn between risking being late and concern for her husband. Did he know something?

But Harlan finished his tea and stood up to rinse the mug in the sink, turning his back, so she couldn't see his face, 'No, there's not enough time now, but it's nothing bad, I promise. Just an idea...'

Alexandra watched him for a second, and then gathered up her things and headed for the front door. As she walked quickly down the front path, umbrella raised above her head, she glanced at the house next door. The *For Rent* sign was nailed up in the garden and had been for three months now since the Smith family had moved to Cornwall. It was almost an exact copy of her own house, with the classic Georgian windows, smart front door.

She knew it was empty, locked up with an alarm system. Could someone have broken in and gained access to her back garden via the shared boundary? The marks on the wall bordering her garden and the damage to the tree suggested it was possible.

The blank face of number eight offered no clues, and she fumbled with her car keys, cursing her lateness, deliberately concentrating on the rush hour traffic. The rain was pouring down, the skies and sea grey and sullen to match her mood.

For now, it seemed, whoever had left the paper bird was content to watch and wait.

The traffic was almost at a standstill from the end of her road right up until she pulled into the car park. She thought if it hadn't been pouring with rain, she might have walked to her destination and still arrived there quicker.

Hove Crown Court was an ugly building, built with lots of concrete and glass, the official emblem on the door and flowerbeds of rather improbable palm trees creating a border between the entrance and the road. She paused under cover at the front entrance, quickly checking her emails, starring a couple of important ones for Melinda to take care of. A client had tagged her on Instagram, and she clicked on the post, fearing retribution from Sam, but it was a sweet post from a local actor praising her work.

Alexandra took a deep, calming breath. Focus. There was nothing she could do about this temporary interruption in her life, so she just needed to ride it out. She zipped her phone securely into her bag and walked into the building. After a moment of panic, when she couldn't find her passport for the ID check, she passed through the main reception area and a court usher greeted her and showed her into the back rooms.

She joined her fellow jurors and the group of them stood like an awkward school party as they were told where to wait, where to get drinks, and reminded of a whole list of things they mustn't do. They were instructed not to mention trials in the press, on social media, to listen and evaluate with open minds. That was almost funny. She was supposed to come in with an open mind, whereas her mind felt so crowded there was barely room for anything else. It was ridiculous to feel so afraid. Her own husband was a police officer for Christ's sake.

But Alexandra had felt guilty from the moment she stepped into the building. Her fellow jurors were fairly quiet too. Her shoes seemed to make a loud noise on the wooden floor as she walked across to the seating areas, passing groups talking quietly, already settling down for the day.

A group of them, including Alexandra, were told they would be in courtroom four by a helpful employee and then left alone. As they waited, she tried to focus on the gravity of the situation, but her mind just couldn't engage with her duties. Instead, she was back to picking over her personal problems. She had still not told Harlan about the possible intruder, because how could she even begin such a conversation? How could she say to her husband that someone had been inside their house, a danger to their children, and she hadn't done what any normal person would do – call the police?

Put like that, she felt sick to her gut. She was putting her family in danger by keeping quiet. But there was a ridiculously faint hope that she had been mistaken, that it was all a crazy mistake, that if she ignored it everything might continue to be okay.

When she had looked up the names from the past, she had read about Thomas Blake first. There had been a piece online in a financial magazine about Matthew Arnold. His company had acquired another, had doubled in size, was leading the way in investment banking. Blah, blah, blah. A photograph of Matthew smiling with another CEO, his rather old-fashioned good looks and immaculate dress sense making him look like he should be on the cover of a high fashion magazine, rather than the financial pages. He lived permanently in Dubai now, with his family. She could find nothing on Mac.

Automatically, she felt for her phone, before remembering she'd had to leave it outside in the jury assembly area. What if the school rang? It was okay, she reminded herself. They would ring Harlan, or Melinda. Someone was talking now and she half-listened, trying to control her tangled thoughts, keeping her expression appropriately grave, concerned.

She *had* been vaguely aware of the Gareth Sellers murder trial that Melinda had mentioned but was too busy to pay any more than a fleeting amount of attention. She knew the murder was big news. Gareth was a local property developer, and his girlfriend had been a photographer. The fact that it had happened on Alexandra's doorstep, so to speak, had made her shiver and move quickly on to other news stories. Crossing her fingers that she was not about to be called for anything more than a boring, routine theft, she reached for her book.

Drifting away from the boredom of courtroom reality again, the voices continued to argue inside her head. She *could* have called the police straight after she found the bird, could have told her husband merely that she had found a strange letter, could have raised hell over a suspected home invasion. He would have found the marks on the wall, and he would have dealt with it via the official channels. But she would have needed to explain the significance of the address, the contents. Or would she? Could she claim to know nothing about it?

She was Alexandra, not Lexy anymore, and she had too many secrets to hide to ask for help. Her kids were safe at school, and Harlan, well, he was safe because of who he was, what he did. She pushed down the niggling doubt about this.

Her husband's long shifts left him exhausted, and his mind had been occupied with doing this security course, which started this summer. It was part of a long-term plan to change career, and he told her he was really looking forward to the pay rise, to progressing sideways through a management course away from the police force.

She had reassured him her business was only set to grow over the next few years. This was true, and she was so proud that Glow now had a waiting list of potential clients. Alexandra pulled her mind back to her present surroundings, trying to force herself to concentrate. All she needed to do was get through this jury business, and then she could get back on with her life and find out who was stalking her. Easy.

Hove Crown Court was smaller than she had imagined, and rather grubby. She realised her perception of courtrooms, of trials and what happened after the perpetrator was arrested, had been almost entirely based on what she had seen on TV and at the cinema.

Surprisingly, given what she had been led to expect from Melinda's experience, there was only an hour's wait before they were called from the holding room, to take their seats in courtroom four. A tiny sliver of fear settled in her stomach as she took her seat near the back.

The defendant was tall, broad-shouldered, and he took his place quietly but with a confidence that seemed entirely misplaced. His legal team shuffled paperwork, and Alexandra glanced up at them, then back down at her lap. She thought of the clinic briefly, wondering how Melinda was managing. And what about her own schedule? Could she squeeze two clients into an evening session? Sophie's show-and-tell at school was tomorrow, and Tom was still upset he'd lost at football... She became aware she was not giving her full attention to the proceedings when people started talking, and the woman next to her gave her a nudge.

Shocked back into the room, she looked up properly, began listening to the conversations, the names bandied back and forth across the courtroom.

They meant nothing to her, except to register that Melinda would be thrilled she had ended up with the Gareth Sellers murder trial, until she focused on the defendant for the first time. She froze, the courtroom spinning around her. The defendant had turned to speak to his legal team and the tilt of the head, the dark hair threaded with grey, brought it all back. His grey eyes were bright and alert, the lines and wrinkles of his face spread across the strong bone structure, the square chin.

It couldn't be the same person, she told herself. It was her guilty conscience calling up ghosts from twenty years ago. But as he moved again, glanced quickly over at the jury, she found herself holding her breath. Older, of course. He must be in his late forties now, but surely, she couldn't mistake the man she had seen burying the bodies. She could see him clearly as her memories shifted like quicksand.

Mac, stripped to the waist in the shadows, with sweat and horror on his face. One girl had been left lying on the dusty floor, her arm outstretched, her naked body dappled with light from the bulb on the stairs, giving a fleeting illusion of life.

'*Lexy! Go!*' *He threw down the shovel and strode towards her, chasing her out of the room.*

Other voices, Matthew pushing past her, shouting for Thomas. Her own shocked question as she spotted the other body, before she turned and ran.

Guilty.

SEVEN

It was him.

Gareth? They had all called him Mac... and here he was on trial for the murder of a woman, standing just a few metres from her. Alexandra stared at him, as though hypnotised. Her body was still frozen, and she was barely breathing. Just one murder? And *Mac?*

She knew there were more victims, had seen the bodies, the graveyard. A lifetime running away from her past, making those choices to create a perfect life, and now here she was, right back where she had started. Maybe Mac had a twin brother? It must be possible, she thought, her mind grasping, flailing frantically to make sense of it. Why, after everything that had happened, everything that they had got away with, would he kill another girl?

The envelope, the sheet of paper without words, and the origami bird made a kind of twisted sense now. It wasn't random that she had been tracked down, nor was it a mistake. Someone knew she was going to be on the jury. Someone was reminding her where her loyalties lay. But did they want her to help him, or help send him down?

'Hey, Birdie, fancy hosting a party tomorrow night? I've got a nice date for you!'

Birdie. Lexy. Alexandra.

The names from her past and present, the names and identities she had shed and gained, now whirled in her brain and she fought to stay silent and calm on her seat. She couldn't make sense of it. Was the bird a threat that she could be up there where Gareth Sellers now stood?

Impossible. She hadn't killed anyone. And yet, they had all known what she witnessed. The hostess who was supposed to keep everything running smoothly, the person who prided herself on taking care of the other girls. It happened on her watch. She had briefly wondered, in those first, terrifying days after the party, if that was why they'd let her live, because she might one day be held accountable.

But what did Thomas, Matthew, and Eddie think of Gareth being accused of murder? At the worst possible time for Thomas. If he became prime minister after the election, could someone discover the connection between a murderer and his old university friend?

Over the years she had thought about exactly why Thomas occasionally turned up at parties with a large gym bag full of cash that he would often leave sitting at the back of the hallway, just out of sight.

From what she had seen, there must have been well over a few million pounds in there, the crisp one hundred pound notes secured in bundles with white tape, smelling of wealth and adventure. Lana had been convinced Thomas had been paying bribes, or money laundering, because who had that kind of money in notes just hanging around.

He is here. Mac... *Gareth,* was so close she could call out to him, could march over and run her fingers over the scar on his jawbone. He had been bleeding that night, the last time she saw him, she remembered, and his right eye had been swelling, bruised, and raw as though someone had thrown a punch. She sat so still, hardly breathing, that she wondered if she might faint. She couldn't. She couldn't draw attention to herself and let him see her. Would he recognise her? What might happen if he did?

Slowly, slowly, as the first bolt of terror settled uncomfortably into a kind of heart-hammering nausea, she began to think. To anyone looking at her, she was a normal, thirty-something woman, with a nicely cut grey suit jacket from Reiss, and a sharp platinum bob. Blending into the crowd was her specialty. At first, she had missed her long, soft brown curls, but now she had been a blonde for so long it had become part of her persona. She was sure he couldn't recognise her. She couldn't tell anyone that she knew him; that would only draw attention to her too. It was safer to keep her head down and hide.

It took a long time, far longer than she had thought, until the first recess, and she spent most of the time trying not to throw up.

'Interesting, isn't it?' A fellow juror, the woman who had nudged her, smiled as they filed out. 'I've been looking forward to this.'

Alexandra stared at her uncomprehendingly, unable to make normal conversation, even to speak, exhausted from trying to contain her conflicting emotions.

The other woman shrugged, apparently sensing her reluctance to enter into any kind of exchange. 'Makes a change from the usual routine, doesn't it?'

'I suppose so.' Her voice came out croaky, unsure, and her mind was whirling still. She licked her dry lips, and to her absolute horror, felt tears springing to her eyes. Sniffing, she swiftly invented a quick, fake cheery line. 'Sorry, I've had really bad hay fever recently. That's how I know summer is on the way!'

'I'll get us a coffee, shall I? My name's Jackie. Do you take antihistamines? Boots do some good own-brand ones,' The woman looked expectantly at her. She had warm brown eyes and a round face, topped by a mop of grey curls, and clearly wasn't going to find someone else to chat to.

'Alexandra.' It took so much effort, but she did it, pulling a tissue from her pocket and blowing her nose, just as though she did indeed have harmless hay fever, rather than poisonous secrets, upsetting her. 'Thanks so much.'

So many questions needed to be answered, and none of them involved inane chat with this sweet stranger. She chose a seat and waited for Jackie to return with the drinks. Oh god, the absolute last thing she needed was anyone trying to engage her in conversation, but it would be so mean to shut this woman down, and she needed to act normally. Just another juror dragged away from work and family commitments. No signs she was upset.

Gareth. Alexandra was sure now there would be another contact, another envelope, now the introduction was out of the way. The bird was a warning and a token, but which way did they want her to jump? It must be Thomas; the timing told her so. But which would be better for him and the skeletons in his closet?

Guilty or not guilty?

When she finally escaped into the cool evening, Alexandra hurried to her car, focusing firmly on getting back home. She had already checked her messages, rung Clara, who was minding the kids, to check on them, and was wondering exactly how many more shocks she could take.

Thankfully the jury had not been called into the court again, but had spent a few agonising hours reading the books and magazines they'd brought with them, chatting, and drinking foul tea and coffee from the machine. The rain had stopped, and the air was sweet with the promise of warmer spring days to come.

It took a moment to register as she pressed her key fob to unlock her car. But as she noticed, the car park, the traffic noise, the puddles at her feet, all receded into a kind of fizzing blackness. Tunnel vision allowed her to see only the three little origami birds nestled in a plastic bag, pinned in place under the windscreen wiper blade.

The birds were larger than the one in the envelope, and each had a handwritten name printed on its wing. She didn't need to bend closer to read them properly. The names were engraved on her brain. And her heart.

Bex, Mina, Jess.

EIGHT

'Christ, Alex, you look like absolute shit!'

'Thanks, Clara, I feel so much better now you've said that.' She smiled and rolled her eyes. 'And thanks for minding the kids tonight.' Exhaustion combined with shock was making her mouth dry and her body weak. She wondered how she was going to get through what was left of the evening. Shoving the plastic bag containing the latest birds into her car, she had gone straight to the clinic, seen a couple of evening patients, and checked in with Melinda, blanking out everything else for fear she'd lose it completely.

There must be CCTV in the car park, but how would she explain herself to security? To anyone else, paper birds were a little bit of an odd choice to leave on someone's windscreen, but not threatening. No damage had been done to her vehicle or herself.

Luckily Harlan had already started his second shift in his run of nights, so she didn't have to face him when she got in, and she had managed a quick, normal-sounding text exchange, ending in the usual heart emojis. If he'd seen her he would have known instantly that something was seriously wrong. And she might not have been able to keep it together, might have blurted it all out, and what would he have done then? She could lose him completely.

She couldn't have hidden this from him, not tonight, but could she fool her best friend? She had to, for Clara's sake.

'No worries. It's lucky my brats are with the grandparents just now.' Clara smiled, even though her green eyes were still concerned. 'Plus, I love chilling out in your gorgeous house, especially with the new kitchen. You have that shiny hot chocolate velvetiser thing, and nice wine, and it's so peaceful.' She laughed, 'Only kidding.'

'Well, thanks again.' Alexandra hoped her friend would get the message and leave. The urge to confide was back on the tip of her tongue, and she knew Clara well enough to predict she would want to help. She would also want to go to the police. There was no way in hell she would put Clara and her family into the danger zone. 'I'll see you at Becca's party?'

But Clara was frowning at her now, fiddling with her long red hair, which was done up in a messy bun with a pink clip. 'I do need to mention something...'

Alexandra felt her heart lurch. Oh god, what now? 'Clara? What's wrong?'

'Nothing really... I just... I don't want to worry you, but I thought I heard someone out the back at about seven. I'd just settled the kids and... well, I checked, and there wasn't anything, but I thought I'd mention it so you could look on the security cameras. There was an envelope stuck in the letterbox in the front door though.' Clara shoved more red curls back from her face with an impatient movement of her elegant fingers, her brow furrowed. 'Harlan left at half five for work, and I didn't like to call either of you, as it wasn't an emergency.'

An envelope. Alexandra glanced at her watch. It was after

nine now. She forced herself to be calm. 'Thanks, you're the best. I'll have a look, but we've had a fox around for the last few weeks, so it's probably just that. Or someone else trying to get photos of our porch.' She gave her friend a shaky grin. 'I might move those potted trees from out the front in case they get nicked.'

'Well, I left the envelope on the table for you.' Clara studied her. 'No address. I don't want to pry, Alex, but you look totally freaked out, and when you came in you looked like someone had died. What's wrong?'

Tears lurked in her throat. She fought them firmly away. 'Nothing... I... The envelope is probably just something from school. I'm just a bit tired. I wasn't expecting jury service to be so exhausting.' She hadn't realised how unsteady she was feeling, and obviously looking, from Clara's expression. 'Sorry. I'm honestly okay. Just had a really tough day.'

'Well, if you're sure.' Clara's tone was still doubtful, concern etched on her face, but she leant in for a kiss. 'Let me know if you need me while you're in court, and we must go and see a film or something soon. Girls' night out with Becca after her epic spring party?'

'Promise.' Alexandra forced a smile and opened the front door, waving at Clara as her friend walked away down the dark street to her car. She remained in the safety of the lit area, but moved to the gate, checking Clara had climbed into the vehicle and driven away.

Number eight was shrouded in the velvety darkness of the spring evening, and the moon hung over the seafront like a gentle silver beacon. Alexandra hurried back up the pathway and closed the front door carefully behind her, leaning back against it as finally she allowed the tears to slide down her cheeks, allowed the sobs that had been clogging her throat to escape.

They had no reason to hurt her friends, but she had no doubt they would do anything to get what they wanted. The question remained. If they did get what they wanted – whether that was to get Gareth sent down and out of the way, or have him exonerated – would they let her live, or would she have served her purpose?

NINE

The house felt quiet, safe, and Clara had left the lights on in the kitchen and living room. The soft glow of a side lamp in the hallway also reassured her and chased the shadows away. Harlan wouldn't be home until around 7am so she shot the bolts on the front door. With the kids, jury service, and the school run, she would have to be up at 5am to unlock everything. There was no sound from upstairs, but she would check on the kids in a minute. She would also move the furniture to block the back door.

For a moment she stood, choking back the little sobs of distress, rubbing her eyes like a child. Her handbag was on the console table where she'd dumped it. She moved towards it and unzipped one of the side pockets. A small inner bag, branded with the logo of an expensive skincare company, fell into her hand. She drew it out, opened it, and shook the blister packs of medication onto the polished surface of the table. Smoothing a finger across the foil, she hesitated only momentarily, before popping a couple of tablets and swallowing them. She carefully returned them to their hiding place and moved slowly and deliberately to the sink, pouring a glass of water.

At last, she felt able to face her tormentor again. Alexandra could feel the stress of the day seeping through her bones, bleeding out into her perfect home, but she went to the table and picked up the envelope that Clara had left there. Her hands were shaking so much she tore the flap and had to take another few seconds to regain control before she finished opening it.

Another sheet of paper, and this time, folded inside, was the missing wing from her original origami bird. The sheet of paper wasn't plain; it had a message, printed:

GUILTY

That was it then. She had been right to guess this was about Mac, or *Gareth*. Alexandra could feel the answers to some of her questions rolling around in her head. Her past was talking to her, threatening her and her life. She did a quick roll call of friends and family, remembering the immense power and reach of Thomas in particular. Who might be delivering these messages? Probably not someone she even knew.

Calling up the security app on her phone, she scrolled through, checking the cameras at the front door. *There!* At seven, just when Clara had mentioned hearing a disturbance out the back, someone jogged up the path and stuck the envelope into the letterbox in the front door. Heart racing, she peered at the pixelated images. But her elation turned to bewilderment as she identified a random kid, probably not more than eleven or twelve years old, wearing a Superman T-shirt and black joggers.

It was clear he was just the delivery boy. Whoever had sent him on the errand had probably bunged him a fiver or something, while they waited and watched further up the road to see the job done. Shit!

Annoyed, but unsurprised, she went softly upstairs to check the kids. Sophie was awake, and she instantly felt guilty.

Normally if she had to work late the first thing she did when she finally arrived home was to pop upstairs to kiss them goodnight.

'Hi, darling. How was school?' Alexandra whispered, as her daughter hugged her with gusto.

'Ah boring. But I'm going to try out for the dance show. You came home ages ago. I was waiting and waiting to say goodnight.'

'Sorry, I needed the toilet, and then I had to answer a message on my phone.' She forced a smile. 'That's great about the dance show. How was Auntie Clara? I hope you didn't wear her out.'

'Tom made her play football and we had beans on toast for dinner.'

Alexandra held her close for a long moment, the child's long brown curls so soft against her cheek, before tucking her in and retrieving the seal from the floor. 'You need to go to sleep now, or you won't have the energy to try out for the dance show.'

'Night, Mummy.'

'Night, sweetie.'

Kissing Tom, who was snoring peacefully, she bent and quietly retrieved the dirty laundry from the floor, before heading downstairs. She could put a quick wash on now, heat something up in the microwave, and be asleep by midnight. If she could manage to dodge the nightmares, she might be able to get enough rest to enable her to make a plan. She had escaped once. Could she do it again?

Niall had said more than once to keep a distance, that Mac (she was still struggling to think of him as Gareth) was one of *them*, and wasn't really as friendly as he seemed, but she had chosen to ignore this piece of wisdom.

Niall hadn't really liked the four men, but he'd been happy enough to take their money for as many jobs as they could give him. Once upon a time, Niall had been that delivery boy. Her brother.

Mac hadn't been like the other three men. He had taken notice of her, looked out for her, and not in a pervy way, although Lana was always teasing her that it was only a matter of time before Mac asked for a date. He never had, and as far as she had seen and heard, he was very selective about dating too, never laying a hand on any of the Candy Girls.

Why would he have murdered his girlfriend? Despite the strict instructions on staying off social media due to the jury service, once she had done her chores she sat down on the sofa with a macaroni cheese ready meal, mug of tea, and her MacBook.

The medication had calmed her, and as much as she hated taking it, it was reassuring to have it tucked away. Once, not so long ago, she had relied on it.

She thought of her mum, in the care home, and wondered if she should call to check she was okay. But that would mark her down as slightly paranoid, especially at half eleven at night. She hoped she was safe. Surely, they would leave *her* alone, especially now. Apart from the small family contained in this house, her mum was all she had.

Friends then. On reflection, she was pretty sure they would not bother with them. They were all new friends, who knew nothing of her past. Good friends, though, especially Clara and Mike, Becca the superwoman with a heart of gold, and even Harlan's idiotic chauvinistic workmate, Bailey, with his constant parade of model OnlyFans girlfriends.

Double checking the rear security cameras on her phone app revealed nothing. She must somehow work out how to point them towards the rear of the house, not the back gate. A thought struck her. Perhaps the deliverer of these messages, or whoever was behind them, had manged to alter the security cameras. It must be possible to hack into the app.

Alexandra finally stopped reading about Gareth's murder trial online, and hesitantly picked her way across the keyboard until she opened a hidden file. She had always intended to delete the only evidence she had, but every time she went to do it, something stopped her. Harlan would never pry into her private files, and this one was purposely obscurely named, buried deep in an old photo collection.

There was no evidence she could have taken to the police without incriminating herself, but she had kept some of the photos, carefully transferred to digital form, and guest lists from two of the parties. Her memory had always been good. Even now, she would very occasionally catch a high-profile name on the news, or on social media, and nod to herself. It was ironic that of all the Candy Girls' clients, Thomas Blake had risen like cream to the top of the milk churn.

It did seem to prove that karma wasn't really a thing though, Alexandra sighed to herself, swigging from her mug as she continued to flick through her past. Why hadn't someone stopped him? She felt sick at the thought he had ever repeated what happened in the pool that night, with anyone else.

The idea that he might have taken his fetish elsewhere had haunted her since that night. She'd prayed that what happened that night was just a one-off, that she hadn't done the wrong thing in walking away without going to the police. She knew it wasn't that simple, that she wouldn't still be here if she had. People had no idea how easy it was to make girls disappear, especially if you were wealthy. There were yachts and homes across the world, storage facilities, and acres of woodland, farmland. The right kind of girl, with the right kind of background, could be erased without a trace.

The parties had been fun, and she had felt safe enough with the Candy Girls, one of Matthew's prized possessions. Mostly. But the darker edge was still present, and Alexandra had heard whispers from other girls, from the men they entertained, those who strayed outside of Matthew's protection, who joined other agencies, who were less fortunate than her, Lana, and Jess. She had deliberately stepped away from the shadows, not wanting to know, not wanting to see.

Although most of the Candy Girls' clients hadn't done anything illegal, as far as she knew, being part of this very exclusive club where you could pay to have pretty girls on tap would be something none of them would want to come out in the media. And then there were the drugs... That *would* have been career-ending for some of them.

White lines laid out openly on polished coffee tables, pills exchanged hand to hand as easily as whispered invitations.

'Come on, Birdie, come and dance!'

Jess disappearing into one of the bedrooms with two men. Lana sitting on the lap of a well-known American entrepreneur. Herself, behind the bar, flirting, laughing, swaying to the music.

Party girls.

Leaving the file open, she checked again on Gareth Sellers, very aware she was not supposed to be doing this. She might have harboured the faintest hope she was imagining the resemblance. The photos on social media, in the papers, destroyed that hope, even if she hadn't received the envelopes. It was him. There could be no doubt that Mac, the apparently genial friend to all the girls, the underdog in the glamourous foursome, the gravedigger and keeper of secrets, was in fact Gareth Sellers.

Gareth Sellers, 42, a Brighton property entrepreneur, faces trial for the murder of his girlfriend, photographer Sara Hayward, 32.

As they had heard in court, he had allegedly strangled Sara after an argument in the road, hidden her body behind a row of recycling bins. Now he was no longer just part of the shadows from her nightmares, but a real man standing in front of her in a courtroom. What a stupid thing to do, to kill his girlfriend and risk the past being brought up. Why would he do that?

She was vague on the law, but it seemed logical to assume that if the police had been investigating this murder, they must have dipped into his past. Did they know about his links to Thomas, Matthew, and Eddie? It was possible they didn't. But it was only a matter of time. University friends, flying high a few years after graduation, right at the beginning of their golden lives. Taking chances and opportunities because they could, and because it seemed they were already wealthy beyond most people's wildest dreams. Family money, she had always supposed, if she thought about it all.

Should I go to the police now? The thought was dismissed even before she had time to turn it over in her mind. An anonymous tip-off then? This, too, she had considered over the years, but again fear had forced her into apathy. The girls were dead. What good could it possibly do to bring their ghosts back into the public eye? Jess and Lana had no family, having drifted around Brighton from foster carer to foster carer. Only Lana's ambition and hard work had landed her on the degree course. Jess had no dreams of a career as far as Alexandra could remember, but she had wanted kids.

The court officials had been very clear that if the jury recognised the defendant, had any sort of link with the defendant, they should come forward. Could she fabricate an innocent link and let herself off the hook? They would check, surely. What could possibly connect her to this man, apart from guilty secrets?

All day she had been wondering what would happen if Gareth Sellers turned and looked at her, but his head had never turned towards the jury. All day she had also imagined being struck down with a sudden illness, of falling down a step outside the courtroom and breaking a bone. A family emergency might suffice, but she couldn't think what she might say to Harlan, to the kids.

The passion, the terror, and heartbreak of that night, and finally the realisation she seemed to have got away with it, had all passed. She had kept her head down, finished her degree, and thanked god her new life allowed her to live without notoriety. But she had lived off her stash of earnings until she met Harlan and had turned her life around.

Her mum. The only other person who knew the whole truth about the last party and the Candy Girls was her mum. Biting her lip, Alexandra scrolled back through her file of photos. Pretty, sexy girls, laughing with their dates. Lana featured in a lot of the pictures. And Jess. Lana's sister had only joined the Candy Girls a few months before the last party. Lana had slipped her sister's pastel-coloured bracelet over her slender wrist.

'I can't believe I'm doing this!'

'It's fun, you get paid well and there are hot men.'

'I'm not sleeping with any of them.'

Lana, laughing, hugging Lexy and Jess to her, snapping a photo before Jess's first party.

If Lana was still alive, did she feel as guilty as Alexandra did?

As she scrolled it suddenly occurred to her. Blindingly obvious. No wonder her previous searches on Mac hadn't ever brought up any matches. He wasn't even called Mac. It must have been a nickname. Tonight's search hadn't thrown up any links with Matthew, Thomas, or Eddie, but she was able to trace Gareth's property development company. Well respected, worth a lot of money. She had expected no less. Despite her exhaustion, her eyelids growing heavy, and her brain slowing, she continued.

Then, just as she was considering giving up and going to bed, she found an online newspaper article from August 1997. She read it twice before she was sure and then she saved it as a screenshot in her secret file. In itself, the article probably wasn't relevant to the current case, or even to the Candy Girls, but it was interesting, shocking, and she could see how Gareth had been left with a fierce desire to achieve. How he had been gifted the money to join his three friends, but his grief might have affected every aspect of his life going forward. No wonder he had never seemed to fit into the power crowd.

Alexandra stretched her arms above her head, rolling her aching shoulders. The house was quiet, comforting, her thoughts anything but.

If they had discovered where she lived, had sent her the bird, they might well have researched her routine, her family. It occurred to her with a sudden chill that somehow circumnavigated the soft comfort of her medication; it was more likely they had just been watching her for the last twenty years. They hadn't really ever let her go. Ever since the night of July 21st, 2004, she had been theirs.

And now they were calling in the favour.

TEN

What does the jury think of me?

All those bland, normal people chosen at random to decide my fate. The evidence is stacking up against me, I can tell. Even though I've done my best to show my legal team that Sara's death was at best nothing to do with me, at worst unplanned, that she must have been attacked by a stranger, another lover, in the alleyway off Beacon Close, for some reason the odds seem to be stacked against me.

Sara was a wild card, which was one of the things I liked about her. I also liked her pretty brown eyes, her way of tossing her hair aside when she was making a point, her youthful arrogance. Sara liked my wealth, my large spacious home, my membership to Soho House, and was happy to tell all her friends she was dating a rich property developer. I told her all my money came from doing up houses, owning houses, renting them out. Which is very nearly true.

Was I crazy to stick around in Brighton when I could have run to a million different places? I was born here, and the city is in my bones. I knew which areas would grow and which would stagnate, and I genuinely enjoyed renovating the old Edwardian villas, the grand Victorian terraces. With each project, my life moved forward, further away from the Candy Girls.

My brief time in Newcastle in the late nineties was forgotten. Five years that changed my life, but five years is nothing in the context of a lifetime, is it?

Not many people know I have a brother. Had a brother. Sometimes I wonder if Jack's death was the reason I threw myself into that cosy foursome at university. I was lost and stupid enough to believe I could fit in, could be someone I wasn't. I would rather have had my family back than had an obscene amount of money.

Anyway, I thought I made it clear to Sara there were spaces in my life she could fill, and others she was not welcome to invade. I didn't spell it out well enough. Sara didn't die because I was bored of her, or because I abused her, or involved her in anything illegal, as the press are suggesting.

At first, I wondered if someone was setting me up, framing me to punish me, or even take me out of play. Given Thomas's current situation I haven't discarded that theory. Could someone be blackmailing him?

I've been living and working in plain sight for many years now, doing work that's legit, and there is nothing I've been doing that could cause Matthew, Thomas, or Eddie any embarrassment. Because those bad boys are right up at the top of the tree now. Funny to think when we met at university, I was the high-flyer, the scholarship boy who had got in on a wing and a prayer. Nobody asked about my early childhood, but it was obvious I hadn't had the same privileges as the boys who became my best friends, and because they were my best friends, they became my secret-keepers. That's where my nickname came from. Mac, who could only afford McDonald's for breakfast. It never bothered me the way they thought it might.

Being drunk, taking drugs, is a sure way to lose your secrets, but I was young and stupid, and perhaps my confessions were the least shocking out of all of us. I was careful after I entered the world of work, but bloody stupid enough to have stayed in the toxic friendship group for a year too long.

I'm pretty sure now that Sara died because she found out about the Candy Girls, which means even after all this time, they've still been keeping tabs on all of us. She triggered an online tripwire maybe. Or found my secret file. And now they've decided to make sure neither Sara nor I can talk. I wish they had killed me instead, and it genuinely makes me feel sick in my heart that an innocent woman has died because of me. You could say she wasn't the first, but I would say it depends how you look at the bigger picture.

Now I'm freaking out about who else they have been watching. I'm so bloody furious I can feel myself coming across just like a clichéd murdering boyfriend. And there's no fucking chance I can be honest with the police, or even my legal team, which is ironic given the circumstances.

And in case you're still thinking it, let me spell it out: no, I didn't kill Sara. But I would say that, wouldn't I? Stuck in my cell with the poxy bars blurring across my vision, with a lifetime of confinement to look forward to, I'd do anything to pick up that get-out-of-jail-free card.

ELEVEN

Day four of the trial, and after waking at 4am Alexandra had already welcomed her exhausted husband home from his shift with coffee and a bacon sandwich, got the kids up, fed and dressed and seen them safely off to school with her friend, left a cash birthday tip for the cleaner, and chased up work emails Melinda had forwarded.

She was now making a second mug of coffee before setting off for court, and thanking god for caffeine keeping her going during her busy days, when the washing machine bleeped, indicating the second load had finished.

Harlan, bless him, would put the washing on and hang it out on the line after he had managed to get some sleep. He had always been great about stuff like that, a proper equal partner. She squashed down the guilt that kept rising up, about not sharing with him now what was happening: the danger she could be in – was putting them all in. She felt she had been jolted out of her routine, her safe little routine, her happy, content family life and her thriving business. Her nerves had been raw ever since she had woken, and before her morning coffee, she had swallowed another couple of tablets from her secret stash. Convincing herself she was being sensible by doing so had been so easy, was something she could push to the back of her mind.

It was all she had ever wanted, to feel safe, but she had never been complacent, never been careless. She probably should have left Brighton, but then she met Harlan and he worked here. The coastal city had seemed safer as the years passed, and her mum had moved down after the diagnosis, understanding that it was important to Alexandra she could be nearby, to look after her mum. She had uprooted her life for Alexandra with a wisdom and stoic attitude her daughter wished she had the courage to mimic.

Hiding in plain sight, they called it. She forced her mind back to her work emails from the clinic.

One of them made her smile:

Dear Alexandra,

I just wanted to let you know how much more confident I feel. It was really tough after the accident, and you were right, I only needed a few tweaks. I recently got the job I was going for!

I'll wait for your reminder re the top-ups, but I'm so happy and my face looks so natural.

Isabelle x

The best side of her work, Alexandra always thought, was the subtle little lifts and tweaks which could change someone's life. Not everyone needed industrial amounts of fillers and Botox, and in her professional opinion, there were far too many charlatans out there peddling insecurity and administering without thought or regulation. The enjoyment came from patients like Isabelle, the fascination of putting together each individual treatment plan, of working in minute detail to create the results she wanted.

Alexandra checked the time and shut her laptop. She felt a twinge of fear as she headed outside, but she could see across the road that there were no notes on her windscreen today, and no letters awaited her on the doorstep.

Naturally the traffic was terrible as ever, and she sat in the queue at the roadworks for half an hour before she managed to get as far as the green traffic light, which promptly turned red as soon as it was her turn to pull out. She pulled out anyway and drove too fast for the rest of the way. She was calmer now, her mind more focused. Having considered all options, she felt sure that the safest thing to do was to wait for another contact. Placing a 'guilty' vote at the end of the trial was the only thing she could do to appease them right now. She was still so afraid of what might happen afterwards, but she reasoned they were hardly going to gun her down in the street. They were all about subtlety.

Finally arriving at the courtroom, she checked in her phone and laptop at security, walked through the metal detector, and sat down with her fellow jurors in the waiting area. Ten strangers, selected at random from the electoral roll. How had she earned this fall of the dice, this probability that she and Mac would meet again under such improbable circumstances? Alexandra had a friend who was a medium, and she knew she would say something about fate, and the world tilting in such a way, or the stars aligning.

Instead, she knew it was just a computer picking her number, but that didn't make it any easier.

'What do you do for a living?' It was a grey-haired lady with a pretty cashmere cardigan who had spoken to her briefly yesterday, and who had been chatting animatedly with another juror, Jackie. She was smiling. 'I'm Anna by the way.'

'Alexandra. I'm a nurse, and an aesthetician,' she explained.

The woman looked dubious. 'You put patients to sleep?'

'No, aesthetician, not anaesthetist,' she corrected, before hastily changing the subject. 'Do you want a coffee?'

She made her way towards the coffee machine, greeting Jackie as she did so. The other woman immediately, sweetly enquired about her hay fever. She could see people walking behind the glass doors and passing through the security area. Was that where the defendants came in? She imagined them arriving in police vans with armed escorts and realised once again that her knowledge of the Crown Prosecution process and what happened in the justice system was rather limited. It was hardly likely to be as dramatic as the TV shows would like her to believe.

Although, there were lots of press gathered in the court-room in the viewing galleries today. The last couple of days had been quiet, but the case was stirring up interest, and Alexandra felt herself dropping her shoulders, walking around with her head down, trying to blend in with the other jurors when they were finally called into the courtroom. Perhaps if she went and had a word with the officials, if she said she'd realised she knew Gareth Sellers, recognised him from... From where? A friend of the family? Work? Ridiculous. No, the only thing to do was to ride it out.

Gareth Sellers was as smartly dressed today, and quietly confident, as he had appeared every day so far, and her eyes tracked him across the room. Glad she was in the back row, Alexandra took every opportunity to watch him, but kept her head down when he seemed to glance their way.

Sara Hayward. Her smiling photo had been everywhere this morning: pretty heart-shaped face and dark sparkling eyes. Alexandra concluded from what she remembered that she was certainly Mac's type, although she had only ever noticed him talking, flirting. Matthew had been careful in that respect too, but Eddie and Thomas had gone all out in their pursuit of fun.

It didn't make sense, and she used the time in the courtroom to switch off, going over the events of twenty years ago in her head. The Candy Girls had shut down, had vanished completely after that last terrible party. She could still feel the terror, the sweat pouring off her body as he slammed the door behind them, pushing her away from the basement room, away from the shouting and the blaze of Thomas's drug-fuelled anger.

As the temperature rose during the hot summer night, and the party exploded into chaos, she had realised she'd made a deal with the undertaker, not the murderer himself. And that had been just one of many mistakes she had made as thunder rumbled along the coast, and rain started to fall in sheets of icy droplets.

The lunch recess came, and Alexandra realised she had been so deep in her thoughts she hadn't even noticed the ebb and flow of the courtroom at all. The whole building stank of fear and disinfectant. Bad vibes, her medium friend, Ella, would have said, with an expression of extreme distrust. This time it was true.

She had made a quick call in the car on her way in this morning, arranging to see her mother on Saturday morning, hoping as she did so that she was not about to put someone else in danger. Her fellow jurors made general conversation and their voices buzzed around the room as she was unenthusiastically nibbling on a sandwich and sipping an energy drink. Just now, she couldn't spare the energy to join in, but she smiled manically at Jackie and Anna and hoped they didn't think she was too weird.

Once the day was over, again there were no gifts left on her car, and she could feel her shoulders sagging with relief. Relieved she didn't need to see any clients tonight, and also relieved she was early enough to catch her husband before he left for work, she was drumming impatient fingers on the steering wheel as she sat in the queue for the roadworks, when her phone rang.

'Hi, Harlan. How's it going?'

'Fine, love... Quick question because I know it's going to be a rush when you get home...'

'I'm actually nearly home, I—'

He cut her off, 'You know we were thinking about a holiday in July when the kids are off school?'

Her head spun; trying to keep up with the minutiae of her family life as well as deal with the ghosts from her past was tough enough, but the sudden intensity in his voice was surprising. 'Yes, of course. You fancied Greece, didn't you?' The lights changed to green, and she sighed with relief as she pulled out.

'Right, we can still do that too. But I've got a friend who's offered us his villa in Provence for ten days next month. He wants a house sitter, and even if we couldn't take the kids out of school for that long, I thought perhaps a week... What do you think?' His voice was enthusiastic, and as usual his impulsiveness, his crazy, generous ideas always made her heart hurt a little with love for him.

'*Next month?* Sounds lovely, but I'm not sure if I could arrange cover at the clinic at such short notice. We'd get in trouble with the school too, get charged for the days they would be away. It's a shame it's not over half term...' She paused, thinking properly, trying to focus. 'And what about your leave?'

'I might be able to rearrange, but I was thinking more about you and the kids taking advantage of a free holiday, even if I could only make a few days.'

As she considered it, something about it made her feel uneasy. It *would* be good to get away – and get the kids away – but France was not somewhere she would feel safe, and right now she didn't want dramatic spontaneous plans, she wanted the comfort of normal routine. If she had any chance of holding it together, of figuring out what was happening, she needed to be in Brighton.

'Thanks, Harlan, that is so sweet of you, but I think I'd rather wait until we can all go away together,' Alexandra told her husband, hoping she didn't sound ungrateful. 'The kids will be gutted if you aren't there the whole time, and it would be lovely if we can spend some time together when they've gone to bed! Let's wait until the summer holidays.'

'Well, have a think, babe. It might be a chance for you to relax a bit too. You've been really stressed the last week.' He paused, and she felt her chest tighten, before he added, 'With jury service and work. See if you can get Melinda and Jane to cover for Provence, maybe? It's a great opportunity.'

Alexandra promised to think about it, and he rang off. She tapped her immaculate pink nails against her phone screen, running over the conversations in her head. Harlan had noticed she was stressed. Her husband wasn't stupid. Laid back, chilled out, but smart. She took a long trembling breath.

The urge to call him back, to run home even and pour out all her troubles was so strong. But it would be the wrong choice. It would ruin her marriage if Harlan ever found out who she really was, what she had done. He was so honest and good. He had even told her he was shocked by his friend's OnlyFans subscription. But France was out of the question just now. She would avoid the whole country, not just Provence. Alexandra drifted back into her memories, hearing Jess's excited voice, feeling the sunshine pouring through the windows onto her bare shoulders.

'Oh, that one. Lexy, did you know he's got an apartment in Marseilles, and a villa in Provence? He said he might take me to Marseilles one weekend, and I've been asked to a party in Dubai too!'

Lexy did know about the villa in Provence. Only last month, when Lana had been away on a yacht with one of her regular clients, she had flown by private jet, with Sean and a couple of other girls, for a party at the stunning villa. She could still smell the scent of lemon trees, the sweet evening air, hear the laughter and splashes as the girls went skinny dipping. A champagne fountain, and plates of delicious exotic snacks.

The lifestyle Lana and, later, Jess had adored. It was addictive, a different world, where you could do what you wanted, go where you pleased, and not answer to anyone. That was what wealth gave you, and Lana had been determined to stay a part of that exclusive club.

TWELVE

She shook herself back to the present, inching along in another traffic queue. Was it the wrong thing not to take the chance to escape? Was she keeping her family in harm's way – could they really be in danger? Surely not. But even so, if Thomas or Matthew was involved, trying to protect themselves, having a police officer as a husband wouldn't stop either of them. She kept saying his name over and over to herself. Unlike Gareth (the name still sounded wrong on her tongue), who had been in charge of the day-to-day business, Matthew was the one who handed out the money, who occasionally spoke to her on the phone. The one who asked her to be hostess at the parties.

Eddie and Thomas had added nothing but their illustrious presence as far as she could see, but she understood from the other party guests that the odd foursome had become well known amongst their circles for arranging the best parties, with the best girls. Networking, Matthew had always called it. She remembered a snippet of conversation, long buried in her memory, but now right to the surface. She had been at the bar, pouring drinks. Matthew had been talking to an older man, and he had been laughing.

'I collect favours. Isn't that part of stepping up? Favours, secrets, and knowledge.'

His company, unsmiling and staring rather too hard at the girls, had nodded. 'I always find it's best to know more about my friends than they do about me, if you understand?'

'And then perhaps the time comes to reveal that knowledge?'

The men had moved away, but eighteen-year-old Lexy, in her black lace mini dress, with her curls flowing down her back, had wondered at the time if Matthew meant he was black-mailing people.

Mac had always seemed very friendly with Thomas, but never quite at ease with him. Part of the gang, but also not? It didn't matter what she had suspected, it was what she had finally found out that night that mattered. The realisation that she had been as part of the murders as he was made the guilt unbearable.

She could have stopped it, but she had turned away when Mina walked out the door, had let herself assume that every-thing was okay. She had been selfish, not wanting anything to rock the boat, or cut off her source of money. This time it was Gareth's voice in her head.

'Money gives you the power to do anything, Birdie. You can give life, and you can take life. I know what you think you saw, but nobody would ever listen to you. These people can make anything go away, and you would disappear. Maybe not today, maybe not next week, but one day, you'd vanish. Run, Birdie, run!'

Niall was dead because of her. They had killed him that night along with the others, she was sure of it. Niall, Lana, just two of the people whose names had slipped into obscurity. Her memories of the night were blurred, which she had always found odd, because she never drank alcohol, didn't take pills or any other form of drugs. She put it down to the shock of girls' deaths, the shock of discovering the dark side of the parties was very real even right here in Brighton, and the realisation she had been complicit all along.

In her life now, she couldn't imagine that people could just vanish, that friends, family, co-workers, and neighbours wouldn't notice. But this was a safe little haven, and on this level she now operated on, nobody she knew had been where she had. And if they had, they would do what she did, and hide that knowledge of another life away.

But it was easy to disappear. Especially if you were a certain type of person. *'Oh, she must have gone off with her boyfriend, her friend, or gone to London/Leeds/Manchester.'* The Candy Girls had not been missed, and not a single one had ever appeared on the news, which told her Matthew, Eddie, Thomas and Mac had chosen wisely. But the graves were still there.

There were probably more girls, those who had gone away on the luxury trips, boarded the yachts from Nice, stepped onto the private jets to Dubai and Barbados. Alexandra thought there might well be a lot of girls who simply never returned home.

It had been an easy world to vanish in. Was that why Sara had died? she thought suddenly. Because she had become entangled in that world? Could it still be going on? The thought chilled her, even though the heating was turned up to the maximum on this cool spring evening. Not here in Brighton perhaps, but elsewhere. If the four men had continued to play with fire, could it be that Sara died because she had simply discovered the truth? Being Gareth's girlfriend couldn't have been easy.

She was deep in thought as she turned into her road, and she missed seeing the van pulling out of the side street to her right, just ahead of her.

She hit the brakes but was too late to avoid the rear of the van, and she stared in confusion at the driver. He made a cheerful gesture and jumped out. He had a navy beanie pulled down low, and a red hoodie. Athletic movements, late twenties maybe? A square chin, stubble, and amused brown eyes. Without thinking she opened her window. He came up to it but instead of shouting at her, or apologising for pulling out in front of her, he smiled. 'Hi, Birdie. I've been asked to give you a little present. I'll check in again soon, so don't start doing too much research, will you? You might get into trouble.'

Adrenalin shot through her body, fear and shock making her tremble, as she scrambled for recognition. 'What the hell? Who are you?' Nothing. She did not know this man, had never known this man, she was sure of it.

A car behind hooted and a woman called out from the pavement asking if they were okay. Alexandra waved in what she hoped was a reassuring way, smiled at her, and turned back to the man.

He was carrying a small, gift-wrapped box, and he passed it through the window as she instinctively shrank back. More vehicles were hooting, pulling out to overtake, drivers shouting.

'See you around, Birdie.' The man winked and moved away.

Before she could react, he was leaping back in his van, reversing, hooting rudely at the other cars trapped by the collision, and driving off at speed. Shaking, Alexandra managed to switch her engine back on and drive the last hundred metres to her parking space. Once she had switched the ignition off, she sat for a few long moments, head in her hands, trying to understand what had just happened. The box was on the passenger seat. Automatically, she extracted the parking permit from the glove box.

The gift wrapping felt expensive beneath her tentative fingertips. It was shiny, pink like candy and neatly secured with a white satin bow. It was stupid to be scared of it, she told herself, and she needed to see what was inside before she got into the house. If it was something horrific, she could stash it in the boot maybe...

Her trembling fingers gradually revealed a cardboard box, and inside was a piece of framed artwork. Her hand went to her mouth, that fight or flight adrenalin pulsing again.

Behind the glass sat a larger origami bird, made with rose-coloured paper. It had two smaller birds arranged behind it, one rose and one white, attached by two white cotton threads. Intricate and delicate, there was no mistaking the meaning. Anger rose in her throat. She would not allow them to threaten her children. It was time to start fighting back. David and Goliath, the fight might be, but the protective rage that spilled into her chest, flooded her body, gave her the strength to emerge from the car and check the damage (fairly minor but the paintwork was badly scratched).

Alexandra shoved the artwork back into the box, collected the wrapping, and stashed the whole lot in her large tote bag. Bastards! Despite her hurry to get inside and see her family, she found herself standing on the side of the road, taking deep shaky breaths, staring blankly at the houses that lined the road. Even as she stared, she wondered if she saw a shadow in the upstairs window of number eight. Was he watching, the man from the van? Was he the same person who had broken in and left the first bird? She realised she hadn't even managed to get the registration of the van.

An idea had slipped into her mind. Perhaps she should go back and visit the house? The venue for the parties, and the location of the graveyard. It might lay some of her ghosts to rest, reassure her nothing had changed. Or she might find out something *had* changed, which would give her more ammunition to fight with. Secrets and knowledge were power. She was no longer a scared teenager.

Composed now, she walked up to her front door and hurried inside. The kids threw themselves at her for hugs, chattering about their day, but to her surprise, Harlan had already left, and it was Clara who greeted her from the kitchen.

THIRTEEN

Saturday morning. Harlan had already left for the gym, and the kids had been dropped off at football practice in the park. Alexandra had two hours to kill and decided to take the chance to check in on her mum. She refused to dwell on the court case, on her husband's odd behaviour; he had gone out early last night, come back late. He had sent messages, and seemed to be still pushing for her and the kids to go to France. They hardly crossed paths at the moment and when they did he seemed distant, almost as though he was avoiding her. He couldn't possibly know... But guilt prevented her from forcing a showdown or going beyond anything but a mild enquiry as to whether everything was okay at work.

The building was light and bright, defying the cool spring air and cloudy coastal sky which echoed a grey and swirling sea. Litter skittered across the road as she parked her car, dancing in filthy whirlpools, skipping over the greasy puddles.

But the care home was in a good area, and it had seemed the least she could do for her mum. The pain of her diagnosis, the shock of her quick deterioration, would never be something she could brush to the side, but at least she could ensure she was well cared for, comfortable.

She pressed her key fob to the white security gate, breathing in the scent of the bright spring flowers, already dancing in the stone-edged borders in the front garden. She entered the building via a set of sliding doors, which also required her key fob for access. Inside, the building smelt of furniture polish and roses. It was one of the reasons she had chosen this place. Too many care facilities she had looked at smelt of stale urine and stale food, and were cramped and underfunded.

'Hallo, Alexandra! Lovely to see you.' A nurse was leaning across the visitors' desk, scribbling on a sheet of paper.

'Hi, Tina. How is she today?' she asked, pausing next to the visitors' book and picking up a pen.

The nurse smiled. 'Catrin is having a good day. She's been in the kitchen doing some baking, and she came to the knitting class in the orangery this afternoon. Still in there reading as a matter of fact. I'm just keeping an eye on the desk for an hour because we're a bit short-staffed. It's that spring flu seems to have got everyone, and we make sure everyone knows not to come in and spread that around.'

Having a good day. A tiny lift inside her heart, Alexandra strode towards the warm living room area. She told herself sternly not to get her hopes up. Dementia was cruel, and seeing her mum so lost and frustrated, sometimes terrified, by something she had no control over, was devastating.

At least she had been able to sell her apartment and pay for this high-end luxury facility. It was the best she could do. If Niall was still alive, he'd want it too. She took a deep breath and headed for the orangery.

'Hi, Mum,' she said cheerfully. 'I brought you a couple of plants for the gardening club.'

Her mum, blue eyes faded, grey-streaked brown hair plaited neatly, hung over one slender shoulder, turned and smiled at her. 'Ellie! Haven't see you in ages.' She frowned, the sadness settling over her brows, before the confusion cleared. 'Shall we go out later? Just us two girls?'

'Sure. Mum? *Catrin?*' Sometimes the use of her name jolted her back from wherever she had vanished to. When she was younger, everyone had said how alike Alexandra was to her mum. The same physical appearance, except her mum's eyes were blue, and Alexandra's were grey, and the same feisty spirit.

A smile and a sparkle before the eyes went blank and glassy, and Alexandra felt the pain, the loss deep in her chest. She would again try before her mum completely disengaged with their conversation. Putting the small box of plants carefully on the floor next to them, she spoke softly, clearly. 'Mum, there's something I really need to ask you.'

No response, although her mum was still staring at her, clearly focusing on what she was saying, even if she didn't recognise her, if the words were making no sense. Alexandra felt she must try.

'Mum, I wanted to ask you about something from the past. Do you remember the Candy Girls?' She had lowered her voice on purpose, but unfortunately one of the carers was walking past, collecting empty cups from the little side tables.

'Hi, Alexandra,' the carer said, moving closer. 'So sorry to interrupt, but I was hoping for a quick word?'

Alexandra stood, walked a few steps away, just out of earshot of her mum, and waited.

'She's been a bit out of sorts the last couple of days, and I wondered if there was anything you knew that might have triggered it?'

'Like what?' Alexandra knew her question sounded too sharp, too defensive. 'Sorry, I don't know of anything.'

'Any recent dates of any relevance, or even the time of year?'

Alexandra knew this particular carer fairly well and she

weighed up her options. Catrin was still staring at her daughter, but she knew from experience, unless something resonated with her, she could carry on staring for ages. She wasn't sure which was more heart-breaking, the fact she no longer recognised her, or the fact her strong, brave, resourceful mum had been reduced to this, was trapped by the disease which engulfed her brain.

Her mum had been her only confidante, the one who had given her the courage to move on, urged her to make the most of her life. Nobody else knew the whole truth of what had happened after the party. She could still hear her mum now, picture her leaning against the sink in their old garden flat back home.

'You were an idiot to get involved, love, but as you say, you made a lot of money from it, so now carry on with your life.' A shadow crossed Catrin's face for a second. 'Have you heard from any of these men again since that night?'

'Mac called to ask if I was okay, and Matthew called to tell me he appreciated my discretion. He said he wanted to give me a bonus to apologise for what I had to go through.'

Her mum's expression hardened. 'You mean a bribe?'

'Yeah. He said he'd leave it in a locker in Brighton train station, and I should just collect it when I wanted. He's messaged me the details. Cash obviously.'

'How would he have access to an Amazon locker? Those are for parcels; you can't just use it for anything. Are you going to take it?'

Lexy took a long shaky breath and scrubbed her sweater sleeve across her exhausted face. She could feel the tear tracks mingling with last night's make-up. She had packed up in the early hours, emailed the landlord that she had a family emergency and needed to get away, paid the lease for another month, and was waiting at the train station by six. 'I am going to take it. They know everything about me, and if this is their way of *making sure I don't talk, then I'm going to go along with it. If I don't, I become a liability. Like Lana. Like Niall.'*

'You don't know they're dead,' her mum said firmly. 'Niall is probably still wheeling and dealing his way through the criminal underworld, and Lana, the poor girl probably ran away to cope with what happened to Jess.'

'Maybe.'

'This Mac bloke doesn't sound like the rest of them,' her mum commented, fiddling with the pretty gold-coloured bracelet on her left wrist, before returning to the subject in hand. 'Do you think they'll come after you, as you were the only other witness?'

Lexy had been so terrified of this, scared when she spoke briefly to Mac, who must have heard from the background noise she was on a train, and had been shivering with fear when she answered Matthew's call. The carriage had been quiet, and he had only reiterated she must keep her promise and she would be safe. Her promise to keep secrets she should never have known.

'Lexy?'

'No, I think if they were going to kill me, they would have done it last night,' she said honestly. 'Thomas wanted to, I could tell, and Eddie wouldn't have cared as long as he wasn't impli-cated. It was Mac and the others who forced them to let me go. And Niall, he was there, but I never saw him afterwards, and when I call him, his phone is switched off. Lana's too.'

The carer was swinging a couple of mugs by their handles, smiling, waiting for an answer. Alexandra blinked hard, drop-ping back into the present with effort. Her mum was still staring blankly.

'Not really... When did you say this happened?'

'Ever since she came in from the garden the other day.'

'Could she have argued with someone in the garden?' Alexandra queried, puzzled.

'I wasn't aware of anything like that. She does have these periods of high anxiety occasionally... She was wearing her favourite gold bracelet...' The carer frowned, thinking, the mugs clasped loosely in her hands. 'Oh, I know! Catrin lost her bracelet that evening, and when we found it again it was wrapped in tissues under her pillow, like she'd been hiding it.'

'Her flower bracelet?' Alexandra couldn't see the significance either. She glanced down at her mum's left wrist. The jewellery was worked in gold with a delicate flower pattern and looked almost Victorian. Her mum had always worn it, for as long as she could remember.

'That's the one.' The carer shrugged. 'I'll leave you to it, then. Catrin, why don't you take Alexandra for a walk in the garden?'

Catrin was staring straight ahead and gave no sign she had heard. Alexandra reached over and held her mum's hand, very gently, so she could pull away if she wanted. But today she closed her fingers over her daughter's, even though her expression didn't change. She made no move to get up, though the glass doors to the garden were propped open in the spring sunshine, the greenness outside inviting.

Another carer brought some cake and fresh cups of tea. 'Catrin helped bake this yesterday. I thought you might like to try some.'

Catrin refused to acknowledge the cake, her fingers picking away at the sleeve of her blue cardigan, her mouth set.

'Thank you. I'm hoping we can walk in the garden, but maybe Mum needs a snack first.' Alexandra took a bite of carrot cake, and she could tell it should have been delicious, but to her it tasted dry, and she had to force it down. It was so wrong her mum had baked this, and now she wasn't enjoying it.

She sighed softly, sipped her cup of tea, ate the slice of cake, kept talking brightly about the business and the children, while her mum stayed locked in her cage. Finally, just as she had given up hope, Catrin suddenly turned and asked if she wanted to walk in the garden.

Alexandra smiled. 'I'd love to, and it's even a bit sunny today, isn't it?'

'Yes, yes, it is sunny.' Catrin stood up, pulled the folds of her soft wool wrap around her shoulders, straightened her cardigan sleeves, and smiled at her daughter. Her expression had cleared again, and she stood easily, shoulders back, the confusion vanishing.

Encouraged, Alexandra slipped her arm through hers, and they headed out of the garden doors, across the lawn and into the vegetable area, where her mum liked to spend time planting seeds, and nurturing the subsequent plants. The air was cool, and the morning shadows still stretched across the dewy lawns, but the space was beautiful.

Her mum paused beside a waist-high raised flower bed, constructed of railway sleepers. She ran her hand through the damp earth dreamily, backwards and forwards as though she was raking through her thoughts. Finally, she turned to her daughter, focused on her face with great determination, and spoke as though she had rehearsed the line. 'Niall was here.'

FOURTEEN

'*What?*' Alexandra felt her breathing stop momentarily, her heart, in contrast, slamming against the walls of her chest in great painful blows. 'Mum, Niall is dead. He died a long time ago.' Normally she would have been more careful about what she said. To her mum, the knowledge of deaths of people she had once known had vanished, and she would grieve all over again, only to go through the same process weeks or months later.

To save her from this, Alexandra had learnt early on in the disease to allow her mum to think people were still alive, even if they were not. And to be fair, she had no idea whether Niall had just vanished or was indeed dead. Over the years it had seemed easier to just accept the latter. Otherwise, it hurt horribly that he had never been in touch. The same with Lana. Losing her best friend, Jess, and her brother in the same night had added to her guilt.

Lana and Jess had not liked Niall, had been wary of him and protective of Lexy. Taking the money would be very much Niall's style.

'Niall was here.' The stubborn folds of Catrin's mouth, the determined expression that met hers, made it a certainty. The blue eyes glittered with intensity, holding hers in a desperate attempt to convey the truth.

'I... When was he here?' Alexandra's voice sounded odd, even to her ears, but she tried to keep the tone even and calm. 'When did you see him, Mum?'

'Last week.' A surprisingly quick answer with no hint of confusion. Catrin was fiddling with her gold bracelet again, but her fingers were gentle, caressing the delicate flower link, rather than fumbling with agitation. She was still calm. That was good.

'Was he here in the garden?' Alexandra could see a few staff tending the apple trees, keeping an eye on the residents in the greenhouses, turning on lights or packing away tools. Her mum must have mistaken one of them for Niall.

'In the garden. He was here.' Again the words were firm.

'Did he speak to you, Mum?'

'Niall was here, and he wants you to know... He wants you to know...' The effort was immense, brow furrowed now, eyes quickly wet with frustration. The movements of fingers on bracelet became shaky, jerky, a sure sign of distress.

'It's okay, Mum, it's alright. Look, sit down here for moment.' Alexandra's heart was hammering, and her palms were sweaty. What if her mum was right? Was it another threat? Surely Niall would never threaten Catrin. But then, surely Niall was dead. How could he have escaped that night and never been in touch?

That last night when she had run back to the flat, dodging through the back streets of the city at 2am, careless of figures that loomed from doorways, of crude offers from staggering groups of partygoers.

She had known if she could make it back to her mum, everything would be okay. And it was. Slumped in a doorway near the train station, she had waited until the first train out of

Brighton, had made it to Gatwick, just to Brighton. Finally, after a long and convoluted seven hours, she reached the safety of her childhood home.

In the kitchen, with the familiar noise of the trains rattling past every half hour or so, they had talked it out. Together they had come up with a plan, and together they had made sure Lexy became Alexandra, hid out until she got her degree and left the Candy Girls behind.

'I never really wanted you to go back to Brighton, you know... I was worried... I thought you might... might get into trouble again.'

'I know, Mum. It's okay and I didn't get into trouble, did I? We're both safe now.'

'Niall was *here*. In the garden with me.' Even as she spoke, Alexandra could see her mum was losing the fight to stay present; the brightness began to fade, like spilt milk running from a cracked saucer.

'Mum?'

With a last effort, Catrin shoved a shaking hand into her cardigan pocket and pulled out a crumpled piece of paper. 'He said to give you this. Niall did.' All at once she was staring stonily ahead again, her face rinsed clean of any expression, her mind once again forced into the darkness.

Alexandra knew what it was even before her hand closed over the paper bird her mum pushed into her palm. A little worse for wear, but still a little origami bird.

One last desperate effort from her mum: 'You used to try and teach me to make these. I couldn't do it.'

She had taught Niall and Lana to make them too. Mac had laughed at her, had seen her twisting her origami shapes while she was waiting for a party to start, sat out in the courtyard, with sun starting to sink into the sea. But he had not been able to make a bird when he tried.

Frustrated and bewildered, Alexandra slipped the bird into

her bag, and shot a quick glance around the enclosed area, at the high stone walls bordering the garden. She knew there was security on the gate, she knew visitors had to sign in at all times, and she had expressed, in writing, that she was the only person to be allowed to visit her mother. And anyway, aside from all of that, why would Niall be threatening her? Why not just call or turn up at the house instead of creeping her out with weird messages?

She gave it one last shot. 'When was Niall here? What did he want, Mum?'

But the energy and purpose, so briefly evident, had vanished. Her shoulders slumped forward; her hands hung limply by her sides. Like a sleepwalker, she rose from the wooden bench, turned, and started back to the house.

'*Mum?*' Alexandra caught up with her in a few swift strides. 'Mum, what did he say to you?' Concern for her mother mixed with her own confusion made her speak more sharply than she had intended, and a tear rolled down Catrin's cheek as she walked.

'Oh Mum, I'm sorry, I'm just worried about you. Niall shouldn't have been here.' No, she thought again, Niall shouldn't have been here. How was it even possible?

No response from her mum, as they reached the doors, re-entered the warm and cosy atmosphere of South Downs House. Alexandra checked her watch and was ashamed by the rush of relief she felt that it was time to leave.

Guilty, she felt so guilty for everything her mum was going through, frustrated she couldn't help more, and now guilty again for upsetting her. She must have been mistaken. And there was the incident with the bracelet... Perhaps that had triggered memories and Catrin had become confused.

On her way out, having left her mum joining a group baking scones in the large kitchen, she popped into the office. Delilah, the manager and matron, was a huge support, and her obvious care and attention to detail meant South Downs House had been the only place Alexandra had been prepared to have her mum living. The sheltered accommodation, ranging from apartments to small houses in the vast grounds, was dedicated to ongoing care and research, and provided the exact bespoke support for each patient.

'What's up, Alexandra? You look a bit lost.' Her face softened, brown eyes ringed with their usual heavy make-up, black curls dropped over one shoulder in a thick braid. 'Is your mum having a bad day?'

Alexandra explained, carefully, that her mum had talked about an unwanted visitor, and Delilah at once shook her head. 'No chance. You know how careful we are. But you're welcome to check the visitor book, and I'll get the girls to check the CCTV.'

'Thank you, if you could, just to set my mind at rest,' Alexandra said gratefully. *Niall?*

There were no names from the last couple of weeks that jumped out at her scribbled into the book. Maybe her mother had seen simply seen another visitor, who looked a little like Niall, and her fragmented mind, jumbled with memories from further back, had put it together wrongly.

It wasn't safe for her mum to even mention the Candy Girls, even now and even here. Not for the first time, Alexandra regretted sharing her secrets, unburdening herself to the one person she completely trusted, and thereby putting her in danger too.

Delilah came back. 'Nothing unusual, I checked the double-checked the trade log too.'

Alexandra nodded. 'Thanks, anyway.'

'You know, if there is a someone you don't want to visit your mum, you just need to give us the details, a photo, and we won't let them in.'

Alexandra seized on this helpful piece of information,

pulled up an old photo, writing down his full name, finding herself doing what she would never have believed possible: giving details of her brother, so he could not visit their mother.

FIFTEEN

Later, much later, Alexandra pulled out her laptop and continued her research as the shadows of the evening closed in, with her children safe upstairs. Concern for her mother had made her phone the facility where she lived once again when she got home. Super-efficient Delilah had already made further investigations, had the CCTV checked for the past two weeks and quizzed the security guards on duty.

There was nothing to raise any alarm bells, so Alexandra surmised if Niall had really been in the garden, he had slipped in one of the back gates, which were locked by staff, but had no CCTV, and stayed in the garden. Hell, maybe he had posed as a volunteer, and been all checked out under another name. Her thoughts were running wild at the idea of his involvement.

It crossed her mind, as occasionally it did, that she had essentially put her mother into prison, and she was in two prisons: the one in her head, and the one her daughter had erected around her physically. The fact that the latter was for her own safety, and that she was receiving all the care and medical attention she needed, still didn't take away the fact she could no longer choose to leave the place she was living in.

Alexandra forced herself to concentrate. Something very real was threatening both her and her mum and the puzzle pieces were spinning in her mind. Mac in a very public murder trial, splashed all over the media, her mum mentioning Niall reappearing after years of silence. Finally, herself on the very jury who would decide whether Mac/Gareth Sellers was guilty of murder. It couldn't all be a coincidence.

Alexandra typed out everything she could remember; clients and girls, every single thing she had shut out of her mind for so long. Dates, places, and even a few short descriptions of what she had witnessed. Having banished the past into a small, locked compartment of her brain, she could now feel it chattering and twittering, rattling the bars to escape. Letting partial memories out was no good, but by opening herself to the past, she was also threatening her present. Although, someone else was already doing that.

Sometimes she did wonder about the whole nature and nurture thing. Niall wasn't her biological brother; her mum had fostered him at ten years old and gone on to adopt him. That was just Catrin. She had so much love to give, and Alexandra's childhood had been full of unexpected arrivals: babies in the night, children staying for a week, sometimes longer. She had never felt resentful of these children, knowing they would not stay for long, respecting what her mum was doing to try and make their lives better.

But it was big brother Niall who had got her into illegal business to start with. He left school at fifteen, just dropped off the radar, but he had been running errands for drug dealers since he was twelve, despite their mum fighting to keep him out of trouble.

'It's not trouble, it's work, Lexy,' Niall would say patiently.

The flotsam and jetsam of the city, the dangerous undercurrent of drugs, sex, and money laundering, Niall found exciting, a business opportunity.

'If we get more money we could get out of here, take Mum away from this. Maybe we could do other work?' she asked Niall once, when she was just ten, riding her bike in slow wobbly circles around the boy she had come to think of as her big brother.

There had never been any friction between them, he the one foster child who had never left, and she the only biological child. They adored each other; Niall opened up to Lexy about his early childhood in care, his parents who he had been told were junkies, and his loneliness. Catrin had seen their bond and wisely let them be.

Alexandra had no wish to drift along, get involved with the same crowd Niall hung out with. She had other friends, and big plans. She thought once she had done an access course, worked what seemed like a million hours in three nursing homes, done the graveyard shifts at the local hospital as a care assistant, and finally been accepted into nursing, that she had broken the pattern, that maybe even Niall might see what was possible with hard work and determination.

How easy it would have been to have a few kids, to stay local, in the close-knit community she had grown up in. It was a good community filled with good people, but it wasn't safe, and the crime rate testified to how many kids went straight out of school into the street gangs. Alexandra was ambitious, restless, and felt stifled, ditching her sweet boyfriend to pursue her dreams of moving away. Niall, also ambitious, was soon submerged into the criminal subculture and showed no signs of wanting to leave their hometown.

Brighton had been a fresh start, even if it meant leaving her mum and Niall up north. But they had both been so happy for her, and so proud. In a new city, she had felt she could start to breathe again, to spread her wings, enjoy a new life, the one she had been planning ever since she was ten years old.

The blue skies, freedom, and new possibilities had all been

hers for the taking. Until one morning, halfway through her degree. She just been introduced to the Candy Girls by her new friend Lana, had done a few dates to pay the rent.

Big brother Niall had appeared on the doorstep of her tiny but comfortable flat share in Kemptown. Lana had been making bacon sandwiches, Jess on the sofa painting her nails, but the smell of cooking had clogged in Lexy's throat when she opened the door and saw him standing there.

'Hallo, Lexy! Are you pleased to see me?'

<h1 style="text-align:center">SIXTEEN</h1>

I'm careful what I say to other prisoners, to the police, even my own bloody legal team. I learnt a long time ago to keep everything locked away inside. That way nobody can use the knowledge, the weaknesses, to their gain.

Sara wasn't the love of my life, because nobody will ever replace the one woman who was, but she was fun, full of enthusiasm for each new experience. She was a photographer, and her photos were edgy and clever: cityscapes, people, abstract images, in a brave and bold new light.

Do I get to grieve for her? On that thought, am I allowed to grieve for the girls who died? The girls whose graves I dug. It's an interesting question, and hell, I have a lot of time to think while I'm locked away.

I think about them sometimes: Bex, Mina, and Jess. Names don't matter to the dead, only to those left behind. You're wondering if I am ashamed, or if I feel remorse? The honest answer is I'm not sure. They were almost strangers, and I was doing a job I had to do, playing my part in the foursome. Someone had to take charge, to control what could have been a fucking disastrous situation for a lot of people.

The graveyard lies not far from here, but I don't visit.

Over the years I've kept in touch with Matthew, Eddie, and Thomas, just a few times, reassuring each other in sharp, coded emails that everything is okay. The deaths of those three girls should have torn our schoolboy gang apart. Instead it tied us all closer, bound up by our shared guilty secrets.

I lost everything when my family died, and I've been grafting like an idiot ever since to try and leave the grief behind. I think of my friends now, as I sit in the prison cell.

Matthew lost his dad very young, and I think he understood. He worked hard and played hard, but his eyes were on financial security after the credit crash lost his family their place in society, and most of their money.

Thomas was always the wild card, cruel in his sarcasm, but drawing followers like filings to a magnet. He never had to worry about the money. His arrogance seemed to make him more attractive to the girls, and he cleaned up in the dating game.

Eddie was a clown, with a temper you needed to watch, but he was generous with his money and most people liked him.

There've been a lot of those times when we kept each other's secrets, have been each other's alibis, but before that final party, I never realised how far we would go to bury the past. Or how bloody stupid we would be.

I have done a lot of things in my life you wouldn't believe me if I told you. Or maybe you would.

But there is one thing I want to make clear: I haven't killed anyone for twenty-five years.

SEVENTEEN

There had been no more deliveries, no shadowy figures on the CCTV at her house or office, but Alexandra hardly slept on Saturday night. She had been so sure he would make contact with her again. It *must* be Niall sending the birds, Niall breaking into her home. It would be easy for him, a career criminal.

The digital alarm clock showed 02:00 as she lay in bed, curled up on her side, eyes wide open in the darkness, listening to Harlan's steady breathing. He hadn't mentioned France again and seemed to be back to normal after his gym session. Tired, of course, but he had played with the kids, cooked dinner, and sat with her flicking through Netflix, chatting about nothing over a glass of wine.

Alexandra hadn't said anything about Niall. Harlan didn't even know she had any other family except her mum. Another lie she had justified to herself, another secret she had kept from him. Her mind racing, she had finally dropped off to sleep and woke with gritty eyes and a groggy head at seven o'clock, totally disorientated.

Her husband had another day off, but he was up unusually

early for a Sunday. She grabbed her phone off the bedside table and checked for messages. Nothing unusual, nothing to make her heart beat ridiculously fast. The morning sunlight streamed in through the white shutters, and she flung them open, desperate to escape her thoughts.

There was another blister packet of tablets now in her bedside cabinet, and without thinking, she slid the drawer open, swallowed two with her glass of water. Now she could face the day.

She almost hoped Harlan had been down to the older part of the house, spotted the furniture wedged against the back door, would start a conversation she couldn't get out of.

But when she made it down to the kitchen, the kids were watching TV in the living room, and he was making breakfast.

'Are you okay?' She glanced at the clock. 'It's a bit early for everyone to be up. You were shattered last night.'

He shrugged, leant in to kiss her. 'Kids were awake at six and I thought you might like a little lie-in. Fresh coffee's nearly ready.'

Alexandra studied him, noting the shadows under his eyes. 'Are you still going to do overtime tomorrow?' She took the mug of steaming coffee that he offered. 'Thanks, I need this.'

'Might as well tick off the overtime.' He smiled, the lines around his blue eyes creasing. He slipped an arm around her waist, holding her close so she couldn't see his expression. 'We need to have a talk about France. I think when we're there we should seriously think about what it would be like to live there. And I was thinking in the future, when we retire, we might look at a place in Spain, or Portugal?'

Surprise made her pull back against his hands, and he stepped away. 'What do you mean, when we're there? Where is this coming from? We're both a long way from retirement. And you were only talking about a holiday in France the other day.'

Harlan kept smiling, but his eyes had lost their sparkle, and the lines on his face were tight. Had he lost weight? 'But what about moving before we retire? The kids would love to live somewhere else. Imagine the weather in Spain in the winter, and they could try new foods, make new friends.'

She set her coffee cup down on the table and stared at him. 'You've lost me. Seriously, Harlan, you have never so much as indicated you are not happy living in Brighton, or mentioned moving somewhere else, and now in your head, you've got us packing up our lives, the kids' lives, and settling abroad. What is going on? We could never afford to do something like that even if we wanted to!' Alexandra could feel her heart pounding uncomfortably again, and her body tense.

But Harlan, after a long moment of silence, simply shrugged and turned away. 'You've got to be in court again tomorrow, haven't you, for the Gareth Sellers case? Word is it might get wrapped up pretty soon. Some issue with the evidence.' He winked. 'You didn't hear that from me.'

She nodded, still stunned by the suggestion of moving abroad intruding on their already complicated lives, and now trying to process this inside information on the trial. At that moment she realised he had hardly mentioned the case, hardly asked any questions until now. He would know she couldn't talk specifics, and he wasn't on the Major Crimes Team, so had nothing to do with the enquiry. But even so he would pick up gossip he should definitely not be passing on to her... She looked at him, at the stubble on his jaw and his tense expression as he turned back to the hob and began scrambling eggs, wondering how well she really knew her husband. She had been so preoccupied with her own traumas that she hadn't noticed her dependable, sweet husband had stepped sharply out of character.

He flinched when his mobile phone buzzed with a message, and pounced on it, almost overturning a half-eaten plate of toast.

'Harlan? Are you sure you're alright?' Concern and confusion made her voice sharper than she intended, and she felt the telltale sting of tears in her eyes. What the hell was going on?

'I'm fine,' he snapped, still looking at his phone. He dragged his eyes to hers with what seemed like a huge effort. 'Sorry, just the boys wanting to go out for a quick drink tonight... Bailey's having woman problems again, you know what he's like. You don't mind, do you? We can talk about things another time?'

'I suppose so...' Alexandra sat down, pushed her hair wearily from her face, and sipped her coffee, keeping her expression bland. Harlan was stressed, and it took a lot to freak her husband out. She did know Bailey, a fellow police officer and Harlan's usual partner on shift, had a tangled love life, with an ex-wife out for vengeance and numerous girlfriends.

As far as Alexandra was concerned, he was a loser, and a patronising git, although she tried to smile at his sleazy asides, and keep him at arm's length without actually punching him. But normally Harlan found Bailey's women troubles amusing, not stressful.

'Just a bit tired still. Anyway, I think I'll head out for a quick run, snap myself out of it, and get on with the day,' he told her, cheerfully, now. His mop of dark hair was tousled from bed, and his bright blue eyes held hers.

'Whatever you want,' she told him, choosing her words carefully, again bewildered by the abrupt mood and subject changes. 'Just, you know... If you need to talk, I'm always here.'

'Thanks, Alex.' It was a swift, guarded brush-off. 'I just need a run to clear my head. You know what it's like.'

She did know exactly what it was like. What the hell was wrong with everyone? Harlan hastily dealt out scrambled eggs, pulled on shorts and a top, and exited the front door for his run, missing Sophie's wails that she only liked egg soldiers and Tom's exclamation of horror when he accidentally knocked his glass of orange juice over his new book.

Alexandra cleared up the mess and told her daughter not to be so fussy. As she turned wearily away to stack the dirty plates, the thought struck her so hard she had to stop and focus on the sunny street outside to avoid a panic attack in front of her children.

Could someone be getting to him too? Or did Harlan also have secrets he wouldn't be keen to share? Oh god, surely not. She felt as if she were sinking – as though her perfect life, all calm and still, like a peaceful sea, had been ravaged by an unexpected storm.

Now the water was cloudy with sand and weed, and the waves were restless as she sank beneath them.

EIGHTEEN

After another sleepless night, not helped by Harlan coming back from his drink with Bailey in a bad mood, Alexandra mindlessly dealt with lunchboxes, reading books and artwork, helped Tom with his shoes, Sophie with her favourite glittery hair slides, and finally hugged them both tight before they left the house. Her anxiety had escalated so much that she needed to be the one to see them safely into school. There was time to get to court. Just. She knew she was being ridiculous, and the kids were perfectly safe with whoever was doing the lift share. But she needed to keep them safe.

Although Tom clung for a moment, and she buried her face in the softness of his springy dark hair, Sophie bounced towards the door without looking back, chestnut-brown curls flying out behind her. Her shiny shoes with the annoying flashing red lights splashed through the puddle by the front gate as she ran to the car.

Having dropped the kids off at school, Alexandra smiled to see them race onto the playground with their friends, but at the back of her mind she also tried to analyse what it was about the conversation with her husband that concerned her the most. It was all kinds of weird, but the feeling that constantly niggled in her gut was that her husband was acting out of character. What the hell was going on with all this sudden desire to skip the country?

Unfortunately, with everything that she had to deal with in her hidden life just now, she really couldn't remember if Harlan's odd behaviour dated from before she received the first bird, or if it had maybe started, or even escalated, since she had been serving on the jury.

As usual now, she hovered a while longer, checking both children had joined the line to file into the school building, checking they were safe, before she pulled away.

She was so deep in her thoughts that she nearly drove into the vehicle in front of her at the traffic lights and had to brake so sharply she felt her neck twinge with pain. King Alfred Leisure Centre, a huge Victorian monstrosity of a building, bordered by scrub land and a mini golf area, loomed in her vision. Alexandra thought of the oily blue of the swimming pool inside the leisure centre and shivered. She never went swimming if she could help it, not even in the sea.

That was a sure way for the nightmare to surface. It had been explained away to her husband as a near drowning when she was a kid, and because her mum had already been deep in the grips of dementia, he would never have been able to find out whether she was telling the truth or not. Not that Harlan would check up on her! He trusted her, had no idea what lies were simmering in her past life. Her panicky thoughts circled back; had she overlooked the fact he might have his own secrets, because she had been so keen to hide her own?

Still trapped in traffic, she reached forward and turned up the heating in the car. It was cold again this morning. Typical crazy British weather. Lots of people had told her to expect longer, and two weeks was short for a murder trial. If that was true she would be lucky not to be stuck on jury duty for longer.

She could hold on until Mac was found guilty and sentenced. But there was still the nagging question of what happened then. If he was found guilty, what difference would it make to her own life?

The rain had started before she reached the doors at Hove Crown Court, and she made a mad dash, arriving slightly dishevelled, but at least punctual.

Her fellow jurors smiled slightly awkwardly as she joined them in the holding area. Today she had brought her current book, a favourite way of escaping the world. Her secret passion was historical romance, and she could devour these chunky, satisfying books for hours, safe in the knowledge she had left her own time, her own troubles, behind her.

The man with the short cropped red hair was already banging on about his last experience of jury service, now in deep conversation with the man with the large nose about legal details. They argued loudly, with obvious enjoyment as each professed expert knowledge of the criminal justice system.

A younger woman sitting on her own in a corner rolled her eyes disdainfully at the noisy bunch and pulled out a tattered paperback. Alexandra smiled when she saw the title. A fellow reader and a fellow romance lover. Normally she would have struck up conversation later, delighted to discuss books, but for reasons she couldn't fully explain and some she could, she didn't want to engage with anyone. It was almost as though she could make the time go faster if she concentrated hard enough.

After two hours of waiting, they were called into the courtroom, Alexandra shuffling at the back to take her seat, avoiding any eye contact, thanking her lucky stars once again that she wasn't in the front row.

When she snuck a peek around the room, she could see that Mac looked serene and in control in another smart suit, and she felt a reluctant twinge of admiration. He was controlling the scene, as he had twenty years ago. Nobody was shouting here, and there was no dust, sweat, and dead bodies, no blood trickling from her nose, but even so, he had it covered. In her imagination, she could march over, push him out the way, take the stand, and tell them all what had happened at the party.

She had spent years hating the other three men for covering up Thomas's crime, but now she was looking right at him, she was forced to admit to herself that Mac hadn't killed anyone. He was just guilty, as she was, of hiding someone else's crime.

Alexandra glanced quickly at her fellow jurors, noting all expressions were sombre, practically shouting out loud that they were serious and committed. But who was totally in the room? If she was being reminded where her loyalties lay, could they have got to anyone else on the jury? She couldn't exactly ask them over the cup of weak tea provided at the break. It was still stupid; she could hardly throw a whole jury with her one guilty plea.

To her relief, the evidence was stacking up against Mac but his defence was doing a good job parrying it. One major issue seemed to be timing. A property with doorbell camera footage from Beacon Close showed a man, purportedly the defendant, following his girlfriend from a safe distance, all the way to the alley where she was murdered. From zoning into the dynamics for the first time, she found herself fascinated by the arguments of the legal teams. They were so concise, so calm. Pokerfaced, she thought, as she tried to figure out who was telling the truth, and who was bluffing. If Gareth *was* guilty, did his team know? They had to defend him anyway. How weird was that?

After a short break, Gareth's team, apparently waiting for an opportune moment, produced evidence of a potential alibi. He had been on his boat at the marina, working on the engine, mending a fault that had occurred earlier that day. More blurred footage, time stamps on a gate pass, mobile phone triangulation data. Alexandra felt like she was dropping into an episode of *Grace*. But this time she wasn't just watching in the comfort of her living room. She was involved, and these were real people, real lives and deaths.

The prosecution hit back. Gareth's DNA was found at the scene, and the prosecution alleged there was enough evidence to show he was in the area at the time Sara had been killed. But his defence team were now pushing hard that all of it could be accounted for, that other evidence was circumstantial.

Back and forth it went, and she felt herself changing her mind at every turn. It was like a game of tennis. She had been to Eastbourne and watched the championships on centre court with Harlan a couple of times, and they loved to watch Wimbledon on TV. This was similar as eyes went one way, then the other, the argument bouncing between the two opposing teams.

She was the only person in this room who knew what he was really capable of, she reminded herself, but even if she had spoken up, even if she had incriminated and exposed herself, would it make any difference?

Today, the poor victim's family were sat in the room, devastation clear in their faces, with slumped shoulders and red eyes. Justice for Sara's family? But she didn't even know if he had killed Sara. She wondered exactly what Sara's death had to do with the events of twenty years ago. This wasn't a coincidence.

What if Thomas Blake was in the courtroom right now, instead of Gareth Sellers? The burst of fear that accompanied this thought made her vision tunnel for a second. Like he would ever get as far as a trial. There was no evidence to connect Thomas to the historic murders, and he would be able to afford the best lawyers, probably bribe police officers, maybe even skip the country on a private jet. Untouchable. That was the word that had been used at the parties. These kinds of men were untouchable, outside of the law, living life on their own terms while others paid the price.

It was still raining, and she could see water gushing down

the window panes. The sound made her uneasy, jumpy. Every sound, every smell, and every word seemed to be magnified a thousand times. If Mac recognised her, would he tell his defence team? Or would he stay quiet, perhaps thinking she could help to sway a verdict in his favour?

By the end of the day Alexandra thought she could feel her fellow jury members moving slightly towards Gareth's innocence. Past crimes couldn't be mentioned in a current trial, she thought, so it wouldn't affect this outcome. But if he was found not guilty... He didn't kill those girls, but he did bury them. On the other hand, she knew who did kill them. Even if he denied it, she still knew. Which made her dangerous.

The swimming pool shimmered and sparkled in the lights. She could see Thomas' hands reaching for her through the shadows. The first party he had attended. She had only been with the Candy Girls for six months, had already met Matthew, Mac, and Eddie early on at a small dinner gathering – just a few girls and a handful of men.

'Lexy, come and play.' Thomas Blake's voice was very smooth, hypnotic, and the water rippled around his naked torso. He was quite a way from the steps, down near the deeper end of the pool.

'I'm not sure... I don't really like swimming.' She could hear her voice sounding weak and rather pathetic. 'I shouldn't really leave everyone. Matthew might not want me to...' It was true, she wasn't a fan of swimming, and water had always frightened her.

'I said come and play. It's my party too, baby.' His voice was colder, but the smile remained serene.

She shivered as she entered the water in her red lacy bikini, despite the fact it was warm in the pool, the ripples on the surface almost a little oily in the half darkness. 'I thought there were other girls coming down here too?'

Matthew and Mac had told her to make sure every girl brought a couple of outfits to each party, including swimwear.

When she and Lana had been getting ready it had seemed so decadent to be attending a pool party in a mansion. Not to mention they were being paid four figures each just for attending.

Thomas shrugged. 'Changed their minds. Gone back to the party I think.'

'But...' Lexy felt her skin prickle with fear, but she still wasn't sure why. He was just a client, she told herself, and Matthew's friend. Matthew never put his girls in danger. She could swim, flirt with Thomas, and then return to the party upstairs. But being alone in the dimly lit pool was triggering panic. The basement room seemed too low and the walls too close.

'Come and swim.' His expression changed, amusement flashing in his eyes, 'Or can't you swim, baby? Sorry, I should have checked.' With a quick, smooth movement, Thomas glided through the water, and took Lexy in his arms before she could escape, 'There. You're safe with me... See? We can go a little deeper and I promise I won't let you go.'

'She can't swim.' Another voice cut through Lexy's panic, firm and calm. She could hear footsteps on the marble tiles around the pool.

Her heart racing, she froze as she felt the anger in Thomas's body, the way his hands tightened cruelly on her arms.

'Mind your own business, Mac. Go and get yourself a drink and maybe relax for once.' Thomas's voice was sharp with annoyance.

The calm voice came again, 'Lexy, Matthew needs you upstairs please.'

Mac had come to save her. Lexy twisted out of the arms that held her like steel and towards the shadowy figure who stood, legs braced, arms crossed at the edge of the pool.

'Lexy, you are the hostess. You don't have time to play tonight.' Mac stood tall and broad-shouldered at the edge of the pool, his face in darkness as the shadows played maliciously across the marble floor and walls.

There was a moment of tension, Thomas still too close, before she could flounder gratefully towards the steps, stagger towards safety.

'Send someone else down.' The man in the pool spoke easily now, but Lexy picked up the underlying anger. He was used to commanding people, used to giving the orders and taking what he wanted.

'Go and find another girl yourself, Thomas.' The careless annoyance in his voice might have been nothing, but Lexy was now close enough to see Mac's expression and she read distrust, disdain in his grey eyes, etched across his square face.

He hustled her away, and when they were at the bottom of the stairs leading back up to the party rooms, he threw a towel around her shoulders. 'Birdie, don't ever go down to the pool with him. Do you hear me? Not ever.'

'How did you know I don't like swimming pools?'

'It doesn't matter. Get upstairs and away from him.'

Shocked and bewildered by his reaction, she had merely nodded, shaking with cold and the underlying menace of the situation.

'Now get changed and go back upstairs. Eddie's just arrived with a couple of friends he needs to impress.' His grey eyes held hers. 'In future, if Thomas wants to talk to you, it's only ever in a crowded room. Do you get what I'm saying?'

Years later, she wondered if all three of Thomas's friends already knew, if there might be others.

Perhaps it wasn't just the final party that had produced the bodies.

NINETEEN

Harlan had picked up the kids and was cooking dinner when she arrived home from court, earlier than she had thought, which was a bonus. He liked to cook, they both did, and shared a love of the best foodie spots in the city. But tonight, there was just something a bit too brash and overdone about his actions. She watched him carefully, trying to seem normal herself. He was too cheerful, too ready to ask about her day, while he added oil, spices, clanked utensils, and turned the TV on low to see the news.

'Oh, and Alexandra, I said I'd pop out for a drink with Bailey tonight. Do you mind?' He added when they had caught up with each other's days, 'I only did four hours on the paperwork in the end.'

'Of course not.' She stuck a finger into the sauce and sucked it, thinking that was a little weird. Normally, overtime was covering either a whole shift or a few hours when they were stretched for additional staff. 'How's his love life going? Is it all sorted out?'

'What?' He turned, looked at her blankly, a jar of sauce in one hand, and half an onion in the other.

'His love life. You said he had some woman trouble yester-day,' she reminded him. Should she be brave tonight and ask him what the hell was going on?

'Oh, yes of course. Sorry, I've got my mind on this sauce. What do you think?' He dipped a spoon into a smaller saucepan and offered her another taste. 'I was going to add a bit more tarragon but I'm not sure now.'

'It's lovely.' She could feel her resolve slipping, so she fudged it. 'Harlan, if there was something wrong you would tell me, wouldn't you?'

He switched off the hob and moved towards her, pulling her into a hug. She could feel the hammering of his heart, feel the kiss he dropped into her hair, before he pulled away. 'I... It's just work stuff. You know how hard it can be sometimes and we had this really awful job last week with three kids who had clearly been abused. Social services are so stretched it might take months to sort out.' His eyes clouded. 'It's okay and we've been offered support, but you know sometimes you can't unsee these things. And it'll take forever to get foster homes sorted. They're all in emergency care now.'

'I know,' she said softly, as he turned away. She hadn't meant to say it out loud, and she spoke quickly to cover her mistake. 'Do whatever you need to, but do talk to me as well. Not about the case, just keep me in the loop, okay? Otherwise, I worry about you.'

For a split second he grinned at her, the old Harlan, before presenting the plates with a flourish. 'I promise, I will. I need to deal with it in my own way, but I won't ever leave you out of things. Now, dinner! Come on, kids, new recipe and it's pretty good if I say so myself.'

Alexandra knew she was good at pretending, but the thought that her husband might be playing the same game was weird. Like finding yourself in a parallel universe where nothing could be taken at face value.

Later, when she had read the kids stories, and tucked them in for the night, Sophie smiled sleepily at her. 'Mummy?'

'What is it, darling?' Alexandra, relaxed finally, and enjoying one of her favourite times with her children, gently stroked a lock of hair from her daughter's face.

'Mummy, who are the Candy Girls?'

The next morning, Alexandra tried unsuccessfully to keep her mind on her job, forcing herself to concentrate. She had barely slept, had been pacing the house, trying to calm the palpitations in her chest, checking on the children obsessively though she knew they were safe. Now her mind was still turning over what had happened, every word that had been uttered, trying to make sense of it.

Her daughter had said a man had spoken to her through the fence at breaktime. He had smiled, like a nice man, and had whispered through the bars.

'Did he ask you to tell me he spoke to you?' Alexandra had tried to keep her voice calm, even though terror knifed through her insides, and she found her eyes darting to the curtains, around the shadowed corners of her daughter's bedroom.

'Yes. He said to tell Mummy but not Daddy.' Sophie had smiled. 'He said I was very pretty and looked just like my mummy before she was a Candy Girl.'

'*Before* I was a Candy Girl?' *Niall?*

Sophie nodded firmly. 'I asked him who the Candy Girls were, and he said it was a secret, but you might tell me.' She didn't seem at all scared, just curious.

Alexandra breathed deeply. Whoever it was, he had been so close to her children, spoken to her daughter... It was unacceptable. She wouldn't let them ruin her life. Whatever was going on, the pressure they were trying to apply to her, it wasn't going to bloody work.

This morning, agonising over what to tell Harlan, she was saved because he had decided to bugger off for another early gym session, evidenced by a scribbled note on the kitchen table. She had hardly noticed him get up, so he must have been careful. This from the man who was guaranteed to fall over his own shoes and make more noise than the kids on the school run, when leaving for an early shift.

She would have to tell him, though; there was no escaping it now their children were involved. She felt shaky just thinking about it. It could be a sanitised version, not the full story. For some reason, she still hesitated to tear her life wide open, and hard on the heels of the fear came the horrible thought that she didn't trust her own husband. Didn't trust him to accept her past, to take her side and understand why she had made those decisions. This could all get very messy.

First, though, she needed to be sure her children were safe. Alexandra picked up her phone and called the school. The headmistress assured Alexandra she would keep a lookout for any strangers near the school grounds, apologised it hadn't been spotted, and asked if Alexandra wanted to make a police report.

Alexandra didn't. From Sophie's rather vague description, the man sounded like Niall, which seemed to prove that her mum had not been talking to ghosts. Could her brother have somehow come back from the dead, inveigled his way back into her life? Why? Why would he come back? He had known about the origami birds, and she remembered how rubbish he had been at making them. How was she going to get her head around the fact her brother was still alive?

Anger flashed through her again and there was a sharp crack as she broke the pencil she was holding. How dare he threaten her through her daughter? How dare he let her think he was dead, and then come back without the guts to approach her in person? Secret origami notes and talking to her mum. Why would anyone do that?

The fury cooled a little as she looked out of the window into the busy street. Her relationship with her brother had deteriorated during the last few months before the final party.

The Candy Girls wasn't for him, although he had liked picking up a few odd jobs at the parties: clearing up, bringing crates of drink and boxes of food into the houses. A delivery boy, an errand runner, and she could see how that must have hurt, how he wanted better for himself. He had hung on to Thomas's every word, and in turn Thomas had seemed to like him as much as he liked anyone who he considered beneath him. Niall had been useful, loyal.

'Why are you doing this?' Lexy asked. 'Why do you have to do illegal work as well as the other stuff?'

He braced his hands on the tiny kitchen table, leaning towards her, his face twisted in anger. 'It's alright for you. You've got a degree to finish, a career, and you can prance around in your little dresses letting those poor blokes think they've got a chance and rake in the cash.' Niall paused, his shoulder-length dark hair framing the sharp cheekbones, the angry, narrowed eyes.

'I've done what I needed to make a life for myself,' Lexy snapped, annoyed at his judgement. Hypocrite.

'So now, I'm doing what I need to do to make my own life. Shit, I don't want to be at the bottom of the ladder all the time; I want some of that money too.' His voice softened. 'I'm just saying, don't go all high-and-mighty on me. We're both ambitious, and we use what we've got. If it means illegal stuff, I'll do it. I don't have to work for just one person.'

She nodded then, turning to look out of the window. Seeing the dirty wall of the block of flats next door, breathing in the stench of bins. There was the usual group next door smoking weed again, and she could feel the smell sticking in her throat, sinking into her clothes, hung out on the broken plastic dryer.

The hot summer made their flat heat up to boiling point, and the stupid fan was broken again. It was Lana's turn to buy a new one, but she probably wouldn't. She'd just wait until Lexy couldn't stand the sweaty nights any longer and made the trip down the road to Primark. Or the charity shop.

Lost in the heat and the past, Alexandra blinked back to the present as a tall man wearing a purple jumper and pink tutu cycled past. She loved the irreverence of Brighton. Her anger at her brother was passing. It was more a question of why Niall seemed to have swapped sides, why he was threatening her... Or was he trying to warn her? The thought struck her suddenly as she picked up her phone again.

What if he was keeping away because he was trying to protect her? What if he knew exactly what was happening with Thomas and his stupid friends, and he was trying to tell her. The man in the van might be working for Thomas, but Niall... Her brother wouldn't threaten her. She was looking at this all wrong, she told herself, not seeing the bigger picture because of her fear.

The day in court passed in a blur, with Alexandra unable to stop staring at Gareth from under her lashes. Despite the threats, despite the apparent evidence that seemed to be piling up against him, she couldn't help but root for him. His team were fighting back, and for every damning statement they had a rational, innocent answer.

In the breaks, she read her book, ignored any chatter, and tried to stop her mind from racing. Now she had made the decision to fight back, she could see perhaps the game plan was larger, more extensive than she had imagined. She was following Thomas's career obsessively and knew that by the end of this week he would be announced as the leader of his political party. Then there was the election. And Thomas was very popular. Very, very likely to be running the country in a few short months. A burst of anger caught her by surprise. If only people knew what he had done, what he was doing right now...

When she arrived home, she had a couple of hours to spare before picking up the kids. Sophie had netball and Tom had chess club at school. She was lucky enough to be part of a parent carpool, and today she had no taxi duties, just her own kids to collect. Her new normal, which had not gone unnoticed by her friends, was to double check every arrangement. To keep her panic under control, she needed to know exactly where her children were at all times. For the first time she regretted not allowing them mobile phones until they were going to secondary school. She could have added a tracker app.

After a quick scan of emails and a phone call to the clinic, she was relieved to discover her business was functioning perfectly well without her. There would be the weekend to decide how to handle telling her husband.

She glanced at the time. She had an hour and a half to kill. Feeling braver, stronger, she decided it was time to visit the house. It was time to face the past.

Grabbing her coat, Alexandra stepped out into the fresh air. The salty seafront drizzle had stopped now, and the fog was rolling away, allowing brief flashes of sunlight to dance across the city. She walked fast, head down, hands in her pockets. Her mind was churning over everything that had happened, trying to make sense of it, put it in order.

After twenty minutes she turned into a tree-lined road, paused for a mere second to get her bearings. The house was in good repair now, transformed into five smart apartments. The elegant street with its wedding-cake-style buildings was considered one of the most sought-after areas in the city. Alexandra walked carefully up to number eighteen. The black and white tiles, the white entrance porch, and the topiary box hedges either side of the path were all in good order.

Unsure, she stood for moment, hand poised to ring the bell, but which buzzer to press? She half intended to look from outside, to anchor her thoughts. Certainly, she had no plans to look inside, until a resident, manoeuvring a double buggy, two shopping bags, and holding tightly to a toddler with her other hand, turned up the entrance path.

Having assisted the slightly frazzled, unsuspecting mum, smiled at the cute kids, Alexandra found herself alone in the entrance hall, breathing in the smell of disinfectant and furniture polish.

Did they use the basement? The house had been just one residence at the time of the parties. A luxurious extravagance, and a far cry from the everyday needs of most of Brighton's inhabitants. Now, the building, with its white-painted walls and clean floors, was only recognisable by the ornate cornicing and the familiar black and white tiling. The staircase was boxed in, still retaining what she presumed was the period structure, but dividing the once grand and spacious area into a more utilitarian space.

Whoever owned buildings like these it must be making a fortune. So, who owned this one? Was it Matthew? Gareth? She knew those two had owned a lot of properties. In fact, she was sure she recalled Thomas referring to Gareth's property portfolio. Where had that snippet of memory come from? And why had she never thought to search ownership of this property? The answer came back to her immediately as she stood in the white, peaceful space: because she had been afraid, ashamed.

Guilty.

TWENTY

There was a door to her left, wide open and showing a flight of steps. She judged the distance from the main staircase, now walled in, with a fat yellow cord fixed either side for residents to hold on to. If memory served her correctly, the basement must be down here.

Without giving herself time to think, she made her way down the back stairs, shivering at the icy breeze that hit her as she stepped gingerly downwards. The steps were wide, easy to navigate, and when she finally stood at the bottom, and her memories came roaring back, she was boiling hot, as though she had a fever.

The first room held recycling containers, waste disposal, and cleaning equipment. It was neat and tidy, and an automatic overhead light flicked on as she peered through the wide doorway.

Another room held piles of furniture, shrouded in dust sheets. More steps down and she reached the lowest floor. She found her hands were sticky with sweat, her eyes darting into shadowed corners. Why hadn't they developed down here? A bolted door stood between her and what must be the pool area. No locks though?

She slid the bolts, hoping there was no alarm system either, snagging a fingernail as she did so and swearing softly in the gloom.

The door swung wide. The pool was still there, empty and abandoned, a concrete shell, with none of the marble tiling and blue silky opulence she remembered. At least nobody else could drown down here now, she thought.

Alexandra stepped carefully around the pool, three steps up in the far corner, and she came to the room where the graveyard lay. There was no door, just a smooth concrete floor, bare wiring, neatly taped, hanging from the ceiling, and a rusty cement mixer sitting in the corner. A few huge canvas bags of sand and gravel lined two of the walls. She took a breath of the musty air.

Above her, she imagined the floors of apartments, the noisy chatter of families, the laughter of date nights, the comings and goings of people who had no idea what crimes had been committed in this building. And this room lay untouched, a shrine to the girls who had been murdered, their bodies given their last resting place here. She pushed her hair back and frowned. They were *untouched*. That was it. Everything above ground had been cleared out, sanitised, the pool scoured clean. The guilty part of the building was safe from prying eyes. And if anyone did venture down here, there was no chance of them seeing anything incriminating, was there?

Almost unaware she was doing it, she bent down, brushing gentle fingers over the rough concrete floor. Under here were the graves. The other girls. And she was the one who got away. Or maybe they had set her free on purpose, knowing she was powerless; they could snare her at any time if they needed to.

She looked past him and saw the body in the room behind him. Long dark hair spread out on the boards, a towel barely covering her naked body. Mina. Her face was pale and her eyes open but unseeing. Bending over a second body, Thomas, his face wet with sweat, his eyes wild.

Unable to stop herself, Lexy started forward, recognising Bex's long red curls, her petite heart-shaped face, even as Thomas stepped back to throw a towel across her body. And along the side of the room, freshly disturbed earth and rubble. Two long trenches started to emerge.

'We have to get them buried!' Thomas whirled, glassy-eyed, grabbing a shovel. Amongst the building site debris, a cement mixer, huge canvas bags of sand and cement, tools and the choking smell of death and brick dust. A graveyard. A mortuary.

'Birdie.' Mac was at her side in two long strides. He cupped a hand under her chin, forcing her gaze to his. It was the second time he had ever touched her, and his grip was just as fierce as when he had rescued her from Thomas. 'Listen to me. Go back to the party. You were never down here; you never saw this. You got it? You will wind up dead unless you forget everything you've seen. You can't help them; you can't do anything so keep your mouth shut.' For a moment his voice faltered.

Trembling, she had been unable to move, standing like a deer in headlights as Niall came in carrying another girl.

Jess.

Oh god, Jess, with her golden hair falling wet and bedraggled, her head lolling. Unlike Mina and Bex, she was still wearing a bikini, but the top was half torn away from her wet skin. Thomas was in jogging bottoms, his hair and torso wet from the pool.

'What the fuck?' Matthew and Eddie appeared from upstairs and suddenly the room seemed very crowded. 'Niall says you need help... Jesus. What did you do?'

Thomas had stopped in his frantic activity, and the shock on his face, his roar of denial made Lexy shrink back in terror against the walls.

'What the hell happened?' Eddie shouted. He started towards

the heaped mound of rubble and mud. 'Are you burying them?'
He sounded incredulous.

His tone mirrored Matthew's cold fury as the taller man
swung around and addressed Thomas. 'Did you kill another
girl?'

'No! It was the drugs! Who got the pills tonight? They all
took the pills...' Thomas was struggling.

'They were all down in the pool!' Mac said furiously. 'I
pulled the first two out while you sat on the edge, you fucking
idiot.'

'Are you sure they're dead?' Matthew leant over to inspect
the girls.

'Of course I'm bloody sure. They're not breathing!'

'We could call an ambulance.' Lexy forced herself to speak,
and they all swung around to look at her. One live girl in a room
full of bodies. Surely this couldn't be happening to her. 'We
could... Thomas said... the drugs...'

The silence told her all she needed to know. A sudden, icy,
calculating silence.

Alexandra edged her way around the perimeter of the room,
studying the floor, biting her lip as she stepped carefully across
the area where she knew the bodies lay. No disturbance at all.
Except, something caught her eye, and a sob of surprise escaped
her as she realised what it was. Not a paper bird this time, but a
little bracelet made of pastel-coloured sweets. This corner had
been swept clean. In fact, as she turned back, shaking, she
noticed the area where she knew the three graves were (possibly
four if they had killed Lana) seemed to be cleaner than the rest
of the room. She wished she had a torch, then remembered her
phone and used the torch app.

A little bracelet of sweets to mark their graves. She bent
down in the gloom, the dust making her sneeze, which sounded
so loud she jumped in fright. The bracelet was so familiar even
before she picked it up. She ran her fingers over the sweets and

brought it to her nose, inhaling the faint scent of candy. Had Niall left these on the graves recently, knowing she would come back? The sweets weren't old, or they would have disintegrated or been eaten by vermin a long time ago. There was no dust on the rectangle of concrete that covered the three girls' bodies.

Bex, Mina, Jess. She had seen them dead. She knew they were here. She had been wrong that Niall was dead. Was it so impossible she was also wrong about Lana? Or was this part of whatever game Thomas and the others were playing? She stood for a moment longer in the silent sad room; its echoes of the past seemed to ring inside her head. Finally, she moved away, hesitated, slid the bracelet into her coat pocket, and made her way down the steps, past the silent shell of the swimming pool, and back up to the present.

Safely back home, Alexandra checked the time. Twenty minutes until she had to pick the kids up, and then there was the barbecue at Becca's house. She should be looking forward to time with friends, and the weather seemed to be clearing. The feeble sunshine had given way to actual blue skies and stronger rays of warmth touching her cheeks as she had walked home. She was relieved the clocks had changed, and the evenings were getting lighter. But she was exhausted, from the lack of sleep and the constant whirlpool of thoughts about the past. There was no escape.

The Candy Girls bracelet she had collected from the house lay on the table, coiled like a pretty, pastel snake on the polished oak. A love letter from her past, or a warning for the future? She needed to get ready, needed to be prepared for the onslaught of excited small children, had a million things to do including putting another load of washing in the machine, and setting the timer, sweeping the kitchen floor, shoving various items into the dishwasher, but she did none of these and simply sat, tipping the bracelet from one palm to the other, thinking and thinking.

Finally, she ran upstairs and slipped it into her jewellery case, cupping it briefly in her hand, feeling the lightness of the sweets, the cheapness. Remembering. Lana had also been wearing her bracelet at the final party. Had the other girls? She couldn't remember seeing anything on their wrists, but she had hardly been in a fit state for details.

As she ran back downstairs, grabbing her keys and purse, she glanced in the mirror. Tired grey eyes, frown lines at her nose and mouth, but her make-up was still in place, and her hair was okay.

A text message made her reach for her phone:

> Will pick kids up – on way over now. Hope
> court ok today. X

Puzzled, but relieved, she clicked on the family tracker and saw Harlan was driving away from Seahawk Estate. What the hell was he doing over there? She pinged him a text:

> Thanks – you been down the gym after work
> again?

No response, and she wished she could delete it. It sounded a bit accusatory. For a moment she stood in the light, bright hallway, undecided. No need to be early for the barbecue. She wasn't really in the mood for chatting, or a party. Now she had half an hour to kill... Almost before she knew what she was doing, she found herself at the kitchen table, opening her MacBook and searching for number eighteen, Acacia Avenue. The party house. A few historical references from blogs, blah, blah. Alexandra wasn't sure whether to be annoyed or reassured by the lack of hits on her search.

Gut instinct told her there was something here. Finally, as she flipped idly down the pages, there it was:

Number 18, Acacia Avenue. Planning permission granted for a basement conversion into three further apartments.

She read further, started pulling up other searches, her shaking fingers flying over the keyboard.

The property had been sold to a private company in 2001. Shit. A little bit more digging, and she found a reference to Gareth Sellers's property development company, Longside Ltd. She thought of Matthew's obviously inherited wealth, Eddie's legacy of acting and the theatre, and Thomas's arrogant connections to royalty and titles. Mac had been different, she knew it, even without her earlier research. Again, the sympathy for a man who had helped cover up murder. But wasn't that exactly what she had done herself?

Alexandra glanced at her watch. Five minutes and then she really had to get out of the house. She glanced back at the screen. The property had been sold again, now converted into flats, four years later, to another company, this one registered overseas. It appeared on various rental sites after that. Not many, because it was a sought-after area. Expensive. If you could afford to be a tenant in that part of town you would want to hang on to your slice of property, even if it was only rented. Nobody had wanted to convert the basement. Until now.

She noted that the two neighbouring properties, numbers seventeen and nineteen (also owned by Gareth's company), had been sold within a year of each other, with the first one changing ownership less than six months after the party. Two different large and anonymous investment companies now owned both properties.

Her phone pinged with a message, and she jumped, cursing herself. It was just a text message from Harlan:

> Had to drop Bailey off too. Me and kids on way to Becca's. See you there? X

She bit her lip, feeling her normally busy but settled world tilt further on its axis. This was the reason for the chaos. The graves were about to be disturbed, just as Thomas was about to become prime minister (if the current polls were to be believed). Gareth had been set up to take the fall, and she had been brought in as, as what? Another scapegoat possibly? It seemed obvious now she considered everything logically.

They had everything to lose.

TWENTY-ONE

My back aches and I swing my arms, walking quickly from the canteen back towards the games room.

Someone shouts and I turn. I've forgotten to pick up my tray, deliver it to the wash-up chute, where other prisoners will receive it and scrub the dirty plates.

I correct my mistake and go and stand alone, leaning against the wall, taking in the scene. A few crazy games going on, the usual cliques forming and breaking and reforming again. Prison, apart from having my freedom taken from my life, isn't so different to working in the world of crime.

The ache in my back has moved from my shoulder blades, around to my left arm, and I do the swinging thing again, irritably. It won't do me any good to show a weakness in here. It's hell getting old, and I'm only forty-two. Not even properly old yet. I work out, eat well, drink a bit, and I've cut down on smoking. I abused my own body when I was younger, and those internal scars make themselves known during the long days and nights in here. But my hair is threaded with grey, and my soul feels over a hundred years old.

I feel weaker, because my own control over my life has been taken away, my own clothes and the routines of normal living. It makes me think of people shut away in care homes, not always older people, but living the same way I am forced to in prison. Freedom is so sweet I can almost taste it, yet when I was enjoying it, I didn't give it a second thought. It was my right to walk down this street or that street, to choose my investments, to choose interesting women to date.

I think I'm beginning to understand, though. This is about what happened back then, not about the men we are now. If someone was going to be the fall guy, it was going to be me. My worry isn't for me, though.

I like to think I saved Lexy twenty years ago, because it had happened before. A party at university, everyone high on drugs, drunk, skinny-dipping in the lake in the darkness. The three of us saw Thomas with the girl that night. They were in the water, and he drowned her.

Later, when blue flashing lights and panic slashed through our drunken haze, Thomas was frantic, gabbling away how he hadn't meant it, hadn't known she was drowning. His whole life could have been ruined at that moment. We kept his secret, accepted that first girl's death as an accident, because it was easier that way. And because by then he had coaxed us all into sharing our secrets, secrets we shouldn't have bloody told anyone.

Eddie, Matthew, and I all have shadows to hide, and these men who were my friends are not people who think twice about breaking promises, about taking lives.

I should know, because I am one of them and I've taken lives too. Now I must wait for the verdict, for a verdict on a murder I did not commit. I bet Thomas is waiting too, probably pissing himself laughing, because he'll think it's a sure thing.

Guilty or not guilty?

TWENTY-TWO

The high, barred gate slid smoothly open. Becca lived in one of the stunning new-builds a few miles along the coast. The development looked more like Miami than Brighton, but Alexandra could still admire the stylish white house set close to the sea. It suited her glamorous friend perfectly – Becca was a polished businesswoman with four children, who still found time to bake her own banana bread and go to the gym every day. In Alexandra's eyes, she was Superwoman.

'Hi, darling, I thought you might have got lost.' Becca, all bright white teeth and shiny spirals of auburn hair, was waiting behind the gate, ready to pull her into a scented embrace. Her pink silk dress caught against her curves in the sea breeze. She looked amazing, and Alexandra smiled at her, forgetting her worries for a brief second.

'Sorry I'm late, I was just trying to find somewhere to park.'

'I would have said come in here, but with the grandparents and Johan's cousins we're packed a bit tightly.'

'Did Harlan and the kids get here?'

'Yes, all present and correct.' Becca grinned, and rolled her eyes. 'The boys have headed for the barbecue and the kids have dived onto the bouncy castle with my lot.'

'Good thing it didn't rain,' Alexandra said, as they began to walk around the side of the house, towards the excited shouts and smell of charcoal smoke. The sky overhead remained a perfect pale blue, although the sun was starting to sink lower over the aquamarine sea. Funny how, in the right light, the water could look such a beautiful blue.

'It is a heavenly evening,' Becca said, 'but I have a marquee and for plan B I was just going to get the caterers to lay everything out in the kitchen.'

Alexandra smiled affectionately. 'Of course you had a plan B. I have never known a woman more organised than you.' She ducked to avoid the rows of twinkling fairy lights that had been hung around the courtyard garden and sparkled in the ornamental trees and shrubs. 'But even so, do you need a hand with anything?' She always felt a bit awkward making small talk, and tonight she really was not going to be able to gossip with Becca's set about nothing. And Clara would be arriving. She needed to stop herself asking her friends for help and work out what the hell she was going to do. Because it was never going to stop at Gareth's trial, and if he was found innocent, would anyone know how she, as just one juror, had voted? She was now convinced that the clock was ticking on her usefulness, and they had another plan for her. Tormenting her, encouraging her to help send Gareth to prison for a crime he didn't commit was only ever going to be part of it. She became aware her friend was still speaking.

Becca was answering her question, apparently not noticing anything was wrong. '... And could you be a love and man the bar while I sign off the catering? I've got someone coming later to make cocktails, but I'd rather it wasn't a free-for-all in the meantime. People can make such a mess when they pour their own drinks.'

'Sure.' She breathed a sigh of relief and even managed to feel a wry twinge of amusement at being assigned bar duties. 'Let me say hallo to Harlan and the kids, and then I'll sort some drinks.'

'Thanks, darling!'

Alexandra made her way off across to the bar, wondering if her outfit choice of soft cotton trousers and a brown silk shirt maybe wasn't quite right for Becca's party. There were so many women in designer outfits, even though it was supposed to be a relaxed evening. The garden was perfect for parties and easily accommodated the six or seven adults and numerous kids already swarming over the play area. There was decking, slate paving, a hot tub, and an indoor/outdoor area where Johan was currently making a big fuss of waving tongs and burgers around. Harlan was next to him, busily slathering sauce on trays of chicken.

'Hi, Alex!' He kissed his wife, and she gave him a hug, leaning into his strength and comforting solidarity for just a moment too long.

Seeing him raise his eyebrows in a silent question, she hastily said, 'Thanks for picking up the kids. I was exhausted after court.'

Johan, Becca's genial husband, a giant of a man with a mane of blonde hair and merry hazel eyes, turned to her. 'Has that bloke been found guilty yet? Harlan told me you were part of the jury. Seems like an open and shut case?'

Alexandra mentally kicked herself for referencing court, but summoned her social skills with an effort and winked at him. 'You know I can't say a word. The rules are very clear and they don't involve gossiping about the case.' Johan was a former rugby player, now sports correspondent, and an adorable gossip. 'I said I'd just look after the bar until Becca's cocktail man arrives,' she told her husband. 'Catch up in a bit?'

He nodded, and returned to chef duties, but she couldn't

help noticing his eyes were heavily shadowed again, and he looked exhausted. Not just the usual tiredness from a run of night shifts, but something deeper, something more concerning. The thought slid through her mind again: had they got to Harlan, and was he afraid to tell her?

The kids, not remotely overawed by the luxurious surroundings, bounced up to their mother, and she smothered them in hugs and kisses, participated in a bit of chit-chat about their day, before they ran off again, in search of Rosie-May and Kayleigh-June, Becca and Johan's twins.

Alexandra walked down the garden to the bar, which of course was not just a table of bottles and glasses, but a proper little pop-up wooden bar. The last of the evening rays were warm on her face, but she shivered as she started arranging the drinks, stacking glasses, pouring iced juices for non-drinkers and the kids. Her position gave her a prime view of the party, and part of her took in the huge unicorn-shaped inflatable, the glitter station, the mani-pedi station, the sweet cart, and the flower wall stuffed with fake pink and cream roses. Another part of her was lost in the past.

Standing at the bar gave her a perfect vantage point for watching the room, Lexy thought. Her off-the-shoulder vintage mini dress might have come from a charity shop, but she knew she stood out amongst the other girls. Less glamorous but also more approachable. She had tried not to be offended when Matthew had pointed this out at first, but she was becoming more comfortable in her own skin, more confident in her ability to make huge amounts of money.

'You look lovely tonight.'

It was Mac, leaning on the side of the bar, with Eddie. Mac looked admiring; Eddie was leering at her cleavage as usual. His dirty-blonde hair flopped messily across his broad fake-tanned face. A contrast to Mac's smart-casual appearance.

Lexy smiled at everyone, chit-chatted about nothing. Nobody expected her to have opinions, ambitions. She could have been thrown back a few hundred years at these parties. The Candy Girls were strictly ornamental. In her purse was the roll of notes Matthew had slipped her with his usual wink. She wouldn't tell Lana how much there was because she had been a bit jealous about the hostess job. Until Lexy had told her Matthew thought she would be better off organising than dating, which wasn't strictly true, but kept the peace.

Thomas had arrived late and pushed his way over to her. 'Lexy, you look pretty.' He held out his hand for a glass. 'Nice crowd tonight. Anyone I haven't met before?'

She pointed towards a couple of newer girls, trying to smile as his cold gaze swiftly assessed them. Something about Thomas gave her the creeps. There was no genuine warmth in his dark, assessing eyes, and as he took the glass she offered him, he slid the other hand onto her bare arm, closing his fingers, trapping her for a moment.

She could hardly be rude and pull her arm away. Instead, she stood, smiling uneasily, noting that he appeared to enjoy her unease. Before he could say anything else, Lana appeared at his side, all big blue eyes and kittenish expression under her tousled mane.

'Thomas! Are you coming to play with me?'

Lexy knew for a fact that her flatmate was highly intelligent, and outside of the Candy Girls was a whirlwind of blonde craziness, and was a bit of a tech geek. Their Xbox gaming matches always led to Lana being declared a winner, and she was often found sitting on their tiny, battered sofa, cross-legged, huge glasses over her freckled tip-tilted nose, immersed in some coding, or, more likely, hacking.

Thomas turned to Lana, removing his fingers from Lexy's arm. 'Of course, sweetheart. Find me a couple of other girls, your pick, and we'll go and watch a film next door.' He winked at Lexy and strolled off with Lana on his arm.

Alexandra poured herself another glass of rosé and sipped it carefully. Her memories were so close to the surface, so raw and immediate. All the little conversations, the happenings, were back in her mind. It seemed like the past was flooding the present, as she stood behind the bar, pouring drinks. Another lifetime.

Automatically she smiled at a few people she knew, and finally, with relief, handed over to the professional mixologist, who was going to prepare cocktails.

She took her own glass and stood for a long moment under a rose pergola, gathering herself. All around her, kids screamed and laughed, and the smell of sweets and early roses was overwhelming. Her heart was beating hard, and she tried to control her breathing. Sipping her drink, trying to look at ease, she made a huge effort to push her worries away. But with each passing day, this thing seemed to be getting bigger, more threatening.

Harlan made his way over, having finally relinquished barbecue duties, with Becca laughing beside him. Alexandra opened her mouth to speak, and then shut it again, her fingers clasped so tightly on the stem of her glass, she was sure it would shatter. Another man was following her husband and her friend. He was slim, wiry, with sharp features, and a thin-lipped smile. She knew his face as well as she knew her own palms, and felt the garden begin to spin.

Becca appeared to notice nothing. 'Alexandra, darling. Thank you so much for doing the drinks earlier. You are the absolute best! Now I want you to meet Niall. He's just moved in next door, and he's relocating from Jersey. His wife and kids are coming to join him in a couple of months.' Becca was all smiles; flirting came as naturally to her as breathing. To those who didn't know her, she was often pinned as just a social butterfly, but to those who did, she was a very genuine person. In that respect she was very similar to Lana.

Alexandra slid a hand behind her and held on tightly to the pergola. The fake flower petals, carefully blended with the real roses woven around the wood, were coarse and unnatural in her hands. Her whole body seemed to be still, breathing stopped, even her heart seemed to miss a couple of beats.

'Alex? Are you alright?' Harlan asked, putting a hand over to touch her arm. His fingers felt warm on her chilled flesh. 'You're freezing! Are you okay?'

'Sorry, just a bit dizzy. I really should have stopped for breakfast this morning instead of just grabbing a coffee!' she managed. How was he here? It was as though her thoughts had conjured him from the past. He did not belong in this sophisticated garden, standing between her husband and her friend. 'Nice to meet you, Niall.'

She couldn't finish her sentence, and she tried with all her heart. *He was here.* Her brother was standing in front of her, smiling the casual smile of a new acquaintance. It was like he didn't know who she was.

TWENTY-THREE

Harlan, who knew she always had something for breakfast, even if it was just a quick slice of toast, was frowning at her, his eyes scanning her face. 'Maybe you're coming down with a bug or something. Do you want to sit down for a bit?'

'Oh Alexandra, you silly thing, let me get you some food.' Before she could stop her, Becca had raced over to the barbecue area, long auburn hair flying out behind her, and was loading a plate with delicious little snacks, topping it all with a hot dog. 'Here you are,' she called, returning at top speed, dress floating in the breeze. 'Sit down and fill your boots, darling. I was just going to show the boys the koi carp pond by the garage. It's Johan's new toy. You just stay here and relax.'

The men left, trailing behind their hostess, clearly for very different reasons glancing back to Alexandra, where she sat silently, her plate in front of her, frozen in time. Her brain refused to work. Maybe it wasn't her brother? Was that even possible? Maybe she was dreaming the whole thing and would wake up and find it had just been a crazy nightmare.

Or maybe he hadn't been joking all those years ago when he said he was going to keep an eye on her. The smell of burgers and chicken wings grilling was making her feel sick. She pushed the plate away, stood up, and made her way over to the elegant summerhouse. It was smothered in wisteria, the purple flowers softening the grey painted walls. The leaves weren't unfurled yet, and she stood, smoothing a frond of the soft plant with shaking fingers.

Niall was here. Older, greyer somehow, but alive, with that same smirk, the same arrogance. And now with a wife and children? Jersey? Was that true or just a cover story? Could he have really been away making a success of himself? To turn up at Becca's party, and show no surprise, no concern for her, told her he was also playing a game. He was part of it. That was the only reason any of this could be happening. She glanced around her in a panic, half expecting to see Matthew, or Eddie, or even Thomas stroll across the garden in the twilight.

Instead, children darted around the garden, a small boy was crying in the sandpit, and two sausage dogs were eating a dropped sausage roll. Having checked both her children were in sight, she leant against the wooden wall, almost glad the shadows had lengthened into darkness. It felt safer, to be hiding in the shadows. The fear left an acid taste in her mouth. How could Niall be right at this moment admiring a very expensive fishpond with her husband? Christ, what might he say? She had been so sure she could get in the game, but now the rules had changed again, and she didn't know what to do. Tears were threatening, and she gulped them down.

The summerhouse was a solid affair, which Becca used as a kind of office when she felt she needed to get away from the chaos of family life. Alexandra ran her finger along the wood, cursed as a splinter slid under her nail. But the physical pain seemed to jolt her back into consciousness.

Niall's sudden appearance was shocking enough, but somehow, he was in her life, in the same place as her husband, her children. Moving in next door to Becca? Surely not... She pushed down the door handle and walked inside, collapsing onto a chair. She left the door open, but the party noise still lessened slightly.

From the safety of the summerhouse, she watched Sophie pulling Tom through the inflatable maze, until they appeared hand in hand through the unicorn's mouth and came down the slide. Sophie waved at a couple of her friends, but Tom was already off, running towards the swings. His cheeks were covered in glitter tattoos and as usual, her youngest looked like he was having the time of his life.

What to do about Niall? Whose side was he on? If it was Thomas's, she needed to tell him she would do what they wanted, she would vote the way he wanted and try and persuade the other jurors to do the same. It wasn't foolproof, was it? He would never know what she was doing in that area behind the courtroom. Unless they had someone else on the jury, unless someone else was watching her. What if he was on her side, though, protecting her the way he had when they were younger? An ally would be really useful just now.

The summerhouse felt far too warm. She tried to get a grip on herself. They were stuck here for at least two more hours. She couldn't do it. She would have to say she felt ill, make an excuse and leave. Harlan would bring the kids home later. Clara didn't seem to have arrived yet, and that was good, because her best friend would definitely know something was badly wrong. She had already taken to texting Alexandra in the evening, with a cheery *just checking in* message. Alexandra had forced herself to respond in the same tone, brushing off concerns with fake work worries, and the stress of jury duty. She could tell they both knew they were lying.

Having made her decision, she left the summerhouse, made herself walk purposefully across the garden; Becca had reappeared with Harlan and Niall in tow. They were headed for the barbecue, where Johan was alternately swigging beer and dishing up food.

In addition to his barbecue, there was a table of grazing platters arranged by the caterers. Becca reached up to peck her husband's cheek, while she waved a hand at the plates of salad and rolls. She was clearly enquiring about the status of the food. Becca liked everything to be perfect.

Harlan seemed to be looking around the garden for her. Alexandra waved briskly, hopefully conveying she was fine and then lost sight of him as a group of laughing teenagers walked past. Back in her view, he waved back, but now he was laughing at something Niall had said. Niall was passing him a bottle of beer from an ice bucket next to the food table. The fairy lights illuminated the sharp angles of Niall's face, danced off his expensive smart-casual trousers and jacket, his shiny shoes. He was the same and yet not the same.

He turned slightly and caught her eye, then, just as she had known he would, just as she was moving through the now crowded garden to tell Harlan her plan, he headed her way. 'Nice to see you again, Lexy. Your husband is great, a really nice bloke, and your kids are cute too. And your friends... well, they're charming.' He was smiling, eyes cool, standing a little too close. His voice was smooth, no trace of his Newcastle accent remaining.

She stared at him, palms sweaty, the music throbbing across the garden and the partygoers laughing at nothing and everything. It was all too much, too much pain to be dealing with right now. 'Did you send those birds? You're working for Thomas?'

The corners of his mouth lifted in a smile, 'You always were a clever girl, Lexy. Maybe they were just reminders of where your loyalties lie. Aren't you pleased to see me, then?'

'It's Alexandra. No. I thought you were dead.' Her voice broke a little. 'Why would you work for Thomas?'

'I didn't say I was. You did look like you'd seen a ghost when we were introduced, and I'm sorry I haven't been in touch before.' He smiled politely, as if it was nothing to him, as if she meant nothing.

'I'm going to do it. I'll say Gareth is guilty and then I want you to leave me alone.' She hissed, 'Don't ever come near me or my family again, Niall.' She found she was trembling with anger now. 'My daughter, my son, and my husband. They are off limits for you and the others. Do you understand? I don't know quite what's going on, but I will find out, and you just showed me whatever game is being played, you are firmly on the wrong side. I hope you've been very happy playing with the big boys, getting rich all these years, but don't you dare fuck with my family.'

'Becca seems nice,' he said, as though she hadn't spoken. 'She happy with her husband?' Someone turned the music up, and he leant closer to speak to her. Alexandra shrank away from the touch of his arm against hers.

'Yes. Extremely happy. Everyone was and is extremely happy and will continue being extremely happy when you piss off back to Jersey or wherever, leaving me to live the life I have worked so hard for.' Alexandra could feel a burning fury rising up in her. How dare he do this to her? She didn't deserve this. Fighting to keep her expression neutral, in case Harlan looked her way, she was speaking through gritted teeth.

For the first time Niall's expression changed, and she caught a flash of uncertainty in his brown eyes. 'Come off it, Lexy, this is work.' He glanced round, then back at her. 'There are things I need to tell you, things I need you to understand. We need to talk, but not here.'

She stared at him, 'Don't call me Lexy! And no, no I don't understand at all. And I can't believe you just turned up like this. You went to see Mum? You went to my daughter's *school*? What the hell, Niall?'

Niall shrugged, but she could see from his expression that she had needled him. 'We need to talk. I'll find you.' He moved closer as though to kiss her cheek, but instead, hidden amongst the partygoers, he slipped a piece of paper into her hand and firmly closed her fingers around it.

'Don't bother.' Shaken but keeping the note in her fist, she scowled at her brother.

As he moved away, her husband joined them, had a bit of banter with Niall, and came to stand next to her, 'Are you really alright? What was that about not eating breakfast earlier?' His expression was concerned, and Alexandra felt her heart lurch for everything she had to tell him, for everything she was going to destroy.

'Nothing, I was just tired. The jury service and work, and you know...'

He looked at her for a long moment. 'You're not... pregnant again, are you?'

She bit back a hysterical laugh. 'No, I'm bloody not.'

'Sorry, just thought... feeling sick, you know...' He changed the subject quickly. Harlan hated talking about what he dubbed women's things. 'Niall seems a good bloke. Becca was quite taken with him.'

'She flirts with the seagulls on the beach given half a chance,' Alexandra said dismissively. 'Do you think we could make a move fairly soon? Or I don't mind taking the kids home if you want to talk with Johan.'

'No, it's alright, I'll catch up with him at a less stressful time. He's been struggling to feed twenty hungry kids for the last hour, and I expect he's looking forward to putting his feet up,' Harlan said, grinning.

As they walked slowly towards the tables, ducking under rose bunting and dodging hyperactive, screaming children, her husband said casually, 'Niall was quite interested in you actually. Asked about your business, all kinds of things. I don't think

Becca stands a chance.' He was teasing, a smile on his face, but a question in his eyes.

Screw Niall, Alexandra thought furiously. 'How funny.' She literally couldn't think of anything else to say, was so aware of the barrier of secrets between her and her husband, a dense wall of darkness she couldn't even begin to try and tear down. And there was something else at the edge of her own darkness; she was pretty sure the secrets were not all on her side.

Haunted by the last party, when Mac had rescued her from Thomas, she had slipped off her high heels and crept down barefoot to the pool. There was no noise apart from the splashes of water, the muffled thud of party music upstairs. In the shallow end she could see Thomas and a girl. For a crazy, panic-filled moment she wondered if she was wrong.

Mac wouldn't give any other reason as to why he had felt it necessary to save her at the previous party. He simply said he thought she looked afraid, and Thomas could be 'a bit rough with girls sometimes'. Nothing else.

But when Thomas turned up tonight, Lexy had kept a close eye on him. When he asked a girl to go down to the pool with him, she gave them a few moments and then pretended to be heading for the bathroom.

Instead, she took a sharp right and descended downwards towards the basement. Lexy peered round the doorway; she could see the entire pool, gleaming in the spotlights. The girl's body floated in the water, just underneath the surface, her short dark hair haloed round her head like a mermaid, her pale limbs marbled with light and shade in the spotlights. Thomas was smoking, propped up on the curving stone steps, lounging as though he was on a beach, ignoring the girl.

She was alive, and Lexy's heart raced with relief as the girl flipped over onto her front and began to swim back towards Thomas. For a long moment she had been so afraid her instincts were correct; now she found herself weak with relief, sagging against the doorway. It was nothing. She had been wrong. Mac had been wrong.

He chucked his cigarette away and took Mina in his arms. Their bodies intertwined as they drifted back into the water, towards the deep end and the shadows that played chase across the marble.

As Lexy moved silently back up to the party, her heart was still beating fast with relief, but the thought still nagged. Why had Mac been so afraid for her?

TWENTY-FOUR

The piece of paper Niall had given her lay nestled in her pocket. The kids took ages to get into bed, hyped up with sweet treats and excitement. Alexandra thought she'd be lucky to get to sleep by midnight herself. Finally, they settled, and apart from the odd giggle, upstairs was quiet. Exhausted, Alexandra went downstairs, sorted out the washing, chucked it in the dryer and make a cup of tea. She ran a hand through her hair, trying to ease a tension headache right above her eyes.

Harlan unexpectedly said he needed to pop out and meet Bailey, which left her alone with her thoughts. When she'd expressed surprise, he had given no explanation apart from the fact that Bailey needed him, was going through a tough time and he couldn't let him down.

Alexandra wondered if Harlan noticed that she didn't make a fuss, didn't get angry about his constant disappearing acts, as she would have done if she wasn't dealing with her own tangled secrets. But he seemed to be completely oblivious to her confusion and anxiety. Which seemed to indicate he was too busy leading his own double life. What could he be doing? Having an affair? The thought didn't concern her quite as much as it should have done, but she pushed this uneasy knowledge away.

She received another short text from Clara:

> I'm worried about you. You sure you ok?
> Missed u at Becca's x

Niall had been taking a big risk by showing up at the party. What if her daughter had recognised him as the man who had spoken to her at school? She supposed the chances would have been slim and he might have been able to laugh it off. After all, he had managed to get past Becca, who always seemed to be able to spot a fraud a mile off.

She desperately needed to discuss it with Harlan, before the school said something, and he realised the sheer number of secrets she was keeping from him. He would be furious, and quite rightly so, if he thought his daughter was in danger and she was keeping him in the dark.

But Niall? He hadn't been able to resist making an entrance, had he? But when they were kids, he had always protected her. She pulled the paper out of her pocket.

I'll find you. Will tell you everything.

Be careful. They are watching us.

A noise outside made Alexandra jump. She scrunched the paper in her hand, as though she had been caught out. A guilty secret. She stood up, nearly knocking her mug to the floor. There was a kind of scuffling noise in the back garden. Something being dragged?

Her heart rate sped up, and her breathing hurt her throat as she slipped back through the kitchen to the rear of the house. Slowly, she inched towards the sliding glass doors, which led to the garden, keeping to the side, peering out through the glass panes. The shadows laced darker and deepest dark blackness all along the patio area, the flower beds, down towards the trampoline. It wasn't a big garden, but it narrowed to a point, and she couldn't see right to the end.

She froze, focusing on the table, illuminated by the security lights. In the middle was a small white shape: an origami bird, bigger than the others, silvered and eerie in the moonlight. There was no breeze, and the paper bird stood firm, beak pointing directly at the house, watching her.

No other noise, no other sound. Alexandra moved her phone into her hand, ready to call for help, mindful of her two sleeping children upstairs.

Was it safe to go into the garden? Biting her thumbnail, she considered. If it was Niall, and she was pretty sure it was, he wanted to talk to her. Could she use this to her advantage? She inched the back door open and stepped outside.

Cool night air touched her face and bare arms with gentle fingers. Silence in the garden. She moved towards the table, picked up the bird.

With all her senses focused on the object now in her hands, she was half expecting what happened next, but it was still a shock. The warmth of a body next to hers, the terror as a gloved hand slipped over her mouth. Before she could do more than lash out and try to take a breath to scream, a voice whispered in her ear, fond, amused, and familiar, 'Don't hit me, Birdie, or I might cry.'

She spun round, and his hands were on her arms, his face carrying that same familiar expression, fondness, world-weary, sarcastic, but always her brother. *'Niall!'*

Alexandra stared at him, emotion rising in her throat, tears springing into her eyes. Recovering very slightly, she snapped at him, 'You bastard. You let me think you were dead and then you pitch up at Becca's. Why? What are you really doing here? And what the hell is going on with the birds and Gareth Sellers, or should I call him Mac still?'

'Sorry if I scared you; it was the only way I could think of us being able to meet without anyone watching.' He seemed more like the Niall she had once known.

'Are you crazy? My kids are upstairs, and Harlan...'

'Has gone out. I watched him leave,' he finished for her. 'I'm sorry I couldn't tell you what was going on at the party, but I needed to keep up a front. You never know who's watching.'

She stared at him through narrowed eyes. 'What the hell? You sound like a bad spy movie. Who is watching? And why did you send me the birds? You broke into my home, Niall!'

He laid a hand on her arm again, gentle this time. 'Wait, what do you mean?'

'The birds.' She took him to the window and pointed to the origami figure on the garden table. 'That was our thing. Yours, mine, Mac's and Lana's.' Hope rose as she turned to him. 'Niall, you need to tell me what happened after I left that night; it's been driving me crazy. And why did you go and see Mum? And why are you pretending not to know me?'

His eyes were fixed on her face, but unseeing, and he was frowning. 'Let's sit down.'

Alexandra led him back inside, into the kitchen, praying neither of the children would wake up and come downstairs. How would she explain Niall's presence? Bubbles of hysteria seemed to be floating around her chest. She was also very aware of how easy it had always been for Niall to switch character, to be the kind and caring brother, and next second the cold-eyed criminal with life and death alternatives.

'Listen to me, really carefully, because we are all in trouble.' He took a breath. 'I'm sorry I had to spring it on you at the party, but like I say, I've been careful, because they watch everything. The only way to see you is by pretending I'm still doing what I've been told.'

Unable to keep still, Alexandra made them both a mug of tea, and sank down onto the chair opposite. 'It has to do with Mac, doesn't it? I knew it was him as soon as I saw him in the courtroom. Mac... Gareth Sellers.' Her whole body was shaking and she dug her nails hard into the palm of her right hand to steady herself.

'Lexy... Sorry, *Alexandra*, you must know Thomas is almost certainly going to be our new prime minister.'

She sat opposite him, hands wrapped around her mug to stop them shaking. 'Short of a political disaster for his party, I had gathered that, yes.'

'They are predicting a landslide victory in the polls,' Niall said, almost smugly. 'But someone is blackmailing him, threatening to expose what happened at the party, and to link that back to another girl dying.'

'Another girl? What do you mean?'

Niall shrugged dismissively. 'A long time before the Candy Girls. The point is, he hasn't been able to find out who is behind this. All the threats have come via email or messages from burner phones. Remember there are very few people who know what really happened at the last party, and even fewer who know Thomas's history.'

She considered. 'Eddie, Matthew, or Mac then?' Realisation hit her. 'Or he thinks it might be me?'

'Is it?'

'For fuck's sake.' Alexandra sipped tea, very slowly, her heart still thumping painfully fast in her chest. 'It's the planning permission, isn't it? That's part of the blackmail?'

Niall leant back in his chair, comfortable in his surroundings, the confident elder brother once more. 'Correct. Because the house has been sold and planning permission granted for a basement refurbishment. Three extra rooms, with underfloor heating.'

'And whoever digs up the floor will find the bodies?' She had been bang on in her detective work.

'Right again.'

There was silence for a moment, while she tried to put the pieces together in her head, failed totally, and looked back at him. 'I didn't know... I didn't realise what was happening. I saw it...' She knew she was lying to herself, remembered Mac's hasty words as she came down the steps on that last night, and saw him burying the bodies, shouting at Thomas, who was standing there with a towel around his waist, bare feet leaving wet prints in the dust.

When Niall came up from the pool holding Jess in his arms, her limp body and fall of wet hair told its own story. Another victim.

Matthew was chain-smoking furiously, snapping out orders nobody was listening to. Thomas was yelling at all of them, threatening them. But as she cowered, disbelieving in the doorway, Mac had met her eyes again. Chucking the shovel to Niall, who had placed Jess tenderly down on the floor, he moved swiftly amongst the chaos to the door. His hands were cruelly tight on her bare flesh as he pushed her away, back up a level, and then towards the door that led to the courtyard.

'You haven't explained why you never got in touch, and why you're working for Thomas. Why should he trust you? He knows you were at the party, that *you* had the knowledge, and he must know you're my brother. We never kept it a secret.'

He shrugged. 'He offered me a lot of money, and he continues to pay me a lot of money as part of his staff.'

'It never occurred to *you* to blackmail him?' It seemed obvious to Alexandra that her brother would have considered it.

He looked hurt. 'No. Okay, I could see how valuable his secrets might be to someone, but he's a winner and the higher his star rises, the higher mine does too. He has a very small, private staff, who he trusts completely, and he made it clear if anyone screws up, he'll make sure we regret it, not him.'

'Nice. What really happened to Lana?' Alexandra asked now. She picked up her phone and checked the finder app for her husband. Annoyingly, it didn't connect. 'Hurry up and tell me everything, Niall, because my husband is going to be back soon, and he doesn't know about any of this.' She looked him right in the eye, immediately noting his slight recoil. 'Niall, for god's sake, tell me how to make this all go away.'

She ran up the steps leading to the French doors and into the main party area, slipping in past the long white curtains. The doors were slightly ajar in the heat, and the music had been turned down accordingly. Desperate to find Lana, she pushed people aside, hardly noticing that many of the partygoers, sensing something had gone badly wrong, were already leaving. Nobody wanted a scandal. Sweat was pouring off her body, and she ducked down behind the bar to grab her bag. Where the hell was Lana? Panic threatened to overwhelm her.

No phone signal as usual. A couple of the other girls approached her, questions in their eyes, and she told them firmly to get home and forget they had been here. Lana must have left already. She couldn't know what had happened, couldn't possibly know about Jess.

Moving to the window, she pulled a corner of one of the huge white blinds aside. Cars leaving. Large, expensive cars conveying powerful people. She moved back towards the French doors. Hardly anyone was left in the party rooms. Lexy slipped out into the hot summer night and ran away, taking her secrets with her.

TWENTY-FIVE

Niall rubbed a hand over his face, agony in his eyes. 'I didn't see Lana. She was dancing upstairs when I left the room. I saw Mac, pushing you away, and I was so scared for you, about what he might do. I was coming down to the basement to see where everyone had gone, and I found Jess on the stairs. She was wet like she'd been in the pool and lying sort of slumped. She wasn't breathing... Fuck, that was awful. The other girls, it was bad enough, but Jess, well, I really liked her. You know I did.' He gave a harsh laugh at the memory. 'She was Lana's sister. One of us, you know?'

Alexandra heard herself make a small whimpering sound, covered her mouth with her hand at the memory.

'Oh hell, it was fucking crazy.' His face clouded. 'I tried that mouth-to-mouth thing, before I picked her up, just to see, you know?'

Moved by his genuine horror at the situation, and by the wave of fresh pain that hit her, she laid a gentle hand over his. 'I get it. You tried, Niall. It wasn't your fault.' She knew he had had a bit of a crush on Jess.

He nodded. 'I know that really, but inside' – he pressed his free hand to his chest – 'I feel I could have done more.'

'Why didn't Thomas just kill you?' Alexandra wondered. 'You were another witness.'

'I guess because I was useful. I was scared, really fucking scared, and he offered me a fortune to say nothing. I've been working for him ever since. Shit, Alexandra, I wanted to get in touch so badly, but I couldn't. Your world isn't my world anymore, and I made my choice that night.' Niall looked up at her. 'He threatened to hurt you as well. I couldn't have that, so yeah, I took the easier option.'

'Do you really have a wife and kids?'

'No! I needed a cover story. But I do have a little place in Jersey.'

'And Mac? Did he kill his girlfriend or is he part of Thomas's current masterplan to make all this go away?' She wasn't sure what to think. 'I assume Thomas must think it's Mac who is blackmailing him?'

'He's the obvious choice, and Thomas says he has evidence.' The words seemed sincere. 'I never saw the bloke after that night.'

Alexandra studied her nails, glossy pink and beautifully shaped, felt the silk of her pyjama top as she moved her arm. Different worlds. He was right, but so much didn't add up. Did she trust Niall? Instinct told her no, but in her heart, he was still her brother, who had looked out for her, had followed her to Brighton, had been instrumental in letting her escape that night, whether he had meant to be or not. There were other secrets he hopefully didn't know about that night too, but he might suspect.

'What happened after you left that night?' In spite of herself, her temper was flaring, and the anger warmed her, gave her confidence. 'Are you sure you never saw Lana again?'

He shifted on his chair. 'We spent a lot of time abroad, on

his yacht, and he trusts me completely. I take care of things for him, but now he's moved on with his career we have less direct contact. As for Lana, no I didn't see her after that last party. She just seemed to vanish.' Niall's brown eyes, thickly fringed with dark lashes, widened in despair. 'My guess is she heard all the shit going on and went off with one of her clients.'

'She would never have left if she saw Jess down there.' This was something that had niggled Alexandra for years. 'If Lana didn't know what had happened to Jess, she would surely have raised hell and heaven to find her. But if she knew she was dead, I suppose that might be why she left... So now we've caught up, what is it that you want from me, Niall?' She was pleased at how calm and strong her voice sounded.

Niall hadn't mentioned the Candy Girls bracelet, and she waited to see if he would. A thought had occurred to her, so blindingly obvious it took her breath away. He was lying. Niall knew what happened to Lana. The big eyes and half-spread hands gesture she had seen so often in childhood hadn't changed now he was a man. He was lying.

Niall was talking again. 'If the police find the bodies, we're all screwed. Thomas reckons they might be able to identify us from DNA on the girls.'

'After all this time? And the girls were in the pool too...' Alexandra was doubtful, but she supposed it did make sense.

'Let's say it's a serious enough possibility and Thomas is at a serious enough stage in his career that even a breath of scandal could ruin him. He's not taking any chances.'

'How the...' Alexandra considered this for a moment. She was a huge Peter James fan and she had seen every episode of *Grace* on TV. 'As the girls were in the swimming pool, surely any DNA evidence would have been washed off. Although I guess anyone who touched the... the bodies,' she choked a little on the word, '...Anyone who touched the girls before they were buried, but after they came out of the pool, will have left DNA.'

Niall's eyes narrowed and his jaw clenched, as he ground out, 'It isn't just that possibility. Don't you see? Once the bodies are found there will be press, people will remember the parties, someone might come forward. Not about the girls because only Thomas, Eddie, Matthew, Mac, me, and you know the truth.'

'Lana? Tell me really, Niall, is Lana dead too? Because her sister died that night and I can't believe she wouldn't have tried to find out what happened, or at the very least got in contact with me again.'

'I told you I didn't see her. We cleared up and cleared out and that was it.' He frowned. 'I wonder if she saw something, or heard something that made her leave. You know, she was always talking about taking off with one of her dates... Lester? Max? She might have known she was in danger.' He shrugged, finished his tea, and set the mug down with a little chink.

Was he lying? She couldn't tell, and it bothered her. 'I should have been one of them,' she whispered. 'I went down to the pool with Thomas one night, but Mac came and took me away. I think he knew, or maybe he was just wary of what Thomas might do.' She could feel tears tracking her cheeks. 'I should have gone to the police that night.'

'You couldn't have known what was going to happen. It should have been the same as every other party,' Niall told her, an odd expression on his face. Part compassion, part something ugly and undefinable. 'Mac was part of it. He buried the bodies, and he knew what happened.'

'And now he might go to prison for murder because Thomas needs him out the way. They turned on him; Thomas turned on him. What if he tries to tell the truth? What if *Gareth* tells the police what happened at the party?'

'It's okay, it's all covered. Thomas has so much power, and as you probably know, Lexy, it's easy to fabricate evidence, to pay off police officers, and anyone else who needs to smooth the path you want to take.'

Alexandra knew it really wasn't okay, and as she sat in the kitchen of her lovely house, with her beautiful children asleep upstairs, she could hardly bear it. This was her worst nightmare, and it wasn't going away. 'And me? What's going to happen to me?'

There was stuff Niall didn't know, and, looking at her brother now, she could tell he really was lying this time. He had always been a good liar, looking into your eyes, paying attention to your nuances. She knew suddenly exactly why Niall was in her house, playing both sides, sussing out how she felt. It made perfect sense. She was the only real witness left, if Lana really was dead, and after the trial they would kill her too.

TWENTY-SIX

Niall was watching her with that curious mix of compassion and anger. He leant across the table and touched her cheek, gently, carefully, and frowned as she flinched away.

'We are not on the same side anymore, Niall,' she said deliberately, feeling her way. 'I appreciate you coming to tell me what's going on, but now tell me what I need to do to keep myself and my family safe, and I'll do it.'

'Just suppose Gareth is found guilty and I promise you, with the case built against him, he won't get off these charges. He'll go down and if anything comes out about the parties, any evidence from the Candy Girls will all be linked to him.' Niall sighed. 'If whoever got planning permission hadn't messaged Thomas, we wouldn't even be in this mess. They want money, of course.'

'You really must be stupid if you think it's that simple,' she told her brother. He seemed so fixated on persuading her to do what he wanted, he was missing the bigger picture. 'This isn't just down to me! You are expecting me to try and convince an entire jury... By the way, just so we're clear, did Matthew and Eddie agree to Mac taking the fall?'

He stared at her for a moment and then smiled. 'Honestly? No, they didn't. But who is king of the castle right now? Thomas.'

'But Mac isn't the one blackmailing him?'

'No.' A moment of uncertainty, before he shook his head. 'There is no proof it's him anyway.'

'Who then? And why can't Thomas bury this planning application if he's got so much power?'

'Do you think we didn't try? It was already granted, and work is starting next month.' He stood up to leave, glanced at his watch. 'Your husband will be home soon, and it might look a bit odd if he walks in on us having a cosy chat in the kitchen, don't you think?'

'You do know who's behind this, don't you? Tell me, Niall!' Alexandra could hear her voice rise in frustration.

He hesitated. 'I can't. But let's just say, this isn't just about tying up loose ends; this is about revenge.'

She looked at him closely, ignoring the painful grip on her arm, her mind spinning. Who? He was laughing at her now, his eyes full of affection, as though they were playing a game, as though they were children again. That was when she knew she was caught up in a far deadlier game than she could ever have imagined. As she opened her mouth to ask again, she heard the sound of a car door slamming shut outside.

She almost shoved Niall outside, letting him out the back gate, and ran back inside, a plan forming in her mind, just as Harlan entered the house.

She crossed the kitchen as he came in and kissed him. 'How's it going? Harlan, I know it's late, but I really need to talk to you about something...' Finally, she felt ready to tell him some of what had been happening. But he cut her off.

'Sorry, I'm exhausted. All this stuff with the case and Bailey is getting to me a bit. Is it important or can we talk another time?'

She looked at him, struggling with the agony of so many secrets, and chickened out again. She waited until he had gone upstairs and into the shower before throwing herself down into a chair and putting her face in her hands. She sat like that for a long moment. When she lifted her face she studied her mum's photo, her brave smile, took courage from it, and then picked up her phone. Like her, Becca was a night owl.

'Darling, how nice. Is everything alright? I was worried about you. You looked awful at the party, and Clara mentioned you hadn't been yourself recently.'

'I'm fine. Sorry, I really need to eat properly and maybe delegate at work more. You know what it's like! Um... Becca, do you remember ages ago you were talking about a journalist friend who exposed a human trafficking ring linked to that fashion designer? She did a documentary on it afterwards.'

'Of course. Kaye Headley. Very professional job, wasn't it?'

'I need an intro.' Alexandra bit her lip, pausing to arrange her thoughts. 'I've got something on a high-profile person, and... well, it's complicated but if I spill this, I need to know it is to someone who has the power to get the coverage and use it, but also someone who won't screw me over. And I can't go to the police, before you even ask.'

Bright, giggly, butterfly Becca was gone, and she was all sharp questions and business. Alexandra had caught glimpses of this other side, had known it existed, but faced with the full force of it, she could see exactly how Becca was a self-made millionaire, with a talent agency full of the brightest, hottest stars.

'You can trust Kaye with anything,' Becca was saying, 'and she'll talk you through how it works... Alex, can I ask you something?'

'Whatever you want, but I may not be able to answer.'

'Are you in danger?' Her friend's voice was concerned.

Alexandra considered this, before she answered with a sigh,

'Yes, I am, but the only way to stay safe just now is to keep running with these secrets until I can offload them.'

'If you need me, you can call me any time at all,' Becca told her gently. 'I don't care what you might have done, and I'm not saying you've done anything at all, but you're a good person, Alex. And you can trust Kaye.'

Touched, Alexandra smiled into the phone, her eyes wet, and the emotion, the gratitude clogging her throat. Her phone pinged and she glanced down.

'Contact details for Kaye,' Becca explained.

'Thank you. You are super-efficient as ever.'

'Of course. Keep me updated, darling. Goodnight.'

The next morning, she woke early, exhausted and gritty-eyed, thinking she heard the front door close softly. Surely not... but she turned and saw that Harlan wasn't lying next to her and there was no sound from the bathroom. Still wired, and adrenalized from Niall's visit, and her idea to break free, she bolted upright, heart thudding uncomfortably, limbs tensing.

She checked on the kids, who were still sleeping, though it was only a matter of time before they bounded out of bed for the day. Creeping down the stairs, she checked the kitchen, smiling with relief when she peeked in the doorway to see Harlan unwrapping a cheeky McDonald's sausage and egg McMuffin. He kept raving about his new health kick, the running and the gym sessions, making a fuss about clearing junk food out of the kitchen. She didn't see anything wrong with the odd indulgence, although usually it was after a night shift, but she didn't want to catch him out, so she stole quietly back upstairs, and sat hugging her knees on the bed.

Although she had talked to Niall for hours, the whole thing was a confused nightmare. None of it belonged in her well-ordered life, and when Niall had dropped the bombshell of what they wanted her to do, it was as though he didn't understand what she would be destroying. That she had already suspected this was the case didn't make it any easier to deal with. But then to Niall, family was Mum and her, never anyone else, so with his tunnel vision, he couldn't possibly comprehend how much she loved her family. His mood swings seemed to be worse than she remembered too. Perhaps he had some kind of personality disorder? Which made him even more dangerous, because he simply didn't seem to perceive things as she did.

And then there was Lana. Alexandra sat in bed and hugged her knees tighter, allowing her head to fall forward, short hair brushing her cheeks. Niall had mentioned the yachts. Lana also knew there were parties on a yacht where anything and anyone was game. She had liked the glamour, been up for experimenting, overlooking the fact she was being treated as less than something on a butcher's slab. In her mind Alexandra had always hoped her friend had made a new life, picturing her far away in an exotic destination. Anything but the alternative: that they had tidied up the other loose end.

She remembered Harlan's amusement over Bailey dating a girl who made her living from OnlyFans, his derision and patronising laugh. When she told him what she had done, who she had been, he would judge her, she knew it. Far from the successful businesswoman, mother, and wife, this was a darkness she wasn't sure they could overcome. But for her plan to work, she would need her husband.

Alexandra shivered as an imagined draught blew in from the window. Or was it someone walking over her grave? She could hear the laughter, see herself offering drinks, feel the press of hot bodies. Choices to make, and a whole life to lose if she made the wrong ones.

There were footsteps on the wooden floorboards, as Harlan came up the stairs, and smiled at her. 'I made you a coffee. Sorry

I nipped out early, but I needed to get a workout in before I go in for some overtime.'

'Thanks. I didn't know you were doing more overtime?' She smiled back, pretending everything was normal. She couldn't say anything, she just couldn't. Not yet. First, she would take action on the first step of her plan, then she would persuade Harlan this was the only possible way out of the mess. That was better, she decided, sipping her coffee, hearing the shower start running. She needed to keep control.

He put his arms around her, pulling her close as he spoke. 'I've got some news too.'

She could feel his heart thumping against hers, the warmth of his body creating the illusion of love and safety. But illusion was all this was and would be after she had lobbed her bomb into their happy family life. 'What's your news?'

He moved away, and she could see he was smiling, more relaxed than she had seen him for ages. 'I bought us a holiday home in Spain.'

Alexandra blinked, confused. 'You did what?'

'It's going to be great. We can start with holidays so the kids get used to it, then we can move out there and retire. I know how much you love Glow, but you could start a clinic over there in the sunshine. It's a lovely place, with a pool and only forty minutes from Alicante airport.'

Alexandra reeled, but tried to focus and reply calmly. 'Harlan, we don't have the money for a holiday home! And you wanted us to go on holiday to France last week. What's going on?' She was breathing fast, studying her husband's face, waiting for him to laugh and say it was all a joke. 'We can't just uproot our lives and disappear to Spain. What about the clinic?'

'I had a bit of a windfall.' He was still smiling, but there was a shadow behind his expression. 'Come on, Alex, most people would love to be told they'd just been bought a new home, a new life. I'm sorry I didn't have a chance to talk it over with you, but you've been so busy with work and the trial... and this was a great opportunity from a friend of a friend, so I took it. For us.'

'From Bailey?'

'What?'

'This great opportunity. Was it something to do with Bailey, or have you been meeting other friends so early and late in the morning?' She was getting angry now. 'What's really going on, Harlan?'

He stood up, annoyance and panic fleetingly crossing his face. 'You are so ungrateful. How can you not see this is an amazing opportunity?'

'I might have done if you gave me some warning, or even talked to me about it so we could make a decision together, like a normal couple,' she snapped at him. 'I repeat, what's going on and how did you suddenly get so much money?'

'Nothing is going on. And if I remember rightly you wanted to talk about something as well?'

She waved him away as she headed for the bathroom, panicked tears blinding her. Tears she did not want her husband to see. 'Nothing important. It can wait.'

TWENTY-SEVEN

As it was now Sunday, Alexandra stuck to her usual routine of taking Sophie to ballet at her dance school in Lancing, dropping Tom off at football, and going for a walk along the beach.

It was a cool day, with the sweet taste of spring in the wind-whipped air, and her hair blew around her face as she stamped across the pebbles, climbed a few breakwaters, and wound up opposite West Pier. She had managed to keep it together for the kids, trying to seem as normal as possible to them, even though their dad seemed to have lost his mind and her own secrets were threatening to destroy them all. This couldn't go on – she couldn't take it. She felt like she was walking on eggshells, with every raised voice, every sudden noise like a punch to the gut. It was time to call Kaye, Becca's journalist friend. It was the only glimmer of hope she could see. A way out. She couldn't go to the police.

Alexandra stood for a while staring at the tangled mass of metal, as strangely beautiful as it was ugly. The waves danced around it, grey and restless under a cloudy sky. It wouldn't be too long before the pier vanished altogether, and the sea reclaimed the structure.

Further down the beach, the other pier was busy with tourists, day-trippers, and locals. She could see people fishing from the end, the funfair had started up, and the kiosks were opening again after the winter. There was the familiar tang of fish and chips, candy floss, and cigarette smoke from the café behind her.

Resolved, she called Kaye and introduced herself.

'Becca said you might get in touch,' said the strong but sweet voice Alexandra remembered from the documentary.

'I have a story I need to tell. It concerns a politician, Thomas Blake,' Alexandra said after the initial chitchat was over. She leant against the ice-cream hut, eyes on the queuing traffic on the seafront by the pier as she explained. Not the full truth, just that she knew Thomas had killed at least three girls, that someone was blackmailing him, and that she was in danger.

When she had finished a quick summary, there was a silence at the other end of the phone and Alexandra supposed Kaye was taking notes. 'Wow. I assume you have solid evidence?'

'I have photos, videos, and I was a witness to a lot of what happened.'

'A lot, or all? I'm not trying to be picky, but this is explosive, and if you are coming to the media, I'm guessing there might be a good reason you are not reporting this to the police first. If I were to start doing some research with the possible intention of breaking the story, I would need to fact check every detail.'

'That's fine.' Alexandra considered. 'Would you need to mention me?'

'I need to think about this. As I'm sure you know, as a journalist I can't just throw accusations around, and I appreciate you coming to me, but we need to meet up. Do you have anyone else helping you with this?'

She sighed. 'No, and Gareth's trial ends tomorrow.'

'I am aware of that... I need to know everything, because

this is huge, and if I put it out there, and I can, I need to know it isn't going to come gunning for me afterwards.'

'I understand.' She stood there on the beach, motionless, phone to her ear, feeling as though she was standing on a ledge, poised to jump. Could she do this? Should she do this? 'Let me know when you're free.'

At a loss now, energy draining away, she walked all the way to Clara's. Her kids were safe and busy at clubs, and although she knew she couldn't tell her friend what was going on, she suddenly needed a dose of normality.

'I made flapjack yesterday, and it's not that sugar-free rubbish either.' Clara sat down on the sofa with her, mugs of tea on a tray, plate of treats arranged on the coffee table. She hadn't reacted to Alexandra turning up without warning, but now she looked at her and said firmly, 'Tell me what's wrong and don't bullshit me; I know there's something going on with you, Alex.'

Alexandra smiled, rolled her eyes. 'Typical I have a best friend who just happens to be able to read people's minds.'

Clara bit into a slice of flapjack, green eyes sparkling. 'Whatever. I'm a healer, not a clairvoyant, but whatever makes you happy.' The sparkle dimmed, intensified, and Alexandra felt absurdly like she was going to cry. She needed to spill something, something safe, or she was going to have some kind of breakdown. There were only so many secrets she could keep straight in her head.

'It's Harlan. He's been acting very weirdly.' She saw the question in Clara's face and shook her head. 'No, it's not like your unlovely, I don't think he's having an affair, although the thought has crossed my mind. And I would hate to ask him outright, because you know if he asked me, I'd be furious he didn't trust me.'

'That's a slightly twisted logic, but I get where you're coming from.'

Alexandra told her friend about the chats with Bailey, the

disappearing, the overtime, and finally the purchase of a holiday home.

'He bought you a house in Spain? What's it like?'

'Clara!'

'Sorry. I agree it's weird he just sprung it on you, but you've said before he had some inheritance and an allowance from his parents?'

'He did. Does. And he can be really impulsive. It's just...' Maybe she was projecting her own guilt onto Harlan, she thought. But no... 'Holidays are one thing, and he's been nagging me to go away to France, but to suddenly say he's bought another house, and let's move to Spain, is insane.'

Are you sure you aren't just stressed because of this jury service, work and Harlan's having a bad month too?' Clara asked hopefully. 'You two always seemed to be rock solid.'

'It's not that we aren't. It's just... He's hiding something.'

'So, he's a twat and should have asked you first, but that doesn't mean there's anything bad there. You said he has family money anyway, but he could have had a lottery win, or poker wins with his mates, and this is his idea of a nice surprise.'

'I don't know... Okay, if I'm honest, because of his weird behaviour, I'm worried the money might have come from something illegal.' There, she had said it, had dragged up another nightmare from her pool of shadows, dragged it out for examination right here in Clara's cosy living room, with the White Company wild mint candles and white lace curtains at the windows.

Clara's eyes went wide. 'But he's a police officer. He'd lose his job! Do you mean like illegal gambling or something?'

'I honestly don't know.'

'Does he normally spend a lot of money? I mean, your house is lovely, and you have nice cars, but you aren't exactly up to Becca's standards,' Clara said.

Alexandra was thinking hard now, realising that had she not

been so distracted, she might have noticed a few red flags. 'No, not quite. I suppose sometimes we've been abroad and stayed at what he claims are villas owned by a friend of a friend, or a family member of someone he works with. Or he'll get the kids tickets to a show, but not buy them online.' The more she spoke, the more she could see her theory had legs. Could her husband be taking bribes? There had been some scandal a few years back about police officers being paid off by criminal gangs, she recalled. But not Harlan, surely not?

The nightmare was, far from fading to black, becoming clearer and more sharp-edged, more plausible. 'Harlan pays cash for almost everything,' she added reluctantly.

'Because it's harder to trace?' Clara suggested, frowning as she considered.

'I suppose. I mean, he does pay some bills online, so perhaps those are the legit things? Our joint account doesn't have any massive amounts going out or coming in.'

They sat in silence, Alexandra feeling her flapjack might choke her. The rich, sugary oats and fruit stuck in her throat when she tried to swallow. She grabbed her mug and took a reassuring gulp of tea.

'Oh Alex,' Clare said sadly, 'I can't even begin to imagine how you would have that kind of conversation with him. Look, I'm sure there is some reasonable explanation.'

'I hope so too,' Alexandra said. 'I haven't noticed anything odd about the financials in all these years, but now I actually think about it...' She sighed. 'He has been so weird lately, and now this sudden urge to run off to Spain makes me wonder if he is in deep with something, and it's all about to blow up in his face. If that's true, I'll let it blow up. I can't confront him with any of this.'

'Well, you know where I am when you need me.' Clara leant in for a hug, and for a long moment Alexandra clung to her friend, her head on Clara's shoulder.

If only things were that easy. Just now she was so confused, caught in a spiderweb of everyone's lies, and she was struggling to find her own path out.

TWENTY-EIGHT

This is it. The last chance for my legal team to sum up my innocence for the jury, to persuade them I didn't commit this crime.

I woke last night with tears on my face, and Sara's laughter in my head. It's more anger than grief that I feel. That and the cold, icy need for revenge. There is no question, if I get away with this, I am going after Thomas Blake. I wonder if he senses this. It will be a huge blow to him if I am let free.

What will he do next? Will he still think I'll keep quiet? Because what I did all those years ago is nothing compared to what he has done to me, to Sara. The problem with Thomas is always that there is never a shred of evidence to tie him to any crimes. And if I blow the lid on the Candy Girls, I will be betraying Eddie and Matthew too, not to mention leaving myself vulnerable to further interaction with the police, and potentially prosecution for my part in the murders. But do I even care, if I'm finally going for justice?

I recognised her as soon as I saw her. To say I was shocked doesn't cover it. But after all these years there was no mistaking the serious expression, the grey eyes. She is no longer a young girl, but I still felt, after the first shock, that rush of protectiveness. Lexy was a sweet kid, and I was fond of her. Now I can only wonder what the hell she is doing on the jury, and if she is once again in danger. And does she recognise me? Will that change things?

The courtroom has an air of tension, and the jury retire to deliberate, leaving me with my counsel. They are supportive, quietly confident. No last-minute surprises were sprung, which was unexpected. Clearly the mountain of fake evidence was deemed to be enough. They underestimated my team, and they underestimated me.

Guilty or not guilty?

TWENTY-NINE

With the end of the trial looming, Alexandra had had plenty of time to make her choices. The sight of Mac, calm and composed – and maybe deliberately avoiding her gaze? Was she imagining that? – coupled with the mounting evidence in his favour, made it easy. It would be hard if there was some kind of last-minute evidence, a bribed witness perhaps, who could sway the jury, but she was confident that the overwhelming vote would be not guilty. How that verdict would affect her own future, she was trying not to think about right now.

Niall thought she would do as she was told, so Thomas would be sure of it. And if she didn't, she was putting her family in danger, her life in danger. What would Mac do when he was free again? He must have considered he had been set up, must know Thomas was in a precarious position, ready to do anything to make the final jump on the chessboard.

If he went free, would Mac be an ally? Why had this not occurred to her before? A rush of energy as she considered finding out where he lived, asking him for help. Surely, he would want revenge too, after what had happened to his girlfriend.

In keeping with her plans, she had also rung her brother last night, so scared she had hardly been able to breathe through the conversation.

Nobody would know what happened during the deliberation, and she would just say she was outvoted. Would they believe her? What if they didn't?

'Hallo, Birdie, I was hoping you'd call.'

'Were you?' She'd tried to stay calm. Niall couldn't possibly know how much courage it had taken to make this call, to enter the game on her terms.

'Of course. Are you okay?'

'Fine.' She hesitated, making it seem as though she was still afraid, tentative, maybe swaying towards doing as she was told. 'Niall, I need to see you again.'

'When's your copper husband next on a night shift?'

'He isn't until next month. There must be somewhere else we can meet.' Alexandra wasn't sure why she was pushing for this, but the instinct which had kept her safe all those years ago told her she could get more information from Niall, that he didn't want to kill her yet.

'How's the trial going? Are you all already for the verdict tomorrow?'

'As you can probably imagine, I'm not really in a position to tell you that. I sit at every session wondering what the hell is going on, and why my life seems to have imploded. There is a lot of waiting around, a lot of time to think.' She left it at that, waiting to hear his response.

'Calm down. You really don't need to stress about this. I'm right here watching out for you, remember?'

'I don't know if that is supposed to be reassuring, Niall, but it really isn't,' she snapped.

He agreed to text an address, a time, to see if they could figure out what to do next, and she felt a flash of triumph. 'Oh, and Birdie, how's Mum doing? I've been over and seen her in the garden sometimes in the summer, just when I was passing through Brighton for work, and she looks good.'

She tried to swallow her angry words, but couldn't help blurting out, 'You never answered when I asked why you went to see her. Why did you go?'

'Just wanted to see her.' His tone was curt, almost defensive.

Was that another threat or was he genuinely still fond of Catrin? And had he forgotten he told her the other night he'd been abroad? For the last fifteen years? Or was this a gentle threat? 'Mum's okay. As you will have seen when you last visited, she has dementia. I'm taking care of her.'

'Did you ever tell her what happened?' There it was, the old Niall shining through.

'No! Of course not. I would never have put her in danger like that, and anyway, if I had, she wouldn't remember anything now. Niall, just leave her alone.' The pain stabbing through her chest made her wonder if she was going to have a heart attack. The stress of pretending nothing out of the ordinary was happening was killing her. Last week she had had to excuse herself and go and sit on the floor of the toilets at the courtroom to sink her head in her hands and have a little cry.

'She's my mum too.' He sounded petulant.

'You could put her in danger, my kids, my husband, my friends. Don't you see? My whole life and everyone in it mean absolutely nothing to someone like Thomas.' She was getting agitated but that was good, that was the part she needed to play with Niall, making him think she was going to do exactly what he said. 'You said you wanted to help me; well, that starts by us working out what we know and what the hell we are going to do.' He needed to feel he was still involved, that she was still uncertain about which way she was going to jump.

'I'll see you tomorrow after the trial. Wait until I text you, and make sure you send that bastard Gareth down for the murder he committed,' he said, and abruptly ended the call.

Back upstairs in her bedroom, Alexandra had taken out the candy bracelet, turning it over thoughtfully in gentle fingers. There was someone who had every reason to have waited twenty years for revenge, someone who was smarter than most people thought, who had the skills to sneak around firewalls, who would certainly know how to manipulate Thomas. And this one person had more money than any of the other Candy Girls.

'Holy shit, Lexy, look at all this money!'

They had just walked in, early so Lexy could help set up, and Lana could hang around gossiping. There was now a stack of cardboard boxes in the hallway near the main entrance. It was the same place where they had often seen a sport bag full of cash. One of the boxes had been slit open, and then loosely closed. Naturally Lana was peeking inside.

'What do you mean?' Lexy stood beside her, watched as her friend flipped the flap of the box. Piles of notes, neatly stacked and held together with white card bands.

'There must be hundreds of thousands right here,' Lana said, picking up a stack of money, and running a fingernail through it.

'Leave it,' Lexy said, backing away. 'We don't want to get involved in whatever's going on.'

Lana knew about the silly origami birds, had laughed as Lexy held one in her cupped hands, letting it fly out of the window of their cramped flat, drifting away on the wind towards the sea.

'Let me try making one!' she'd said.

Alexandra felt a snap, and, looking down, realised she had been clenching her fist over the bracelet far too hard, breaking the largest pink candy charm in the chain. As she smoothed the sugary powder away, a tiny roll of paper fell out. She straightened it and saw a phone number with shaking fingers. Shit. Her heart was beating hard as she fumbled for her phone and keyed in the number. She figured she had nothing to lose. If it wasn't

Lana, it was some stupid game Thomas and Niall had planned to torment her further.

The phone rang, and she waited, almost holding her breath. And if Lana had gone off with a rich client? A genuine sugar daddy, without the kink, was what she had often called a few of her favourites. Although she knew about Lana's family set-up, and knew that nobody would be calling to check if she was okay; she had checked with college at the time. The admin had told her Lana had dropped out and they were not concerned about her whereabouts. That said she had voluntarily left, which tied up loose ends, didn't it?

The phone was still ringing out, and she sat on the bed, shoulders hunched, body tense with hope.

Finally, someone picked up, and when she heard the familiar voice, she felt a rush of emotion so strong it nearly winded her. 'Hallo, Lexy.'

'Lana?'

'I've been waiting for you to call me.'

It was the voice that had answered the phone, when she finally worked up the courage to call, that had given her the strength she needed to come into court today fighting. The prosecution was winding up, and it was time for her to make her final decision. Ever since she had made her choice last night, she had known it was probably the most dangerous thing she would ever do. But it was the only choice she could make.

As the jury were escorted away from the courtroom to consider their choices, she thought for a second that she caught a flash of recognition in Mac's grey eyes. Next moment she was walking between Anna and Jackie, moving one foot after the other to decide the fate of the accused man.

She had already decided her strategy would be to let everyone else argue, make their points, before she made hers. So she sipped the poor excuse for coffee and waited, heart beating fast. The majority seemed to be swaying towards not guilty, when the red-headed man gave a persuasive speech from the opposite point of view.

Alexandra waited, running things over in her head. She and Harlan had been perfectly polite to each other, communicating mainly via text message. He hadn't mentioned the move to Spain again, but she had noticed his passport out on his bedside table yesterday morning and wondered for a wild moment if he was thinking of just leaving her and the kids and heading to Spain on his own. Was this what their life had come to? Had their marriage fallen apart? Alexandra ignored the stab of heartache and pushed the thoughts aside. She had to move forward with her plan.

The jury filed back in, and the judge took her place. Alexandra was light-headed with relief. Not because she had done as she was told, but because she had made the right choice. She had people on her side now, and there was a flicker of hope.

The verdict rang out across the room, echoing into the corners, clearing out the shadows.

Not guilty.

THIRTY

Suddenly it was over, and the next day she was back in the clinic, dealing with a full set of appointments, trying to enjoy her work as she usually did. And failing because she needed to get on with her plan. This wasn't normal jury service, this didn't end once the verdict was read, and she knew she was now in more danger than ever. She needed to get the kids out of Brighton, and she needed her husband on her side.

Melinda was full of gossip and trying to make her laugh with a story about her latest online dating fiasco, and she forced herself to act normally.

'... And I said if you're going to ghost me, you can piss right off! Imagine, he said he wanted us to go on holiday to Tobago and asked me to pay for both of us, then when I said no, he cut off all contact for two weeks.'

'Maybe he thought you would have missed him so much you'd be desperate to pay for his holiday after that?' Alexandra suggested, checking her supplies of gloves and hand gel. 'I need to order some more of these... So, are you seeing him again?'

'What do you think?'

'I think you kicked him all the way down the road.' Alexandra grinned at her office manager.

'That too. I also took out an ad in the free paper, the online one, with his number and the classic "Free puppies for a good home" ad.' Melinda was laughing as she made the coffee. 'I don't know who started that but it sure is a good way to get revenge on an arsehole!'

Jolted out of her thoughts, Alexandra managed the day better than she had thought she would. A few minor celebrities, regular clients came in, plus others who were new but took a sensible attitude to aesthetics. Sam, she could see from her Insta profile, had unfollowed the clinic, and was showing off the most horrendous, sore-looking, overfilled pout.

She showed Melinda, who agreed the girl was on a destruction course. 'I just don't get it. She was a pretty girl naturally; why does she want to look like Barbie? I mean, to be fair even Barbie looks more natural.'

Alexandra agreed. 'It's really sad.'

Ridiculously, because she didn't actually care what these stupid girls were doing, she felt the need to head off to the toilets for some privacy. What the hell was wrong with her? She was tougher than this, stronger in every way. All she had to do was outthink the men who she thought she had escaped years ago. They might be power players, but she had come from nothing, had built her own success. Alexandra slipped a hand into her bag, removed the blister pack and popped her daily dosage. She was now back on the maximum dosage, and it had taken months to wean herself off these before.

She hated herself for going back to relying on medication to help her cope, but there really wasn't time to consider any other options and she needed to be at the top of her game to navigate out of this.

. . .

Alexandra met Niall again late the next afternoon, telling Harlan she was popping out for some groceries. He seemed more than happy for her to go; in fact, he informed her that when she got back he was off down the gym. He seemed to be so anxious to avoid her, and she was beginning to wonder if he was getting suspicious.

Maybe it was easy, and her husband was just having an affair? If she was honest a simple infidelity would mean nothing compared to the shit show raging in her own head right now. If fact, she longed for it to be something so mundane and seedy.

Alexandra walked down the seafront towards the colourful beach huts, the breeze lifting her hair, the sea calming her crazy thoughts. Niall was standing at the tideline, trying to skim stones. He looked relaxed and tanned, she noticed. And his clothes were expensive. So was his watch. Thomas Blake was clearly a generous employer. But what price luxury goods? And how much money bought silence and murder?

'What do you want, Niall? The trial is over, and I tried my best. Everyone else voted him not guilty.'

'Hallo to you too, sis. You're looking good today.' His expression said he was not happy with her. 'Maybe you didn't try hard enough to convince everyone Gareth was guilty?'

'Piss off, Niall. I pushed for him to be found guilty, just like you wanted, but that's the point of a jury: you don't always get the verdict you personally want. Now you can just leave me and my family alone.' She could feel Lexy, the hesitant young woman she had been, slipping away, as the woman she was now stepped up to flex her muscles, fill in the blanks, fighting her corner.

'I can't, actually. It is unfortunate he was found not guilty, and because of that you need to do something else for us.'

'What if I say I won't do it? All I want is for all of you to go away and let me live the life I've worked really hard to build.' She knew she sounded defiant, aggressive even, but she didn't care anymore. 'Why can't you go and bribe the owner of the building, or the council, or something? There must be another way of dealing with this.'

The sea was flat and gleaming in the late afternoon sunlight, a few lazy ripples reaching towards their feet and a tiny burst of foam stroked the slick of sand with bubbly fingers.

He spoke slowly, his eyes narrowing against the glare of the sea and sun. 'Do you really think we haven't explored all the other options? We want you to go to the police and tell them Gareth is a murderer, that he killed the three girls at the final party, that you witnessed it. But you don't know anyone else involved. I will coach you through it. Thomas doesn't want anything linked to him, and naturally Matthew and Eddie feel the same. This whole situation is a fucking nightmare! You and your family will be taken care of, and you'll have plenty of money tucked away somewhere to do whatever you want with your lives.'

She opened her mouth, and he pressed his fingers against her lips; they were salty but gentle. She shoved him away. 'I have everything I want right here, and I've worked bloody hard to get it.'

Niall continued as though she hadn't spoken. 'Just do it. It won't harm you and as you were there you can just describe what happened but say only Gareth was present. Not Thomas, Matthew, Eddie, or me.'

'I can't do this. It would implicate me! It would ruin my life, and I'd have to lie that you weren't involved. I can't tell lies to the police!' Alexandra found she was furious. This was not part of the plan; instead of getting information out of her brother, she was thrown another curve ball. 'Don't be so stupid, Niall. What about Mac? Do you not think when he finds out his so-called friends have dropped him in the shit that he won't tell the police exactly what happened that night?' She almost choked on her words. 'The police will find out everything that went on *after* I've lied about it.'

'Birdie...' Amusement warmed his icy expression for a swift moment. 'You could get away with murder; we just need to get Gareth banged up for all of it. You leave out certain parts, you fabricate others. It's easy.'

Her head was spinning, and she spoke carefully, choosing her words, knowing Lana was safe, but wanting to buy time. 'Wait, who owns the house now? Get Thomas to put in a massive offer for the house. Buy it, bury the planning permission, keep the secrets in the basement and none of us has to wreck our lives.' God, she needed to buy some time. Time to act out on her plan, time to put things in motion.

His face was impassive, the way it went when he was trying to control her, to make her do what he wanted, see his side of an argument. 'We've planned this very carefully...'

'What, just like you framed Gareth in the first place? It didn't work, did it? Your stupid plans, all your money, did not have the power to send an innocent man to prison. You just murdered an innocent girl in the process. I wonder who did kill Sara? Was it you, Niall?'

His face was contorted with anger. 'Don't be ridiculous.'

'I'm not doing it. Niall, come on! No way. It means he gets to go free. I don't care about the pathetic mutual blackmail between those four bastards.' She shoved a finger in Niall's face. 'Thomas could have killed me too. I went down to the pool with him once, and Mac saved me, told me to go back upstairs. It could have been me in the graveyard in the basement.'

'You mentioned. I don't understand why you didn't tell me?' Niall's eyes narrowed again. The sea breeze whipped his hair across his face. 'We were always a team, Birdie. Us against the world.'

She fought the wave of sadness and anger his words triggered. 'You were already so far in with Thomas you probably wouldn't have believed me. And he didn't do anything to me that night. It was only at the last party when I realised what he was, what he had been doing.'

Niall was looking at her curiously. 'Did you sleep with Mac, Lexy?'

'Oh go to hell!' Before she could stop herself, she had slapped him hard across the face. The sting in her palm, the redness on his cheek didn't cancel her own indignation.

Niall gave a quick, involuntary movement, which he checked even as Alexandra moved slightly away. He brought his own hand to his cheek, glanced down at his fingers as though checking for blood. 'I don't think you quite appreciate what might happen if you don't do this, Alexandra. I've been trying to protect you. Always, I've tried to protect you. If I hadn't put in a word, it might have been you who was murdered in that alley off Beacon Close, instead of Sara.'

She stared at him, trying to control her emotions. '*What?*'

He stared back, eyes cool and assessing. 'You are only alive because you were going to be useful. You need to help us. Mac is going to take the fall one way or another.'

'But I know he didn't kill them.' The words were out before she could stop herself, and she saw anger blaze again in his eyes.

'The truth doesn't come into this. It's a case of tying up loose ends. You've forgotten how easily people disappear in Thomas's world, how powerful these people are.'

'And you? What do you get out of this? Apart from *protecting* me?'

He scowled at her. 'I'm doing my job, making my way in the world, just like we were all those years ago. This is my path, and you chose yours. For fuck's sake, Alexandra, you're lucky you're still alive now. You witnessed everything, and I've been covering for you ever since.'

She wasn't quite brave enough to frame her thoughts, so she

just stared at him, memories tossing in her head, horrors and half-truths reforming, just like her picture of her brother.

'Think about it. You've got forty-eight hours, because quite frankly we are out of time on this.' His voice was cool, controlled, and she wondered how she could ever have thought of him as her brother. Her mum had often taken in the lost kids, given them a home, gave them meals when their parents were off their heads, taken them in when they had been beaten.

But Niall had started calling her Mum and pretty much moved in by the time he was ten years old. Alexandra had loved having a brother, had enjoyed the open house, with a constant flow of friends, had not understood until much later in her life how much her mum had risked providing a safe haven for these lost children.

He turned without saying anything else, and jogged easily up the beach, leaving her stunned, frozen to the spot, far too close to the incoming tide. She didn't come to until the water ran icy cold over her trainers. And she still had to get the milk and bread. *Shit!*

Harlan kept up a constant stream of chatter with the kids over dinner when she got back, and she couldn't help but wonder if he, too, was acting. He was normally great with the kids, of course, but this was... slightly over the top.

When he left for the gym, she locked herself in the bathroom for a few minutes to check her messages. Kaye, the journalist, was cautiously optimistic about turning this into a big story. But she added that the police would want to talk to Alexandra if she admitted she was a witness. There was no way around that; she needed to tell the truth and trust that by breaking this via the media instead of the legal route, it would break the stranglehold Thomas had over everyone.

Later, when she had popped the kids into bed, read stories,

soothing herself as well as them with the nightly routine, she came downstairs to find her husband was back from the gym, had poured them both a glass of wine, and was flicking through Netflix.

The next part of her plan was to remove her kids from the danger zone. It needed to be done as soon as possible, after her conversation with Niall. She just needed the right moment to mention it to her husband.

Harlan looked up from the sofa as she took her glass off the kitchen counter with a little chink, called through the open door. 'I thought we could find a movie? At least the trial is over now, and I can tell how stressful you've found it. You haven't been yourself at all.' He hesitated. 'Perhaps we can discuss the future? I'm really sorry I didn't tell you about the house in Spain, but I wanted it to be a surprise. I think I was just so excited I kind of ran away with myself.'

It was her chance, her opening. Alexandra sat down, sipped her wine, approved film choices without really thinking, and finally said, 'Harlan, is something wrong? It just seems like you've been a bit weird lately. And... where did the money for the Spanish house come from?'

He laughed. 'I bought a scratch card at the garage. I know, what are the chances?'

She smiled like she believed this. Surely there was no way Niall would have got to him already, not when they wanted her to do this... this terrible thing, but her guilty conscience seemed to be screaming out her secrets across the room.

Harlan turned to look at her, puzzled, a little frown line between his brows. 'I'm fine, and it seemed like such a great opportunity. I can study and work from home doing consultancy for that security firm, and you... you can take your skills anywhere. You don't need to sell the clinic; get Melinda to run it and pop back occasionally. You could even commute! You know I mentioned that case. It just knocked me a bit, you know?

But I'm honestly okay now. You look so serious, Alexandra. Lighten up.' He was laughing at her now, but in a weird false way that made her body freeze. She pushed through the reaction and laughed too.

Her genuine, loving husband was lying about something and she needed to know what the hell it was. She needed to navigate her way through this, somehow hold her family together without exposing her secrets, or falling prey to Niall and the powerful forces at work behind the scenes. Her first instinct had been correct. She needed to take them all down.

No pressure at all then, she chided herself, settling back into Harlan's arms to watch the movie, still feeling her days were numbered before she was exposed. But for now, she was safe.

Although she laughed in the right places in the movie, fetched more wine and a bowl of fancy salted nuts she had bought ages ago and forgotten about, talked and joked with her husband, she felt all the time she was acting a role, waiting for the inevitable destruction of her life as she knew it. One of the worst things was she could tell he was acting too.

As they walked upstairs, she said casually, 'I was wondering if your parents might like to have the kids for half term? I hate to send them away in holiday time, but you don't have any leave, and the clinic is way behind because of the trial. We could have some time together, talk about Spain properly.'

He paused on the stair above her, turning so she could see the relief evident on his face even in the semi-darkness. 'I'm sure they would. Actually, that might be a very good idea.'

THIRTY-ONE

Alexandra drove the kids up to their grandparents in the Lake District on Thursday morning, as the school broke up early for half term to allow for two days of teacher training. It was a long drive, and she kept thinking she was being followed. The blue truck, the white van, the red Mercedes, all making her jittery. But the kids were delighted to be going to see their grandparents, and when they weren't glued to their iPad, they played I Spy games out of the windows. Every time she caught sight of the two smiling faces in the rearview mirror, her heart filled with protective love, and determination to make things right.

Stopping at a motorway service station for Nando's, and to stock up on jelly sweets, Alexandra allowed herself a little respite. She was in control; she was moving forward. Nobody accosted her, Niall did not appear behind her in the queue at Nando's, and the weak spring sunshine was filled with warmth as they sat on a picnic bench on a ratty strip of grass. Thankfully the children were still young enough to be oblivious to the tensions around them, and they chattered away.

She turned the radio up to listen to the news. Thomas Blake was now party leader, well ahead in the polls and the race for the election. The radio announced that he was 'way out in front thanks to his promises to help everyone from the NHS to smaller, diverse groups across the country'. She shivered and bit her lip. His power was like a tidal wave just about to crest. And she would be killing the process right at the worst moment.

They arrived in the afternoon, and she was once again filled with relief that she had such lovely in-laws; Jocelyn and Stan were the kindest couple, had welcomed Alexandra into their family with open arms.

'How's your mum doing?' Knowing her grandchildren well, Jocelyn had food on the table: sandwiches, a huge fruit cake, scones and cream. 'I hope she's better on that new medication?'

'Seems to be a little better, thanks. And there is a new clinical trial Delilah has put her forward for.' Alexandra tried hard to act normal. Jocelyn was a doctor, and before she retired had specialised in Alzheimer's, so she was always keen to know what was going on.

'That's good. Do you know who's running it?'

'A team from America, I think. I'll email the details over to you in case you know anyone.' Jocelyn kept abreast of the latest developments even in retirement, fitting in reading and writing medical journals and scientific papers between her other loves of gardening and cruises.

The kids tucked into the huge meal, but Alexandra found her mouth was dry, and she had to fight the urge to check her phone every ten minutes. So much for the respite. 'But she's doing okay. Good days and bad days, you know. I hate that there is no cure, no medication that can make her recognise me, recognise she has two grandchildren.' She said the last softly, to Jocelyn, making sure the kids didn't hear, knowing she would understand. Her mother-in-law slipped a hand on hers, giving it a firm, but sympathetic squeeze.

After Sophie and Tom had run out to play in the big wild garden, she managed a cup of tea, managed to chat normally.

'Thanks so much for having the kids,' she said.

'We love having them... Alex, is everything alright with Harlan?' Stan looked concerned.

Immediately she felt a flash of panic run across her chest. 'Yes, as far as I know. What do you mean?'

'Don't look so worried. He just seemed a bit off, and he didn't phone last week like he normally does,' Jocelyn explained, pushing a strand of silver hair behind her ear.

Alexandra knew her husband was obsessive about his weekly calls to his parents, and they were very close. He was the golden boy, the only child, and he basked in their love and admiration. 'I think he's had a tough shift; you know one of the bad ones he doesn't like to talk about.'

'How's the clinic doing?' Stan changed the subject.

She entertained them with a few snippets of gossip, no names of course, but she loved that they were so interested in what she did as well as Harlan. All the while she was looking around the beautiful stone house, the expensive furnishings, and thinking how lucky Harlan had been to have such kind and generous parents.

'I don't suppose I'll make that much when I eventually sell the clinic and retire,' she finished, 'but it's doing well at the moment and the income is pretty stable.' She wanted to introduce the subject of Harlan's money, but she wasn't quite sure how to broach the subject without causing concern. More concern.

'Well, if you've stayed solvent and enjoyed having your own business that's the main thing,' Joceyln said. 'I mean, we went bankrupt our last venture, didn't we, Stan?'

'It was a tough time,' he agreed.

Alexandra stared at Jocelyn. 'You went bankrupt with the furniture business? You mean the antique shop?'

'Yes. We sank everything into it. It was a foolish idea, to retire and start a business, but we, well, we got caught up with everything and it seemed like a great investment idea. As I'm sure Harlan has told you, we ended with nothing, no savings, no pension, until he stepped in.'

'But it looked like such a beautiful shop,' Alexandra choked out inanely, still trying to understand.

Jocelyn looked at her closely. 'He didn't tell you, did he? He doesn't like anyone to know how generous he was, but he had a couple of properties before he became a police officer and he sold all of them to buy this place, buy your house, and give us money to live on until we got back on our feet.'

'I...' Alexandra tried to smile, shaking her head. Harlan had never mentioned owning properties. 'Sorry, no he didn't, but you're right, he is very generous, and he doesn't ever like to be thanked for anything, does he?'

'I'm sorry, Alex, I shouldn't have said anything.' Jocelyn looked guarded. 'Don't tell him, will you, if he hasn't already let you know the whole sorry story? He was a proper entrepreneur right from when he was a little boy.'

'Of course, I won't.' She forced herself to smile. 'He, um... he did tell me about selling apples on the side of the road, and doing up cars for his mates, so I do know he worked hard.'

What the hell? Harlan had told her his parents were wealthy, and they had paid for everything. He had never mentioned owning property. He had always reiterated how kind his parents had been to pay for everything. But he had made her promise never to speak to them about it, said they would be embarrassed. The extravagant wedding, their beautiful house in Brighton, the nights out to see shows, the holidays, none of which would have been possible on a police officer's salary, even when he was promoted.

He had told her he had an allowance, had seemed embarrassed about it, told her he wanted to share it with her, had seemed hurt when she insisted she must pay. He said he liked to treat her, was lucky to have such supportive and wealthy parents, and enjoyed spoiling her and the kids. But then, according to Harlan, he had also just won a fortune on a scratch card and bought a Spanish villa with it.

Feeling as though her head might explode, Alexandra hastily called the children to say goodbye, hugging them tight even as they wriggled to go and find the pygmy goats, who were housed at the bottom of the garden.

'Bye, Mum!' Sophie yelled as they ran away down the garden, the peachy evening sky arching above them.

Tears filled her eyes and she had to swallow hard before she could answer. But she was sure this was the right thing to do. They would be safe here, out of Brighton while she played dangerous games. She was hit by a pang of fear that she might not come out of this alive. What might Thomas organise? A traffic accident? A mugging? Would Niall really kill her? It was inconceivable.

Her and Niall running down the road, dodging through the scrubby playground with rusting swings and health hazard slide, nipping into the corner shop to spend coins clutched in grubby hands, scanning the side of the road for dropped pennies to spend on sweets.

For a long time, she hadn't understood why Niall never wanted to go home to his dad, but she loved him, almost idolised him as a little girl, so when he moved in, it seemed like a logical step.

The long drive home gave her time to think properly. The news was full of Thomas and his plans for a radical overhaul of the country and its politics. Meanwhile the clock was ticking. The election was in two weeks, but Niall had only given her forty-eight hours.

She was so deep in thought that she almost missed the exit to the A23. A police car blasting up behind her as she neared Pyecombe, lights and sirens blaring, made her pulse race. Almost as though they were after her. The guilt was making her feel sick again. She wondered how Gareth had felt when he was arrested, when he was going through the trial, and then she wondered how he was feeling now, about his friends, about Thomas about to become prime minister.

If she were him, she might be thinking of revenge. Perhaps even thinking along the same lines as Alexandra herself?

THIRTY-TWO

When she got home, she went straight to the boxes at the back of her closet and finally pulled out an old mobile phone. The battery was dead, and it took so long to charge she began to panic it was broken.

But under her trembling fingers the texts, the photos, everything from that time in her life appeared. Her and Lana, her old life. Over forty text conversations remained, and they were excellent examples of what Kaye needed as evidence.

Her memories, released into the safety of her warm kitchen, engulfed her, bittersweet, two teenagers taking everything life had to offer. Tears trickled down her cheeks even as she smiled at some of the wilder pictures. The beach parties, first day on their course, the club nights, the wild walks on the Devil's Dyke, the sweet pictures of them cuddled on the tatty sofa in their flat in Kemptown. More photos after Jess joined them, arms around each other, cheeks creased with laughter.

There were profile pictures for the Candy Girls, each girl approving the other's before they went ahead and posted them. Alexandra looked for a long time at hers. The girl in the photo wasn't classically pretty, but she had a sweet round face, dimples in each rosy cheek, and with pink lipstick highlighting her best feature, her 'pin-up lips' as Lana had always called them, and a light touch of mascara on her dark lashes, she looked, well, she looked like perfect bait for a sugar daddy. She also looked much younger than nineteen.

Her eyes were wet with tears, and she almost felt a shadow pass over her kitchen at the thought of the men handpicking which girls they wanted for the parties. It had seemed fun, had made her feel carefree, had made her richer, enabled her to save for the future. Had it really been so bad, what they were all doing?

Next to the phone there had been an empty cash box, the wads of notes long gone, firstly paying for her to finish her degree, later helping to pay for her mum's accommodation and care. Alexandra had worked extremely hard, and by the time her secret stash had dwindled to nothing, her clinic, along with Harlan's money, was more than enough to pay for everything she and her family needed. Oh god, where was he getting his extra money from?

Harlan had insisted on buying them the house. The deeds were in both their names, but he had been quite hurt when she wanted to pay half of everything, including their property. So hurt that she had given way, even though she made sure the bills were divided equally between them.

At this thought, and the thought of money, her mind spun back to her conversation with his parents. She made herself a mug of coffee, forcing herself to deal with things one at a time. It was a habit her mum had got her into, and she could see her, standing, exhausted from a night shift at their front door in Newcastle, still finding the time and energy to comfort her daughter.

'You don't have to sort out everything at once. Get up, have a shower, make a mug of tea.' That sweet, exhausted, but still

sparkling smile. 'Then you've already accomplished three things on your list, haven't you?'

Her phone rang and despite the situation, despite the stress, she smiled at the caller ID. Lana. Since she had rung the number hidden in the bracelet, they had spoken several times, carefully filling in the gaps, rebuilding the trust.

'Hi, Lana, how's it going?' It was comforting how quickly they had fallen back into their old friendship, if rather strange given the circumstances.

'All good. Did you get any more information from Niall?'

'No, I haven't heard anything since the bastard issued his deadline. Did you hear about Thomas?'

'Of course.'

'I've been looking through my stuff and I've got quite a lot more evidence.' She swallowed hard. 'Pictures of all of us at the parties that I took without anyone noticing, that kind of thing.'

'Any with Jess?' The voice was hard, controlled.

'A couple.' She heard a noise on the front path. 'Shit, my husband's home, I've got to go. Text me when and where you want to meet up. We've only got until tomorrow before Niall thinks I'm going down to the police station to tell them about Mac.'

'Bastard.' A harsh laugh. 'I can't wait to see what happens to him after this is done.'

'Yeah, well...' Alexandra bit her lip, uneasy but resolute. She had made her choice. And she hoped she might potentially have another ally. She would have to work out how to approach Mac.

Harlan, apparently back from the gym once again, dumped his bag in the hallway and came in for a quick kiss.

'How was your day?'

'Good thanks. It feels funny not having the kids around.'

Alexandra waited. Normally he would have suggested a date night, be full of enthusiasm for a new restaurant, a new venue opening that they just had to check out. Especially with the kids away, he should have been eager to head out. They often joked about getting old and bedtimes getting earlier, so when they did have free time, they should have indulged themselves. He was keen on the glitzy high-end side of Brighton, whereas she preferred the smaller venues. The food was often better, and she was unlikely to bump into any of her clients.

He was silent for a while, busying himself with making a protein drink, unpacking his trainers, and setting them carefully on the shoe rack. 'I might get an early night. I'm pretty tired, but you go ahead and watch TV or whatever. I would like to talk about Spain before you go and chill out, though.'

'Actually, I've got some admin work to catch up on.' She knew this would annoy him, and she childishly felt like needling him. He didn't ever like her putting work in ahead of him. In the early days of the clinic, when she had been putting in insane hours to get the business up and running, they had frequently argued about it. He had even suggested she be grateful he had enough money for her to take a career break, stay at home to raise the kids. Because they had the money.

But Alexandra loved using her skills, loved her enterprise, and had managed to juggle everything. She could never entertain the thought of not being independent, financially or otherwise, no matter how much she loved her husband.

Come on, Alexandra! she mentally admonished herself. She needed to discover what was going on with Harlan and prepare him for her imminent revelations. The clock was ticking, and by this time soon, on another normal evening, she could even be dead. 'But yes, we should talk. I'll make some pasta, shall I? We can chat about the house then.'

'Fine. Actually, that sounds good. I'm just going to take a shower,' he said.

'Didn't you have one at the gym?'

'No, the water was off... Some problem with the heating

system,' he called back. She could hear his feet thumping on the stairs.

As the bathroom door banged, she jumped at the sound of something sliding through the letterbox. She almost ran to the door, saw the white envelope on the mat, caught the name on the front, and swung the front door wide.

The light rain sprayed her face as she ran outside, careless of her bare feet on the icy stone steps, desperate to catch a glimpse of who had delivered the envelope. A kid on a bike was cycling along the road, two teens were lounging next to the bus shelter, laughing, heads bent over a phone. A few cars went past, and an elderly woman, yellow umbrella up, turned and looked at her curiously, before hurrying on her way, shopping trolley bumping over the pavement. Nothing, or rather, it could have been anybody.

She bunched her hands into fists in frustration and went back inside quickly. The envelope contained another bird, just the one, and perfect in every way. A single sheet of paper:

Birdie,

Just a little something to remind you that you have 20 hours left.

I'll be watching,

N

Stuffing the envelope and contents into her bag, she hastily started cooking pasta. There was nothing else she could do but go ahead with the plan. And she was back to trusting nobody but herself again. It was as though the last twenty years had never happened. She reminded herself she was no longer a teenager with no qualifications, no longer a terrified twenty-year-old with a secret stash of money, working her butt off to get her degree.

But as she rummaged in the fridge for a packet of fresh sauce, her mind was taking her back to that time. Back to when she was hiding away in another rented room, this time in a small village outside Brighton. Henfield had been a perfect bolthole. She had rented a room off an elderly couple, got the bus back and forth for classes, cut her hair and dyed it, and worked and hid until she was done.

Alexandra stayed there even when she graduated, just while she worked out how she was going to get started with her career, how she was going to bring her mum down to Brighton, pay for her care when it became necessary. There had been a lot of cash stashed away – all of it earnt, and all of it illegal.

All in all, over half a million pounds. At first she had been worried the notes might be stolen, maybe traceable to the police, but gradually, and she was so careful, she had been able to spend them, buying her flat, working up to paying for her mum's care.

She had been so careful, she never splashed the cash, never went out clubbing, but worked all the hours she wasn't studying at the local fish and chip shop. She worked and read in her room, her one luxury a small bookcase stacked with hard copies of her favourite novels. The historical romances with the sprayed edges, the signed copies she had sneaked into book signings in Waterstones and Goldsboro to get. No social media. She hadn't dared.

Her secret life. And then she met Harlan at a bar. A quick drink with some other girls who worked at the same clinic as her, that she normally refused. A cancelled bus and the rain had led her to be in exactly the right place at the right time to meet her future husband. Finally, she was safe to reinvent herself again, to take on another name, to become Alexandra Marshall.

Twenty long years working up to becoming the person she thought she should be, the one she had always hoped she might become.

And now all was going to be destroyed.

THIRTY-THREE

The house seemed unusually silent without the kids. She had wanted to get a dog, but Harlan had dissuaded her, saying with him at work, her at work, the poor thing would be fed up, or in doggy day care half the time. Which was true, she supposed.

The sounds from upstairs indicated Harlan had finished in the bathroom, and she hastily gave the pasta a stir, added grilled chicken, and poured a couple of glasses of wine. She would think about it later.

'So, do you want to see the photos of the house?' Harlan said brightly as they tucked into dinner. His hair was still damp, but he looked brighter, happier than he had for a few months.

'Sure.' She glanced down as he slid the iPad towards her, flicking slowly through the photos. A stunning white villa on the outskirts of a town, with views of the sea. There were four bedrooms, three bathrooms and a swimming and outdoor party area. 'It's beautiful.'

Harlan beamed, sipped his wine, and proceeded to tell her every single detail about the house and area. 'I know I kind of sprang this on you, but I reckon if the kids finished school for the summer here, we could maybe even transition over there in August.'

'I'm not dead against the idea, but I just think we do need some time to consider it,' Alexandra said slowly. 'You would have to give notice at work, and I didn't realise you'd finished the online security course? And then there's the clinic. I would need about six months to try and figure out a workable plan for the future.'

He was nodding enthusiastically. 'Yeah of course. That's all fine. It's just a great opportunity and I want us to make sure we take every chance we get to... to enjoy life.'

'You're not sick, are you?' Panic suddenly flooded her body, and she grabbed her wine glass, gulped the alcohol down. What if that was it? All the signs had been there and she...

'No! Of course not.' His dark blue eyes held hers, surprised. 'You know how much I've been struggling at work. It just seemed like a fresh start would be perfect. No more child abuse cases, no more night shifts trying to help people caught in the social care system.' Harlan sighed. 'It's heart-breaking to keep seeing these people time and time again and they're caught in an endless merry-go-round of being passed from us to the ambulance service, to crisis lines and social workers who have two-year waiting lists.' He caught sight of the TV on in the corner of the kitchen.

The sound was turned down, and Alexandra turned to see what had grabbed his attention. 'I really hope Thomas Blake gets in as prime minister. He seems like a bloke who gets things done, and most politicians are so full of crap.' Harlan laid his fork down. 'Did you know he's coming to Brighton tomorrow?' He chuckled. 'They make me laugh travelling round the country with their entourage, but as I say, he's my choice this time around.'

He stood up to clear plates and luckily totally missed Alexandra's reaction. She was clinging to the table, aware only of the rapid thump of her heartbeat, her body frozen in fear. When she could speak again, she hastily poured another glass. 'I didn't know he was coming to Brighton.'

Harlan was washing up. 'What? Oh, Thomas. Yes. It's all over social media, I'm surprised you missed it, but you've never really been into politics, have you?'

She had been planning on trying to find out more about Harlan's reasons for leaving the country, being really subtle and clever and trying to find out where the money had come from, but instead she cleared her throat. 'I might go and have a bath. I'm really tired.'

'We can both get an early night.' He winked at her, and she kissed him as she went past, feeling absolutely nothing but a kind of frozen fear. Thomas was coming here, to her hometown.

Alexandra almost laughed when she considered how easy her life had been before the arrival of the first paper bird. Sure, she had secrets, but who didn't? Now, she was constantly aware of time passing, almost as though she was carrying one of those glass timers, with sand slipping through to indicate the *time's up* moment.

She didn't have many grains of sand left. At least the kids were safe. She had ordered them both those kid tracker phones, which had a few games on as well, as extra reassurance. As she ran her bath, she messaged Lana and Kaye.

An address, a date, and a time on their group chat. Nothing else. Adrenalin fizzed through her veins. She was getting closer to the showdown, and now it looked like Thomas was going to be right here in Brighton for it. Lana would be pleased. It was only as the thought occurred to her that she realised Lana probably already knew.

She had been meticulously planning this for twenty years; of course she bloody knew. From the very first time she had called her former best friend, the slip of paper from the candy bracelet trembling in her fingers, she had realised Lana knew far more than she was letting on. Her cautious approach to making contact with Alexandra was in direct contrast to Thomas and Niall's scare tactics and bullying.

After seeing Harlan off on a day shift for more overtime, she was driving along the coast road by nine-thirty, turning up the radio to drown out her thoughts. She quickly reached Worthing and began to search the maze of streets.

The address was in a nice area, much like her own: leafy treelined streets and townhouses. Coffee shops and a glimpse of the grey sea on the smudgy skyline. She parked, checked the permit sign, and decided she was okay for two hours. Who knew how to decipher the stupid things anyway? Her husband had been in a good mood still this morning, apparently thinking his wife was seriously considering his crazy plan to up and leave the UK. They had even FaceTimed the kids, who were off for a hike with their grandparents.

Alexandra found her palms were sweaty, her heart was pounding as she walked up to the front door. A weird thought occurred to her, followed by a flash of irrational panic. Was it really Lana in this house, or was she walking into a trap? Niall hadn't been back in touch, but she could feel his eyes on her everywhere. He was in the queue at the grocery store, in her garden, in court... He wasn't, but the pressure was simmering in her chest as the deadline ticked closer.

The door opened and Lana peered quickly out, indicated she should come inside. The hair was almost the same, but more groomed, polished. They could have walked past one another in the street and Alexandra might have needed to look twice. But up close, the woman Alexandra now faced in the hallway was indeed the same girl she had once considered her best friend.

'I thought you were dead.' Alexandra spoke softly, unsure whether she was going to cry, holding herself together, because, surprisingly, Lana was now looking nervous. Maybe she was having second thoughts.

But then she smiled, and her dimples popped out, eyes warmed, and she held out her arms. 'Bloody hell, Lexy, it's been a long time!' She felt her own heart beating alongside her friend's, and when they finally drew apart, she could see the tears she felt on her own cheeks, mirrored in the wetness in Lana's eyes.

'I can't believe you're really here. I couldn't think how to contact you, didn't want to in case it all went wrong... I've been dreaming about this for years, but now I'm so scared...'

'Me too. Kaye's going to be here in half an hour. Is that still okay?' Nervous, unsure whether she had done the right thing, she followed Lana into her living room. Most of the furniture was under dust sheets, and although everything was clean, it was apparent the house was uninhabited. 'I told her we needed a quick catch-up first, just to make sure everything is clear. Did you *know* Thomas is coming to Brighton tomorrow?'

'Yeah. Ever since he started climbing the ladder, I've been watching, waiting for the right moment to cut his balls off.'

'Ouch.'

'Right,' Lana agreed, with a degree of satisfaction. 'Do you want to go first?' she asked quickly, after they had perched slightly awkwardly, facing one another, on the sofas.

'Lana, I have less than twenty-four hours before my life is destroyed; I need to know as much as you can tell me before it all kicks off.' She could feel her voice wavering. 'I didn't have a choice in any of this, but now I'm committed, I'm bang in the firing line if anything goes wrong. I trust you, but you need to have my back.'

Lana looked contrite. 'I'm so sorry, Lex... Alexandra. I really am, but we can't let him get away with what he did. I... I suppose I didn't really think of anything but Jess, and I knew you'd feel the same. You never told your husband about me?'

Alexandra struggled with the rush of fear. 'No. Do you know the first thing I felt when I heard your voice, knew that you were alive?'

'Tell me.'

'I felt I wanted to hug you, cry, kiss you, and shout at you all at the same time. Lana, we were best friends, until that night. But when you never got in touch, I thought you had died with the rest of the girls, but I hoped, I really, really hoped you might have hopped onboard a private jet and flown off into the sunset. I wanted you to be somewhere sipping cocktails on the beach, living your best life.'

Lana's blue eyes softened slightly, and her mouth trembled. This wasn't exactly the reunion Alexandra had imagined, but like it or not, they were firmly on the same team.

'And I'm so sorry about Jess. I should have said that first. That was another thing I couldn't understand. If you didn't know she was dead, you would have been searching the whole of Brighton for her.' Alexandra leant over to squeeze Lana's hand. 'How did you find out?'

'I went down to the basement. I was in one of the bedrooms with Ahmed, and I'd gone to the toilet. I saw you run back upstairs, looking absolutely terrified and beaten up. I was on my way over to you, but you disappeared through the French doors.' Lana was speaking softly now, her shoulders hunched, hands clenched in her lap. 'People were leaving, and I could hear shouting downstairs from the pool area.' She looked up, met Alexandra's concerned gaze. 'I saw them burying my sister under the rubble, and I screamed at them. I didn't know what I was doing but I found myself clawing at the rubble, the dirt, pulling her body back into my arms.' Tears were suddenly streaming down her cheeks, her shoulders shaking as the grief poured out. 'I was drunk, and I'd taken some coke too, so everything was a blur. I even wondered if I was hallucinating.'

'What did they do?'

'Thomas hit me, dragged me away from Jess, and he had his hands around my throat. Mac and Eddie stopped him from killing me. I was so angry I didn't care if he did kill me too, but the others calmed him down, and Matthew went out the room, came back with a rucksack full of cash. Do you remember those boxes in the hallway?'

'Yes. He gave you a bribe to keep quiet?'

'I didn't know you had seen the bodies too, but I could guess from the state of you that something bad had happened. It was just the four of them, and Niall down there. Niall was in bits, but holding it together, Thomas was coming down from whatever made him high this time and he apologised, said it was a terrible accident, that all three girls had taken some dodgy pills. There was a long moment where nobody spoke and then Matthew took me back upstairs and told me to get out of there.'

'I can't believe they just let you go,' Alexandra exclaimed.

'I was sobering up, realising I guess that the only way to get revenge would be if I could get out alive. Ahmed was still upstairs, waiting. It turns out Matthew had texted him, asked him to take me away.' Lana paused, wiped her eyes, and added, 'Would it be weird to say that as soon as I could think straight, I was already planning to hurt them so badly for what had happened to Jess? It was literally my first reaction, and that has never changed.'

'You loved Jess, and she was killed metres away from us. It's not weird, it's strong and brave.' Alexandra studied her friend carefully, trying to remember Ahmed.

'Ahmed was a nice guy. Very wealthy family, wife and five kids, and he often kept a few girls on the side. I'd been on a few dates with him, and Matthew must have seen us together earlier that evening.' She sighed. 'I saw him pay Ahmed something, and that was it. I went outside and got in the car with nothing except my purse and the rucksack full of cash. My heart was torn apart, but you had run away, Jess was dead. I didn't know what I was doing.'

'Oh Lana!' Alexandra hunched forward, taking her friend's cold hands and squeezing them gently in her own. Lana returned the pressure.

'You'll be pleased to hear some of the lavish lifestyle bit did happen. It was the weirdest thing, like I was floating. I kept seeing Jess everywhere we went, and I dream about her almost every night. I have been living abroad as Ahmed's girlfriend ever since... ever since the party.' For the first time Lana sounded less sure of herself, even glancing down and picking at the sleeve of her flowered dress, a gesture Alexandra remembered.

'Was he kind to you? Have you been happy?' Alexandra was trying to imagine what Lana's life had been like, as mistress to a billionaire. To think they used to joke about finding a sugar daddy.

Lana gave a little dry, bitter laugh. 'Happy? God, Alexandra, life isn't like a fairy-tale. There is no happy ever after when you know you're lucky to be alive. Actually, that's not true, there are times when I have been happy, and Ahmed is a good man. He looked after me, was horrified that Thomas had hit me that night. I've had my own place, I've travelled, shopped and after the shock had worn off, I studied, got a business degree, and settled into my new life. I also started to plan. Because on the outside I know I seemed fine, but on the inside, Jess was with me twenty-four-seven.'

'I tried so hard to find you,' Alexandra told her.

'I wanted to find you too, but I knew it was dangerous. If I saw you, I knew I'd tell you what happened to Jess and that would put you in the firing line as well. I still wasn't sure what had happened to you that night, if you knew, if they had black-mailed you too. Ahmed might have been shocked at what Thomas did to me, but they were all still in touch, still friends.

It's like a ridiculous secret society.' Lana pushed her hair back behind her ears, drawing a long shaky breath.

'And you trusted Ahmed enough to tell him about Jess?' Alexandra said gently. Her own shock at what had happened to Lana made her blink back tears of anger. All these years.

She shook her head. 'I never told him what I saw, because I never knew how much he was feeding back to Thomas, Matthew, Eddie, or Mac.' She leant forward, a strand of hair falling over her left cheek. It was only then, as her movement threw her into the light streaming through the windows, that she smiled and Alexandra thought that she was still beautiful as ever, still the same brave, smart girl she had shared so much with.

She drew the candy bracelet from her pocket, and held it in her palm. 'I had an idea on the way over. Kaye needs more evidence and I think we need more help.'

'I'm listening.'

'Mac. Gareth. Whoever he is now, I want to talk to him. They tried to screw him over, and I think he'll be on our side. It doesn't matter that he's been cleared of murder; they killed his girlfriend and destroyed his life without even thinking. Plus, he saved me from Thomas. Twice.' Alexandra tried to keep her voice steady, confident, but the truth was she was shit-scared about approaching Gareth. What if he didn't want to know? Or thought she had somehow been part of setting him up?

Lana stood up, staring blankly at a grand piano encased in a dust sheet. She was quiet for a long moment. 'Maybe. It's a risk when we have so little time.'

'Everything is a risk. If Gareth will talk to Kaye as well, we have a powerful ally. She's a journalist, and she has to have indisputable evidence, or she'll be ruined too. It evens the odds, having someone else on our side, Lana. But I need to do it today if I can. If he doesn't seem receptive, I'll just back off, I promise... Do you trust me?'

Lana was tapping an elegant fingernail against her lips, eyes distant, mulling it over. Finally, she nodded. 'Do it. I also want you to know two things. Number one, I have had limited choices in a life I never wanted and number two, I knew I would one day get justice for Jess, and that meant I needed to stay in that inner circle. They might be watching me, but I was watching them too. Who better to be mistress of than Ahmed, who happened to be friends with my sister's murderer?'

THIRTY-FOUR

Alexandra stared at her. 'Okay. Kaye will be here any minute. We talk to her, do the initial interview and make sure she has everything. As soon as I can, I'll go and find Ma... I mean Gareth.'

'Do you know where he lives?'

She smiled. 'Of course I do. If he won't help it doesn't matter. He's hardly going to warn Thomas that I contacted him, and I'm not going to tell him what we have planned.'

Lana nodded, as though Alexandra had just made a valid point in a business meeting. Her blonde hair was long, beautifully set in bouncy curls, and these moved softly as she turned her head. The likeness to her sister was painfully hard to ignore. But the difference was the hardness, the set of her jaw, and the wrinkles none of them had worn twenty years ago. Battle scars.

'What about Ahmed? What will he do when all this comes out?'

Lana shook her head. 'He won't care. It won't touch him or his family. He's based in Dubai now. We still keep in touch, but we haven't been together properly for a couple of years. I invested everything I earned, and I sold the gifts he gave me. I'm a wealthy, educated woman, just like I always wanted.' A shadow crossed her face. 'I set up corporations, limited companies, invested money, bought and sold properties, until I was secure, and ultimately in a position to buy the party house when it came up for sale.'

Revenge. Lana had admitted she was doing this for revenge, and Alexandra was shocked at the respect she felt for the other woman. She was fighting back, not just watching Thomas take over the world; she was planning to take him down. 'I still can't believe it was you who applied for planning permission for the basement.' She had been right: for all their wild partying, Lana had always had a razor-sharp, analytical brain.

'I wasn't sure what I would do at first. Thomas had been going on about dodgy pills, but nobody else at the party died, and all three girls were in the bloody swimming pool. I kept going over and over it in my head, how the other men almost didn't seem surprised...'

'I'm sure Eddie said something like, "Did you kill another girl?" when he and Matthew got to the graveyard room,' Alexandra told her. 'It didn't really occur to me that Thomas was telling the truth.'

'Over the years I did my business management course, my degree, and watched Thomas. When it became clear her was going to get away with everything, that karma had just backed off, I knew I had to do something. I got his private contact details from Ahmed's phone ages ago, and I created a random email account to tell him all about how the graveyard was about to be dug up, and that I knew the three bodies were victims of his.' The anger in her face made Alexandra reach for her hand again. 'Jess should be enjoying her life, not rotting in a basement.'

'I know.'

The doorbell made them both jump, and Alexandra hurried to peek out of the window. 'It's okay, it's just Kaye.'

Kaye, dressed in expensive sportswear, and trailing two adorable little French bulldogs, shook hands with them both and Lana escorted her into the living room. 'I hope you don't mind the dogs, but they go crazy if I leave them at home alone.'

'They're cute.' Lana was already stroking the small velvet heads.

'Nice place,' Kaye said, smiling at both women, 'and it's great to meet you at last, Lana. I'm so sorry about your sister, about everything that happened, but I'm honoured you trust me enough to share your secrets.'

'Kaye, we've decided to ask Gareth Sellers if he might have anything to add to the story,' Alexandra said.

'Okaaaay... That's an idea, but he has just come out of a murder trial,' Kaye said doubtfully.

'He's all tied up in it, and we think that's why he was even on trial.' Alexandra added hastily, 'We don't have proof and we aren't trying to complicate things, but if he comes over to our side, there's no doubt this is watertight. Gareth was there when the girls were murdered.'

'He'll land back in trouble with the police for helping to cover up the deaths of three girls,' Kaye pointed out.

'I know, but I want to try,' Alexandra said stubbornly. 'Oh, and Lana, Niall's putting the pressure on. I did tell Kaye one of Thomas's lackeys was threatening me.'

'*Bastard.*' The anger in Lana's face was painful to see. 'It's a shame he isn't dead. I saw him on the floor as we left. He was covered in blood. Thomas beat the shit out of him.'

'Really? *Why?* That's not what he said.' Alexandra felt the room spin a little. 'Sorry, Lana, but the way he told it, after he tried to save the girls, they pretty much all became best buddies.'

'They all seemed to be fighting, but Thomas was definitely taking a lot of anger out on Niall.' Lana, recovering, gave a little thoughtful nod.

Alexandra caught her eye, responding swiftly. 'Sorry, we'll talk about Niall later.'

Kaye was taking notes, frowning, occasionally putting a quick question as they talked.

Alexandra nodded slowly as she spoke. 'Niall and Thomas want Gareth Sellers to take the fall for all of this, and they want me to go to the police and be a witness.'

'I don't understand.'

'They set up Gareth, and they failed, so I suppose the fall-back is me. If they knew where Lana was, and I would bet they've asked Ahmed a million times, they might have tried to get at her too.'

'I've got tea and coffee if anyone wants?' Lana offered, wandering towards the kitchen.

'It's a hell of a story,' Kaye said, sitting down, talking firmly to her dogs, who lay down on the wooden floorboards.

'And you're positive we can put it out there?' Alexandra asked bluntly. She glanced at her watch, aware she still needed to get over to the other side of Brighton to visit Gareth. 'Because this can't go wrong.'

'I'm putting my neck on the line, my professional reputation, so don't worry, if I didn't think it would fly, I would be backing off right now,' the journalist said firmly. 'Did you get the photos?'

Lana came back with three mugs and sat down opposite. She took a sip of tea and frowned. 'Will the photos be enough?'

Kaye nodded. 'Every piece of evidence is crucial. The photos are time stamped and dated, so they place Thomas at the party, with the girls.'

'And we're witnesses.'

'Yes. You have to remember you didn't actually see Thomas drown these girls, so the story is about how Thomas Blake has skeletons in his closet,' Kaye explained. 'It links him to a scandal, to the drugs – that photo is great, Lana – to the girls, to you and the house and the other men involved. We aren't accusing him of anything, we are just causing a splash by saying Mr Perfect is not Mr Perfect.'

The two dogs sat panting at Kaye's feet, and she leant down and fed them each a treat. When she sat up, she faced Lana and said, 'You have planning permission. When are your builders starting?'

Lana looked at her. 'Tomorrow. They only have to make the area safe and dig through the concrete in that one place. We could be looking at three open graves by tomorrow night.' A flash of pain darkened her expression. 'My sister's bones.'

'Okay.' Kaye was eyeing her carefully. 'That will help when we break the story. We can link it to the news that bodies have been discovered in the alleged party house.'

Lana stared at her, licked her lips quickly, and continued, 'I have other names, lists, so many photos, after I worked out who was at the parties. It wasn't all rich playboys; these are men in power, in charge of billion-pound investment portfolios, politicians, a member of the royal family even...'

'Keep everything, and we can look through the other pictures, see what we can use, but stick to the basics. We aren't accusing, merely breaking a story the public needs to know about. Lana?' Kaye looked hard at the woman opposite her and then at her phone, which had started to ring. 'Are you alright if I run with this, with what we've got right now? I've already started on the main story outline, and if Gareth comes through, it will just strengthen the evidence. If not, we have enough. Be prepared for it to get extremely messy though, and the police will want to interview you both.'

Kaye stood up, the dogs trotting obediently at her heels, and headed for the front door. She pulled her baseball cap firmly down over her face and turned back briefly. 'I'll put the schedule on our group chat, so you'll know when to prepare yourselves or anyone else you want to know before the scandal hits. Thomas is in Brighton tomorrow. It's a two-day visit for meetings and shit. We'll break the story on day two.'

Lana shut the door firmly behind her, and suddenly said, 'What about your husband, Alexandra? Will he stick by you?'

It was the first time she had asked this, maybe even the first time she had considered what Alexandra had to lose. 'I don't know. I hope I could tell him the truth and he would understand, but I... I don't know.' She had no idea. Before Harlan started acting so strangely, she might have thought, when she did eventually tell him, he would help her, protect her, because they were a team, a unit. But now? Now he had money she never knew about; he had lied to her about where it was coming from, and seemed to be doing everything he could to get out of the country.

'Alexandra?'

'Sorry, just thinking. I really need to go and find Gareth now.' Even the thought was making her knees weak. But look at what Lana had been through over the years. She could do this and find a way out.

'Having a family, anyone you care about, is a weakness,' Lana told her, almost as though she was reading her thoughts. 'It means people can hurt you.'

Alexandra hugged her arms across her chest and tried not to let tears fall.

'Oh, Alexandra, what a bloody mess.' Just for a second, she sounded just like the old Lana who had shared pizza nights on the beach, who had done her eyeliner in huge flicks before they went out clubbing, who had giggled with her over the assignments they had been set and drunk coffee late into the night revising for exams.

Without either of them seeming to move, suddenly she felt Lana's arms around her, and they were clinging together, both sobbing great gut-tearing rasps. She could feel her friend's fragility but also her strength, and it just felt so good to let it out, to be with someone who understood the secrets because they shared them.

Finally, they drew apart and Alexandra said, 'We are going to be helping to bring down a government minister, and causing the scandal of the decade. Shit, I'm terrified.'

The significance of this seemed to hang in the air, to echo through the stale and empty house. Traffic passed outside, a baby cried from the house next door, but both women stood motionless.

'Are you having second thoughts?'

Alexandra sighed, 'I can't, can I? Either Niall and Thomas wreck my life, maybe even literally take my life, or I choose this way out and do it myself.'

'I'm sorry.'

'It's for Jess,' Alexandra said softly. 'I'm in. It's okay, I'm still ready for this. It's just... I'm scared.'

Those were exactly the same words she had used twenty years ago when Lana had proposed working for the Candy Girls. She was doing what she had to do to survive, now as she had then, and she had no idea if her family or career would survive the bombshell that was shortly going to be dropped. But she had no choice. She was out of luck and out of time.

'I'm scared too.' A last hug and Lana smiled. 'Love you, Lexy.'

THIRTY-FIVE

Alexandra drove quickly along the coast road. Before she'd left Lana, Kaye had already sent through a schedule, and the name of the paper that would get the exclusive. This did nothing to help her nerves, and as she sat at the traffic lights at Portslade, she wondered how the hell she had managed to get into this mess. The prospect of brazenly turning up at Gareth's place and asking him to wreck his life was terrifying, but what choice did she have?

Her phone rang and she answered on the hands free. 'Hi, Harlan. I'll be about an hour. I've got a few errands to run. Do you want me to do dinner? Make the most of our child-free nights?' How would her children react to the story? Her friends? Her clients?

'I really need you to come home right now. I've got something we need to talk about.'

No, no, no! Not now. 'Can we talk over dinner. I've just got an appointment...'

'Please, Alex, this is urgent. Honestly, I... I need to talk to you right now. I've found out something... I can't quite believe it's true, but I need to talk to you.'

He must know. How could he have found out? Perhaps Niall had told him, just to give Alexandra less choice about going to the police. If her marriage was already destroyed, she had less to lose. That was exactly how Niall would see it. And oh, god, he sounded terrible, she noted as the pain twisted in her heart, and the sharp stab of betrayal in his voice made her agree to go home.

She would still have to see Gareth, but she needed to make her peace with her husband first, however that might turn out.

As soon as she was through the door, she took in his distraught expression, and knew it was time. Before he could say a word she blurted it all out, from the Candy Girls, to what happened that awful night, how she'd tried to outrun it and focus on building their life together – the life she loved so much and wanted so badly to protect – and how it had all hurtled back to the surface with the trial. After all the years and weeks of hiding she was surprised at how coherently she managed to say the words, and how unafraid she felt, now that it was finally out in the open between them.

'I'm so sorry that I didn't tell you all of this, but I was trying to protect you and the kids, trying to see if it would go away, I suppose.' It was as she finished speaking and saw his expression settling into a look of total shock that she realised she might have made a terrible mistake. Her guilt had driven her to assume this was the awful news he had found out about, and wanted to discuss with her, but everything about his expression told her he had no idea.

'You shouldn't have gone looking for trouble,' Harlan told her, as she sat ashen-faced, gripping her woollen cardigan around her for comfort. 'These people are dangerous. You have no idea what you're dealing with. You should have come straight to me. I can't get my head around this at all. Were you ever going to tell me?'

It was worse than she had imagined. When she had touched on her involvement with the Candy Girls she had watched his face change from a mixture of fear and exhaustion to absolute disgust. A few things she had held back. Mindful of her commitment to Lana and Kaye she kept quiet about the story, about Niall, about Gareth. Okay, most of the story she held back, she admitted to herself as she watched his face. He might try and stop them, and that left her at the mercy of Thomas. He wouldn't understand; he had never been around these kinds of people.

'What do you want me to say?' Alexandra asked. Her voice was soft, and the pain was deep. 'It was a long time ago and we have built a whole life together since then.'

He gave a dry, sarcastic little laugh. 'A life based on lies. You were an escort, and you slept with men for money.'

'What?' Her head went up and she blinked at him in confusion. 'I didn't sleep with them.'

'Does it even matter? You were still part of it.' There was hurt in Harlan's voice, but she couldn't tell if it was pain from the hurt, or just that she had been proven to be damaged goods, not quite as top shelf as he thought she was. If you put someone up on a pedestal, there was only one way for them to go, wasn't there?

'Harlan, this was a very long time ago. I was nineteen, trying to support myself and study at the same time. I had three crappy jobs and I still couldn't pay the rent. My landlord was going to kick us all out!'

His expression said she was disgusting, but she ploughed on. 'I never had sex with any clients, but yes I occasionally sent them videos and pictures, which they paid for. Me and my flat-mates all did.' She paused. 'It seemed like just a bit of fun, and a way to pay the rent. It's how I turned my life around, dammit. I would never have had the money to buy property, start the clinic if I hadn't earnt so much with the Candy Girls.'

'It's shocking that you would have done something like this. You were a prostitute.'

'I wasn't!' She slammed a hand down on the table. 'Shit, Harlan, this was more about serving drinks and running a bar than having sex. This is no different to any other job. It paid my rent, let me eat, let me save to finish my degree. Are you telling me you never did anything remotely silly when you were younger?'

'Not like this!' He raised his voice too, and instinctively glanced at the ceiling, before apparently remembering Sophie and Tom were at their grandparents'.

The gesture caught at her heart. Their children, their lives. How could she possibly explain? But a little part of her was angry. Why should she need to explain something she had done years before they met? She hadn't done anything illegal, and she was telling the truth. Sort of. A little bit. He was never going to accept what happened next, but she couldn't bring herself to tell him any more. She was just so exhausted, lacking the strength to keep explaining, to keep juggling.

Harlan moved away from her, almost as though he was afraid she might contaminate him. 'Anyway, Alex, I didn't call you home because I knew about any of this, and I don't quite understand what's going on. I called you home because something happened at work. Your little secrets and lies, they don't really matter, because I'm not going to be around much longer.'

She stood, frozen in shock, unable to speak, to form any words that could possibly make this better. Harlan's phone rang, and he frowned, picked it up, walked into the kitchen. She thought she could tell by the tone of his voice it was a work call.

He was *leaving* her.

The sun poured in through the shutters, the sky was Mediterranean blue, a hint of the perfect spring day outside, and she was standing in her perfect kitchen watching her perfect marriage disintegrate like a tissue in the wash.

Harlan had finished his call, but he was now standing silently, shoulders dropping, his back to her so she couldn't see his face. Ignoring her? She considered walking past him and taking her drink into a room that was echoing with stale arguments but couldn't muster the energy. Instead, she went back to her usual position at the kitchen table and braced herself for what was to come.

He said nothing.

After a few minutes she said softly, 'Harlan? What's going on?' For a crazy moment she thought Thomas might have something to do with whatever had gone wrong with her husband. But Niall had given her a time frame and there was still time for her to go to the police with the fake story. They would be banking on that. Or was this extra pressure? Her brain felt foggy and her mouth clumsy when she tried to speak. There were too many pieces of the puzzle, and nothing was currently fitting into the bigger picture.

Still Harlan said nothing.

He did turn towards her then, but his face was so pale, so shocked, and his demeanour so crushed she forgot everything and ran to put her arms around him. Her husband didn't push her away; in fact, he drew her close, and just for a moment she could pretend it had all been a nightmare, that they were safe, and nobody had been lying.

For a long time, they stayed close together, until he finally, gently moved her away, holding her forearms loosely. 'Alexandra, there's something I need to tell you. Before you get upset, before you start hating me for ruining our lives, I want you to know I did this for us.' His eyes were dark, his face pale. *Guilty.*

'I still don't quite understand what you were trying to tell me about your past... But this is what I called you home for. Because we don't have much time left and I need to explain.'

She stared at him, heart beating wildly. 'You did what for us? You're scaring me now. What the hell is going on?'

Guilty.

THIRTY-SIX

'Hang on, he's actually been *arrested*?' Clara's voice on the phone was incredulous. 'He can't be arrested; he's a police officer!'

'I... Shit, I can hardly even begin to get my head around this, but he's been accused of taking bribes from criminals, making money on the side in exchange for looking the other way when they deal drugs or whatever on the Seahawk Estate.' As Alexandra said the words, she could hardly believe they were coming out of her mouth. She was reeling from this latest blow, but now the initial shock had worn off, the clock was still ticking on her deal with Lana and Kaye, Niall's deadline, and Thomas's arrival in Brighton. She would have to deal with the fallout of Harlan's mistakes later. 'Did you have a good time on your last night?'

'The best. Don't side-track, Alex. How can you even ask that after what's happened to you? Shall I come over?'

'No, honestly, I just need to sort out what's going to happen, talk to Harlan's solicitor, and oh god, the kids are supposed to be coming back from the Lake District. What the hell am I going to tell them? And his parents?' Alexandra paused, pressed her fingertips to her forehead. 'Actually, Clara...'

'Yeah, I can have them. Look, I'm not trying to pry but this thing with Harlan is shocking and I'm your friend, so lean on me a bit.' She sighed down the phone. 'I leant on you, cried all over you and slept a few nights in your bed when Joe left me, so let me give something back. The kids can stay with me for as long as they want. Mine love a sleepover, and then you just need to deal with the in-laws.'

'Thank you,' she whispered, before she ended the call. Then she sat with her head in her hands for a moment, taking deep, slow breaths. *Think, Alexandra, think.*

As she tried to get her head straight, her phone pinged with two messages. The first was from Lana in response to her text after Harlan had been driven away in the back of a police car:

> Shit. I'm so sorry. I wonder if the bastards set him up? Hold on and let me know when to call.

The second was from an unknown number:

> Hallo, Lexy. Long time, no see. I think we need a little chat. Tomorrow. Niall will be in touch.
> Thomas

Holy shit! Ice seemed to be filling her stomach and she glanced at the windows, afraid he was outside. Was the message really from Thomas? If so, he must have got wind of something. Desperate men did crazy things. She called Lana.

Her friend's first words were soft, concerned. 'I'm so sorry about your husband.'

'Thanks. Thomas sent me a text.'

'What the hell?'

'I've just sent it to your phone.' There was silence as Lana read it. 'What do I do?'

'I take it you haven't seen Gareth yet?'

'Been a bit busy,' Alexandra said with a wry shake of her head.

'I'll ring Kaye and ask her. I'm thinking, though, you say yes and arrange a meet.'

'Are you crazy? He might kill us both?'

'Of course he won't, not now, not yet. He more likely wants to buy us off. Let me talk to Kaye. Go to Gareth's.'

'Alright, I'm going...'

'Lexy?'

'What?'

'Stay safe, babes.'

She glanced at her watch. Still time to drive over to Gareth's place. They needed him on their side, and now it looked like she might be on her own with the kids, more than ever this had to work. Her phone pinged again, and as she read the words from her mother-in-law, she swore. No, not right now. Sophie had broken her wrist on the trampoline at a kid's party, and they were on their way to hospital. They wanted a video call.

Sophie had tinsel in her blonde ponytail and Tom was clutching a goodie bag and a balloon. Alexandra's heart ached as she saw their faces, Sophie's a little pale as she supported her injured wrist with her other hand. 'Sophie! What have you been doing?'

'They think I broke my wrist.'

'Oh, baby, does it hurt very much?'

'Not as much as I thought it would. I've never had a cast before. I'm going to get all my friends to sign it,' her daughter informed her stoically.

'Hi, Tom. Are you taking care of your sister?'

'I found her when she fell and I went to get help,' he informed her.

'Good boy. Can you put Gramps on?' The camera moved erratically, towards the passenger seat.

She scrabbled in her bag for tissues as tears leaked out. Why did she only have a useless half packet of mini pocket tissues?

'Mummy? Are you crying?' Tom asked anxiously. 'Sophie will be okay. It's just a bone. She'll probably grow it back in a few weeks.'

'No, sorry, kids. I've got terrible hay fever,' she lied, forcing a cheery tone into her voice.

'Where's Daddy?' Sophie asked.

'He's just gone out, but I'll tell him how brave you're being and how well Tom did,' she promised.

She talked briefly to her in-laws, who reassured her they would keep her updated, that there was no need to rush up there. They were hugely apologetic that something had happened to one of the kids on their watch, and she found herself reassuring them, before blowing kisses to her babies. She couldn't possibly tell them about Harlan, she just couldn't.

In the downstairs toilet, she gave herself five minutes to sit and sob, quietly, before she wiped all her make-up off, brushed her hair back into a ponytail and reapplied waterproof mascara.

She hated lying to them, but what else could she do? *Hey, my precious babies, your daddy just got taken away because he's been accused of corruption, and he's mad at Mummy because she was once an escort and witnessed the deaths of three girls. And Mummy's best friend, who was also an escort, is right now about to blow the whole thing apart because one of the dead girls was her sister.*

Put like that, no wonder she felt like hiding away in this cool airy room and getting senselessly drunk.

She was proud of them both, loved them both so fiercely and protectively. But how best to protect them now? The press hated dirty coppers. Harlan's colleagues would turn on him, and quite rightly so. He had confessed to her, hadn't said he was innocent, or had been wrongly accused, he had said he had taken bribes. Because he loved her and wanted to give her everything.

There was so much she needed to do. She must ring Harlan's solicitor again to find out what was happening. Would he be back home tonight? The solicitor had sounded doubtful. The severity of the offence, she told her, meant her husband was a flight risk, and they knew he had money stashed away, contacts. It was more likely he would be kept in custody for thirty-six hours and probably charged.

This was not what she had wanted to hear. How bloody ironic that she had just severed her links with the courtroom, only to find Harlan was now the guilty one. Perhaps, when the story broke and the bodies were uncovered, she would also be down at the police station. At that point she would probably realise she had made the wrong choice.

There was still time to visit Gareth and persuade him to help. As she drove along the brightly lit seafront, she let her mind reel back to happier times. It had been fun, a laugh, and until the last party, she would have said she had no regrets.

Lana was laughing as they got ready, spraying perfume, playing with her expensive little gifts, her jewellery and her dresses.

'I might just carry on with this job and ditch the degree, you know. Come on, Lexy, don't look like that. I'm making more money than everyone I know, and I get to go to all the best places. Shit, this is bloody brilliant.'

'What the hell?' Jess was making up her own face in the mirror, and she stared at her sister. 'Lana, this isn't real, and do you know what, the more I see of it the more it freaks me out. I mean, it's very pay to play, isn't it?'

Lana slipped a silky lilac dress over her curves. With her luxuriant blonde curls, and curvy figure, she looked incredible. 'I don't see why that should bother you. We have ground rules, and they have ground rules. How much playing you do is up to you.'

'I think they break the rules.' Lexy was slicking on a bright red lipstick. Snapping the gold top back on, she dropped it back into her cosmetics bag, 'And when we're a couple of years older, they'll be wanting younger models. It's hardly a career.'

'Says the girl who hasn't made six grand this month. Come on, you love it, admit it.'

Lexy walked over to her friend. 'I don't. It's a means to an end, and yes I'm hiding money, stashing the gifts, but I'm doing that because I know this thing is going to end soon.'

'How do you know?' Lana's expression changed. 'Oh, did Niall tell you? Babe, I know he's your brother but he's weird sometimes. Sorry, but he is.'

Jess added, 'He keeps coming on to me. Can you drop hints I'm not interested please? He's too intense.'

Lexy shrugged, dragged on a white pleated skirt and knotted a white silk shirt high on her tanned midriff. Her own hair fell in long brown curls to her waist. 'Why don't you tell him?'

'I did, I do, but he's not taking it in.'

'Okay, I'll talk to him. He gets a bit obsessed with a particular girl sometimes but take it as a compliment.'

'Whatever.' Jess held up her camera to snap a picture of all three flatmates, pouting, laughing. 'Stay safe tonight, babes.'

Alexandra's hair blew across her face as she got out of the car. It was dark now, and the wind was cold. Sore and tired eyes, an exhausted face reflected back at her from the glass doors of Gareth's building.

She was just so very tired of pretending, of being someone she wasn't.

THIRTY-SEVEN

I never felt especially comfortable with any of the Candy Girls. Don't get me wrong, it was fun, and we were young, rich, and stupid, and I dated as much as anyone else. But nobody stood out until I met Lexy. It wasn't a sexual attraction. It was because she was resourceful, and sweet and had this air of innocence.

In a funny way she reminded me a little bit of my brother, Jack. He was ten years younger than me, and I enjoyed being the older brother, teasing him, helping him, watching him grow. Maybe because of the age gap.

Jack was so young when I killed him. Him and my parents. I was driving; I'd been drinking with the boys, swore I was fine to pick up my family from the airport and chauffeur them home. Instead, I destroyed my family. It was an accident, and I panicked in the aftermath of the crash. When the emergency services arrived, it looked as though my dad had been in the driver's seat, and nobody ever questioned it.

Thomas also swore it was an accident – the drowning in the lake at university. A party gone wrong. Another accident, but I knew better. I checked the party footage back on my phone, on Eddie's phone; I could see what had happened.

Thomas had enjoyed every minute of it, had lived out a sick and dangerous fantasy. No witnesses. When we started the Brighton parties, Eddie suggested I had little cameras installed in the ceilings, just in case. The others agreed, and it had been a mutual agreement between the four of us to use the tiny, discreet little cameras, but they were not to be placed in bedrooms or down in the pool area. To protect us all, I had installed the cameras in the forbidden areas.

Thomas was a loose cannon, and after the girl at university, it was only a matter of time before he killed again. There was no way I was going to be implicated. Hilarious when you think what happened in the last couple of months.

I believe I am the only person who knows what truly happened the night of the last party. I know Thomas only killed two girls that night, and I know who killed the third girl. All this time I have waited, watched. I probably would have left it alone, because what good could it possibly do? The girls were dead, and it wouldn't bring them back to life any more than I could resurrect my brother and my parents.

The car crash was my fault, but different, I tried to tell myself. Because I never intended to kill anyone, never intended it to happen. It was in a wooded area with a steep drop on one side of the road. Rural, isolated, and we were nearly home. A deer ran across the road.

It might have happened anyway, but all I know is that it might NOT have happened if I'd kept my temper. They all died. Jack was dead there and then from a broken neck, and my parents died later in hospital from their traumatic injuries. I will never forget the silence, the hiss of the engine, the cracking of branches, and the smell of blood, as I lay upside down, squashed against the airbag.

I never had any illusions about my group of uni friends. When we were young, the thing that united us was ambition. We all wanted power and influence, our definition of success. When we were older, the thing that divided us was that imbalance of power. And the secrets we had sworn to hide.

The funny thing is once I realised what was happening, standing trial for murder, when I saw that the bastards had decided I should take the fall, I had already swapped sides. Screw them all! When Lexy came to me for help, I had no hesitation in joining the side of the angels.

I was finally telling the truth.

THIRTY-EIGHT

It hadn't been hard to find out where Gareth lived, and Alexandra pitched up at his building bang on nine at night.

For a long moment she thought he wasn't going to answer the buzzer, but eventually she pushed the heavy door open and started for the lift. The hallway was plush and spoke of money and luxury.

When he opened the door, looking older, greyer than she had expected, his expression gave nothing away.

But the grey eyes were the same, and the curve of his mouth as he smiled took the years away. 'Alexandra.'

'Can I come in?' She smiled suddenly. 'You know my real name.'

'Of course.' He moved to the side of the doorway and waved her through.

'How do you know my name?'

A large top-floor apartment with views of the i360 and a panoramic view of the coastline. She had expected no less. Now she was here she found herself at a loss for words. Instead, memories crowded her mind, so many memories she had tried to forget. So much had happened today that, to her horror, tears were lurking behind her eyes, her throat tight with emotion and her head aching with plans she must complete.

'It doesn't matter. You can be Birdie, Lexy, Alexandra or whoever you want, but you're still... you're still you. Do you want a drink?' He switched subjects abruptly.

'No, thanks. I... Look, this is awkward but I need your help.' She forced herself to focus.

'I saw you in the courtroom.' He sat down on a large black leather sofa, and leant forward, hands on his knees, giving her his full attention.

'I should have stepped down.'

'Why didn't you?'

She sighed heavily, finally giving in to weariness, and sat down opposite him. 'Actually I think I will have a drink. Just the same as you, thanks.'

'Are you in trouble, Alexandra?'

Alexandra looked at him and took a deep breath. She was screwed either way, but Gareth was the one person she could maybe get on her side, on the side of justice. Hell, she had nothing to lose. Everything she had was lost already.

'They set you up, didn't they? Thomas, Eddie, and Matthew?'

His gaze was steady, a clear grey fringed with dark lashes. Encouraged by his silence she began to talk, to explain. When she had finished talking, she couldn't stop nervously twisting her wedding ring around and around her finger.

Gareth had kept his eyes on her face while she spoke, but now he moved slowly towards the window, staring out into the light-speckled darkness of the city.

Finally, she said, 'Well? What do you think? Will you help us? I know it's a lot to ask, and you just got through a murder trial, but we need you. Thomas will be here tomorrow and I'm... I'm so scared, Mac... Gareth.'

He turned, and his face was full of concern, gentleness. She felt an unexpected pang of compassion.

'I will help you. I've heard of your journalist friend, and you're right, the only way to take Thomas down is to use the media. Otherwise, it's impossible to know who to trust, as my murder charge has proven.' He did smile now, a little sadly, and in the dimly lit room, the shadows smoothing his face, he could have been the man she knew. The man she had liked, genuinely liked.

'Okay, that's good. Thomas wants to talk to me tomorrow, so if we can get everything in place with Kaye by then. She'll need to check stuff out for credibility and to make sure Thomas can't wriggle out of it, but...' She rubbed her eyes and pushed her hair back behind her ears. 'Gareth, why did you ever go along with it?'

'It's not something we need to discuss now, but let's just say Thomas, Eddie, Matthew, and I were friends for a long time, and perhaps unwisely, okay definitely unwisely, shared each other's secrets. Thomas was particularly good at getting people to share what perhaps they shouldn't have, so that he could use it against them.'

'I'm sure he was,' Alexandra remarked.

'I believe Thomas was genuinely shocked at the first death, but it became a dangerous compulsion for him. The girls were like toys; you play with them, and it doesn't matter if they get broken. It was a chance to indulge his sickest fantasies and have us cover them up for him.'

Alexandra was feeling nauseous. 'The first death?'

'When we were at university. It was a summer party, near a lake... It doesn't matter. What matters now is keeping you and Lana safe. And your family.'

'Lana and I have photographs and we both witnessed, individually, what happened at the party.' Alexandra frowned. 'I hope it's enough.'

Gareth was silent for a moment, as if he was thinking it over. 'Alexandra, the whole house was rigged with cameras. Even the swimming pool.'

She stood up quickly. 'Shit! Have you got the footage? Of the murders? You mean he did kill them?'

'Yes.' He smiled grimly at her. 'Give me Kaye's number and I'll give her what she needs. Just a couple of things, though: I feel the less Thomas is prepared for any kind of retribution the better. I haven't contacted him or the others since I was arrested. Matthew and Eddie both live abroad and I imagine they will keep a safe distance from the fallout. If you feel you can reply to Thomas's message, even speak to him if you have to, you need to act as though you are about to head to the police station.'

Relief swamped her and she felt light-headed. 'We can prove he killed them.'

'Yes.'

'And Niall?'

'He's a loose cannon, but after tomorrow you won't need to worry about him. Stay away from him and let him believe you are doing what he wants. Make sure your kids are safe and stay with a friend if you have to.'

'Okay,' Alexandra told him, getting up from the leather sofa. 'I need to go. Here's Kaye's number, and Lana's if you need it.'

As they stood in the doorway to his apartment, Gareth said, 'Look, Alexandra, there is one more thing...'

She had known it was too good to be true. Were there strings attached to his offer to help?

'You need to know that Thomas only killed two girls that night.'

Her chest hurt suddenly, breathing fast. 'Who killed the other girl?'

There was so much sadness in his eyes. 'Niall killed Jess on the stairs to the pool.'

'He what? Why?' She remembered her brother's obsession with Jess, her jokingly asking Alexandra to tell him to back off.

'The footage isn't great, but it looks like they met on the stairs, he grabbed her and she pulled away, and she fell...' Gareth sighed. 'He strangled her.'

The door frame propped her up. She opened her mouth, but no words came out.

'I'm so sorry, and I really wasn't sure whether to tell you, but when I show this footage to your journalist friend and then, later, the police, I didn't want you to think I was lying to you.'

'I... I appreciate that.'

She felt weird leaving him after their conversation. As before, all those years ago, she'd felt so comfortable in his presence; he was so easy to talk to, it was hard to believe he had done what he had done. Oh god, Niall, though... As she thought about it, it was as though she had known all along.

The roads were clearer now it was nearing midnight, and she put the radio on to distract her. Green Day were playing. Great. Was it a sign? She had to park further down the road, because some idiot was in her space. Cursing, she grabbed her bag and began to walk.

The shadows lengthened as she approached home, and she felt her breath quickening, pulse accelerating. If Niall had been going to kill her, he would have done it already. A text from Kaye told her to start a conversation with Thomas but tread very carefully. A wave of relief made her shoulders sag as she turned up the garden path, followed by the pain of the knowledge Harlan wouldn't be at home, cooking, in bed already if he had an early shift, texting her sweet emojis if he was starting a night shift. For a moment the pain in her own head was too much to cope with and she froze, heart racing.

She couldn't do this now, couldn't succumb to a panic attack when so much depended on her keeping a level head. Alexandra reached out and her trembling fingers encountered the wall. It was rough and cold against her skin. She squeezed tight, then released. She was okay, she would deal with things a piece at a time, and they would all be okay. They would.

Finally, she arrived at her own front door, let herself in and shut the door behind her, the relief leaving her weak-kneed. She checked every window and door was locked, made sure the old back door was secure, and slipped upstairs. Before she went to bed, she again texted Lana and Kaye.

Just one message back from Lana.

Thomas texted me too. He's got my number. WTF???

THIRTY-NINE

It was such a risk, but Alexandra felt safer knowing Gareth was just outside. Gareth was sure the other two would turn on Thomas when the news broke, and it would finally all be over. Lana, at her side, was shivering, and Alexandra felt the other woman take her cold fingers in a gentle squeeze.

'What happens if he just kills us?'

'They won't. They can't. It's gone too far for that,' Alexandra whispered to her. 'Remember why we're doing this.'

'Justice for Jess.'

'Right. And to show the world that it doesn't matter if you're the big man on a TV show or a politician, you can't get away with murder.' Alexandra felt her own heart speed up just hearing the words out loud as they walked upstairs.

'Nothing to lose?'

She gave Lana's hand one last squeeze. 'Nothing to lose.'

The top room in the townhouse was large but unpretentious, and Thomas himself greeted them. There were no staff that Alexandra could see, but she imagined the conversation was being recorded, that many people would be listening, perhaps even watching remotely.

'Ladies.' Thomas smiled graciously but she could tell it was killing him to do it. 'Take a seat and let's talk.' He glanced at his watch and motioned for them to sit down.

The ridiculousness of the situation made bubbles of hysteria rise in Alexandra's throat. She took a sip of water from the glasses on the low table in front on them.

His voice changed. 'Let's not mess around, girls. I believe you are both somehow trying to blackmail me with an event you believe may have occurred twenty years ago.'

'Let me be clear.' Alexandra was pleased at how strong and confident her voice sounded. She felt the warmth of Lana's body next to her, drew courage from her friend. 'We are here because you asked us to come, and because Niall led me to believe you have created some kind of deadline for me to give false evidence to the police.'

'I'm really not sure why you should think that... I'm here because I am concerned about you. Niall... He was employed by me, but I had to let him go.' A swift, smooth upward look. 'His behaviour was increasingly erratic, and he was prone to... psychotic episodes. I tried to get him help, but he didn't want it.'

Alexandra had imagined he was going to try and lie, but this was a new and interesting slant. Did he suspect Niall had killed Jess? She hadn't actually found a way to tell Lana this bit of news yet; she had asked Mac to do it for her. She hadn't slept at all, going over and over what Lana might do when she discovered, okay, she was about to take down a murderer, but that person was not responsible for her sister's death. Alexandra hauled her tumbling thoughts together.

Meanwhile, Thomas, blissfully unaware that Mac had the footage from the swimming pool, was actually going to pretend he wasn't a murderer at all. Beside her she felt Lana tense.

'You surely aren't going to tell us Niall killed those girls?' Lana's voice was gentle, mocking, and Alexandra felt herself jump.

'I have no idea,' Thomas continued confidentially. 'I admit I was a party boy when I was younger, myself and my friends, but this talk of dead girls is shocking. I really don't remember which party you are referring to.'

'Are you denying you were involved with the Candy Girls?'

'The Candy Girls was a little venture set up by Matthew. A name given to the many girls who partied with us at the time. It was nothing seedy,' Thomas pointed out. 'You two were there, having fun with us, I remember. And now, perhaps you regret some behaviour from your past? Alexandra, I know your husband is in rather hot water at work, and Lana, you have been seeing a therapist for the last couple of years. This fantasy about dead girls... A blackmail opportunity, or revenge maybe, for Ahmed ending your relationship, Lana?'

Surprise flickered in her face, but Lana sat up straighter. 'No, this is revenge for you murdering my sister.'

Seemingly genuine confusion crossed his face. 'Your sister?'

Lana nodded. 'Jess was only seventeen. She ran away from her foster home and ended up with me and Alexandra. She was wild and excited for what her life might be if she managed to turn it around. You killed her at that last party, along with the other two girls.'

Thomas leant back in his chair, eyes narrowed. 'I really have no idea what you are talking about. I don't remember a girl called Jess.'

'Why did you want to see us?' Alexandra asked. 'What was the point of this meeting?'

His expression changed, and he smiled again, all smooth, cold good looks and expensive aftershave. 'I am suggesting it would be wise to stop trying to blackmail me. Stop this right now, and if you apologise, I can make everything go away. Alexandra, what your husband has done is dreadful, but I'm sure he was under a lot of strain; I can help him.' He turned to Lana. 'I'm so sorry you lost your sister, but believe me when I say I had nothing to do with any deaths. I think, I honestly do think that perhaps Niall may have been responsible for whatever may have happened. I tried to help him for years, as I would any employee, but as I say, he became increasingly unstable. Perhaps this, coupled with a guilty conscience, led him to develop an obsession with his sister, with Alexandra's life. A life perhaps he would have liked for himself?'

Alexandra sat rigid, turning all this over in her mind, feeling out his defence, wondering if he could use it as a viable option. She knew Lana, frozen beside her, would be thinking the same. Ironically, given that her brother had probably killed Mac's girlfriend, Sara too, it was something that could work. Kaye had said not to mention the footage, just to get a feel for what Thomas wanted, might offer.

Thomas, clearly confident that business had been concluded, smiled again, and rose to his feet, reaching for his suit jacket. 'Thank you both for coming, and I do hope I've managed to straighten things out for you. Now you have aired your concerns you can tell me if you would like me to go to the police with your suspicions.'

'What?' Lana blurted out.

He adjusted his tie and buttoned the jacket. 'I am happy to tell them what I know about Niall if it will set your mind at rest. And Alexandra...' His eyes rested a little too long on her face, a faint shadow of confusion in his own. 'Let me know how I may best help your husband.'

FORTY

Lana had slept over at hers, and the two women had stayed up all night, waiting, watching to see what might happen. Kaye, calm and professional, had kept to her schedule, read the copy back to them, sent over the finished spread. All in all, she had allowed them final approval, even though if they had decided not to go through with this, she could have run it anyway.

The journalist's integrity had soothed Alexandra, but Lana had become more and more jumpy as the hours wore on. Mac had called, spoken to Lana and she had cried tears of frustration that Niall, her sister's killer, was still out there. 'What have I done?' she whispered to Alexandra across the pillow, as they lay side by side as they had as teenagers.

They were watching the news when the story broke. The red banner screaming of a Thomas Blake Scandal running along the TV screen. Social media erupted with a million different views. But the main publication ran the full story, just as Lana and Alexandra had approved. Kaye was interviewed, immaculate, tough and professional, saying she believed people needed to know the truth and that was why she had uncovered this story.

Thomas Blake was pictured leaving the townhouse, being driven away, stonily announcing 'No comment,' to a growing crowd of reporters.

Another camera crew filmed the party house, running the story of three bodies discovered within the last twenty-four hours during renovations to a Brighton townhouse, linking this straight to Kaye's story.

The police issued a statement, saying they were investigating.

'Are you okay if I go home and pick up some stuff?' Lana finally asked at 6pm.

'Sure. I hope Gareth is okay.' He was at the police station again, but voluntarily this time.

During the day, Kaye had kept in touch, as she'd promised. Lana and Alexandra were not named in the article, also as promised. By evening they had achieved what they set out to do.

Lana slipped away into the evening and Alexandra wondered briefly if that was the last she would see of her. After all, she had accomplished what she had set out to do. Maybe she would just cut her losses and disappear again, not stay to face questions from the police, the inevitable and stressful fallout over the coming days, weeks, probably months.

Harlan was still being held in custody. The scale of his deception was extensive, and she couldn't believe how he had been sucked into the criminal underworld thoroughly.

The kids were still with their grandparents, and Sophie was making everyone sign her cast, both of her babies unaware of the huge changes in their lives. It broke her heart whenever she thought about how she would navigate all of this. How could she tell them Daddy had done a bad thing, and could be in police custody for a long time before he was even tried and sentenced? The family she had worked so hard for was shattered forever by that alone. Having experienced the media reaction to Thomas, it wasn't hard to see how Harlan might easily become a hot topic on the socials.

She was curled on the sofa in the living room, watching the fallout of Thomas's fall from grace, the media frenzy, when a noise made her jump. Grabbing her phone, she moved cautiously, heart racing. Hesitating in the doorway to the hall, she could sense someone was there. An intruder inside her house.

Another step, with adrenalin spiking and her other hand curled into a fist, before Niall erupted from the shadow of the bannisters, snarling at her.

'What the fuck do you think you've done?'

'What do you mean?' She tried to dial 999 but he pushed her hard against the kitchen doorframe. She dodged and moved to the other side of the table.

'You've ruined my life. You and bloody Lana.'

'Why are you doing this?' she asked, trying to control her terror, her shock as she edged slowly, barely breathing along the side of the table. If she could only get to the door.

'You set me up! Thomas is blaming me for all the deaths.' Niall was staring at her in disbelief, one hand gripping the kitchen knife, the other the edge of the table. 'He won't take my calls but one of his staff told me he's telling the police I killed those bloody girls and Sara.'

It wouldn't do any good to tell him she knew he had, so she tried for a calming tone. 'I know you always looked out for me.' Alexandra took a breath, her heart pounding so hard she could barely force the words out. 'I like to think I did the same for you, but Thomas is facing an enquiry now, his career will be over, and he decided to try and blame you. Not me!'

'I worked so hard for him.' Anger in his voice and the knuckles of his hands grew white, jaw clenched. 'And I blew it by trying to help you at the same time. That was bloody misplaced loyalty, wasn't it? You and that bitch Lana, laughing at me, when really you were just fucking escorts.'

'I want you to go, Niall. Go now while you still can. You told me you had money, contacts, and now you can use them to get away.' She knew he wouldn't, but if she could just get him to leave, she could call the police herself.

He studied her for a moment. 'Do *you* think I killed anyone?'

This mattered. She bit her lip – she had to lie or he'd lose it completely. 'No, Niall, I don't. It was all Thomas, and he's trying to get out of it. Go, quickly, before anyone figures out where you are.'

'What if I told you I did kill someone? Not long ago, either.'

She stared at him for a beat longer, absorbing the information, remembering how she had defended him, hidden the truth from herself. 'What?'

His eyes flickered, as if he was amused. 'That confused you, didn't it?'

'What are you talking about? You killed Sara?'

He made a dismissive gesture with his hand. 'Yes. But at the party, I killed someone too.'

So it was true. She closed her eyes and saw Niall arriving in the graveyard room with Jess in his arms. Niall had killed Jess that night because she had turned him down. She had been on her way down to the pool, to join the other girls with Thomas, when she ran into Niall. How bloody ironic.

'Did Mac know?' she asked, though she knew that he did.

He seemed to deliberate for a moment, then admitted, 'Nobody else knew. There was the panic about the others. Thomas was off his head, and it was easy to let everyone assume all three girls had died in the pool.' Niall studied her. 'You should have just let Gareth take the blame, then all of this would have gone away.'

'It would have been wrong, and you're stupid if you think it would have gone away. My life would still have been ruined. You need to go, Niall. Just go and run and get away. I won't say anything, just leave me alone.'

'Yes, you will be alone because the fucking big man police officer was caught with his hands all dirty, throwing blood money at you. You made another bad choice there, Alexandra. I know all about that, and he won't be coming home to you.'

He moved so quickly she barely had time to make two strides towards the door, before he grabbed her arm, twisting it painfully, so they were cheek to cheek. He held her close and ran the blade of the kitchen knife along her collarbone. She could feel the sting, the wetness of blood.

'Sorry, I'm sorry.' He paused and, for a tiny second, she thought she felt his regret. It was all she needed. She flung herself backwards, pushing both of them onto the floor, and when his grip loosened, she scrabbled for the knife.

But his hands were no longer tight on her body, and he was lying still. Grabbing the knife, still filled with that primeval terror and instinct, she leapt back with the knife in her own hands, ready to strike. With the other she was fumbling for her phone.

He wasn't moving. There was a growing pool of blood on the dark tiles around his head. Was he breathing? Confused, she watched for a moment, but then he pushed himself slowly up onto one elbow, wiped blood from his eyes and looked at her with such hatred. She ran from the room, into the old larder, phone in her hand, knife in the back pocket of her jeans. Before Niall could recover, she slammed the door shut, yanking the chest of drawers she had wedged against the outside door, and shoving with all her strength. It slid across the tiles with a shriek and sweat poured down her back, her muscles cramping.

She slid the knife out onto the cool tiled floor, and slumped with her back to the door, shivering, whispering to herself

'*Please, please, please...*' It seemed to take forever for her 999 call to go through, and she watched the signal on her phone fade and then, thank god, strengthen.

The call handler was still on the other end of the line but she was shaking so much that she dropped her phone Slow footsteps along the tiles, the hiss and metallic twang as another knife was drawn from the butcher's block on the work surface.

'*Come on!*' She strained her ears, trying to hear sirens, praying for sirens. He would know it was too late then; he would run away.

Footsteps in the kitchen. Slow and shuffling but coming towards the door.

'Hey, Birdie, we aren't done yet.'

She stayed silent, shaking.

'*Alexandra?*'

Fury mingled with terror. He had stalked her before and now he was hunting her down in her own home. It would be madness to open the door. She stayed where she was, praying she would hear sirens, that the police would be coming to end her nightmare.

'Come on, let's talk.' His breathing was laboured, but he was still able to notch it up as anger flared again. '*I said talk to me!*'

He was banging on the walls with his fists now as he approached the door, and finally, thumping on the old wood. 'Time's up.' Niall tried to push the door open, but the chest of drawers held fast. Perhaps weaker because of his injury, the door and furniture only moved a couple of inches.

But finally, blessedly, she could hear sirens in the street outside, see the flash of blue lights through the high window in the old larder. There was a pause and a scuffle outside, before the footsteps began to retreat. She tried to track them, tried to hear where he was going. Upstairs?

Hammering at the front door, shouts, and a bang as the door was opened from the outside.

Only when she could hear sounds of a struggle, of her brother shouting it was all a mistake and that she had attacked him, did she force her stiff limbs upright, and walk towards the door.

FORTY-ONE

She stood alone in the house she loved. The house that had been bought with the money made from prostitution, from drugs, and from violence. How strange that she could have believed she was the one with secrets to hide, when all along her own husband had been part of the world she had been running from.

Alexandra ran light fingertips over her wooden kitchen table, over her marble countertops.

'You have to believe me when I tell you I did it for you and the kids.'

She didn't. Well, she did partly, but the other side to Harlan, the one she had only recently seen, showed how much he cared about appearance, about what people thought. It mattered to him that she was beautiful and successful, that the kids were adorable and cute, and he had a very narrow idea of what being beautiful and successful was.

Harlan's parents had been shocked, horrified when they too had discovered their house had been bought using dirty money. But they had remained supportive of Harlan, maintaining he had only been taking the bribes so he could support his family. Alexandra knew it was deeper than that.

He had enjoyed playing the game, had been drawn into the criminal world just as she had been, with promises of money and power. But she had been young, naïve, had moved on, while Harlan had been on an opposite timeline, moving further into the darkness, realising far too late he was caught in a web of blackmail and broken promises.

The woman standing next to her was silent, supportive.

'I'm sorry I didn't tell you about Niall. It was just too much to process, you know. And we were never going to back down on the plan, were we?'

'It's okay, I understand.'

Alexandra covered her friend's hand with her own. 'What will you do now?'

Lana shrugged, her eyes distant for a moment, and then she smiled. 'I'll live in the house in Worthing. It's a peaceful place, and I can still dabble in my business portfolio. And I'll be near to you. Maybe...' It was said hesitantly. 'Maybe you could introduce me to your friends. I'd love to see your kids. They look beautiful.'

Alexandra smiled too. 'I would love to have you close. I've missed you so much,' And she knew she had, that the part of her that had shared the dark times had come back, the missing piece replaced. It was as though Lana was lighter, younger; the obligation she had set herself twenty years ago had been achieved.

Thomas had been brought to justice in the only way he could be. He would never regain any kind of political footing, and he would be prosecuted. His life's ambitions, dreams, and reputation were now in tatters.

Niall was facing two murder charges, but Alexandra knew Lana was only concerned with the one girl. It was a kind of justice.

· · ·

Alexandra gripped the green railings tightly as she watched the ebb and flow of the waves. The day was hot, and she could taste the sweet promise of summer in the salty air.

'What will you do now?' He was next to her, leaning his forearms on the same railings, also staring out to sea.

'You mean now my husband is up on fraud charges, and my brother turns out to be a murderer... I still can't even begin to get my head around this.' Alexandra gave a bitter laugh. The salty spring breeze was lazily lifting her long hair. She knew her brown roots were showing, but she didn't care. She wondered if she might return to her soft brown curls, just as she wondered why everyone in her life had been lying to her. She closed her eyes and repeated the mantra she'd told herself, over and over, to remind herself what really mattered. 'My kids are safe, my mum is safe, and Lana is and always has been my best friend.'

'You did the right thing, made the right choices in the end,' Gareth said gently. 'And Niall, he was never your brother, not through blood and not through friendship. He was going to destroy you one way or the other, Alexandra, and he would have killed you.'

She didn't answer.

'Alexandra, do you want me to stick around for a bit?' Gareth turned to look at her, and she felt his gaze on the side of her face. It reminded her of Lana's hopeful hesitancy earlier. Did she want people from her past to be part of her new life, in whatever shape that might take?

She found that she did but kept her gaze on the sea as she answered, 'I would like that... But are you planning on leaving?'

'I was thinking I'd go to my place in France. I've been planning to live there for years, sell the property business, and relax a bit, but I'll stick around until you've worked things through, and it's easy enough to visit.' As she finally turned to face him, he smiled. 'But only if you want to stay in touch.'

'You didn't kill anyone, Gareth. It was an accident. The car went off the road and it was just a terrible accident.' Alexandra's heart went out to him, after he had confided that Thomas had threatened him with blackmail, threatened all of them so they were tightly bound together.

'I had been drinking. It could have been prevented. I've spent so many years keeping secrets, feeling so guilty, it's hard to let go.' He sighed. 'That was the one reason the police didn't press charges, you know. I kept some of the emails between us. It shows they were blackmailing me, and it shows Thomas threatening to ruin my business, my life. That was my main concern and my main reason for staying quiet. I felt I deserved to be punished for driving the car off the road, for killing my family.'

'I know what you mean. About family. I would do anything for my kids, and for my husband... I still would. I mean, I hate him for taking bribes and letting us think everything was perfect, when he didn't need to, but I still love him, and he's still the father of my kids.'

'I'm sorry about Harlan.'

She said nothing.

'You can call me if you ever need anything at all. If the kids need anything. Or, when I've gone across the Channel, just turn up in Toulouse, day or night, and you will be welcomed.' His grey eyes were very dark in the coastal light, almost matching the black lashes. 'All of you would be welcome.' He pointed at Sophie and Tom, happily building sandcastles with Clara and Becca's kids.

'I need time to think, and space to work out what I'm going to do.' Alexandra faced him properly. 'Thank you for being honest with me, and you never know, we might just turn up at your French place one day.' She felt the corners of her mouth curve upwards despite her mood, despite her confusion.

'Please do.' He hesitated, and for one awful moment she

thought he might go in for a hug. But he seemed to reconsider and held out a hand instead. 'Friends?'

She took his hand, warm from the sun, and they stood for a second, palms clasped, until she laughed at the ridiculousness of the situation, and he did too.

Alexandra watched as he walked away. He didn't look back; instead, he climbed the steps and finally disappeared into the busy streets.

From her pocket, she produced the last little paper bird that her brother had sent, stared at it for a moment, thinking of Niall, who would be in prison for a long time, of everyone whose lives had been torn apart by that final party twenty years ago. A shout from behind made her turn. Lana, blonde hair flopping on her shoulders, beach bag over one arm, was making her way towards her. She waved, and even from this distance Alexandra could see the smile lighting her face.

Shaking her own hair loose from its clip, feeling the strands float around her face in the sunshine, she waved back and pointed to their spot on the pebbles.

The paper bird sat on her palm, rocking slightly in the sea breeze. The sounds of summer surrounded her; the warmth of the sun gave her hope. Slipping a lighter from her bag, she knelt down on the pebbles and clicked. The flame flashed brightly, engulfed the bird until all that was left was a tiny pile of ashes. As the breeze swirled, the ashes took flight and vanished into the blue sky.

Quickly stripping off her dark hoodie to reveal a pink striped T-shirt, Alexandra ran down the steps to join her family and friends.

Not guilty.

EPILOGUE

Alexandra stood hand in hand with her best friend as they watched the flowers dance in the wind.

They had come up to the very top of the Downs, Devil's Dyke, where the great slash of chalk drove a slice through the grassy hills. Poppies and other wildflowers dotted the country-side. Brighton could be glimpsed in the distance, but just the city edges. The evening sky had cleared to a soft blue and gold, and the weather was warm enough for Alexandra to still feel the touch of sun on her face.

They walked a few miles, slowly, down to a copse of bent hawthorn bushes, their growth stunted by the high winds of winter, trunks twisted and gnarled, but the green leaves of early summer, still beautiful, unfurling with fresh promise.

Lana laid the little wooden box underneath the trees, scratching her arms, but ensuring it was hidden in the dense thicket of thorns. Even in winter the place would not be found. In time the box would rot, spilling the three bracelets out onto the chalky soil. And in time the Downs would bury the memories gently, relentlessly beneath the ancient grassland.

'One last thing,' Lana said. Tears were drying on her face

and her voice cracked as she spoke. 'I want to do one last thing...'

She brought out a photograph of her sister, of the three of them, taken at the flat before another riotous night out, and tore it into pieces. From her other pocket she pulled out a bag of rose petals. Alexandra watched as she stepped forward and released the petals and fragments of the photograph into the wind, watching them swirl over the gulley, dance with the wind, and, just as the paper bird had done, vanish into the blue sky.

The women linked arms and turned to make their way back up the hillside, just as dusk fell and the skies turned pink and gold. Overhead the gulls wheeled and called, but they were alone in the vastness. Alexandra kept her gaze ahead, kept looking forward, and beside her, Lana whispered in her ear. A little word, but one that meant so much.

Alexandra smiled and whispered back, 'Thank you.'

She could have sworn she heard Jess's laughter just one more time, but it was probably just the birds in the evening sky.

A LETTER FROM THE AUTHOR

Dear Reader,

Huge thanks for reading *Everyone Is Lying*. I hope you were hooked on Alexandra's journey.

If you want to be the first to hear about my new books with Storm Publishing, you can sign up to my newsletter here:

www.stormpublishing.co/d-e-white

And if you'd like to hear about all my new releases, pre-orders, and more, please click the Follow button on my Amazon author page:

www.amazon.co.uk/stores/author/B07LDTXBZ1

Or follow me on BookBub:

www.bookbub.com/profile/d-e-white

If you enjoyed this Brighton-based thriller, you'll love another, *You Know Her*, which is also available as an audiobook. Fancy something darker? The first book in my South Coast Gangland series, *Blindsided*, set on the fictional Seaview Estate, is one I would definitely recommend!

Leaving a short review, or star ratings, helps other readers across the world to find my books. I would be so grateful if you could take five minutes to do this.

Thanks again to all the wonderful readers, bloggers, booksellers, librarians, and my fellow writers for being part of this amazing journey with me. A big shout out to my brilliant editor Vicky, who always makes my books a hundred times better.

Keep following – I have so many more stories and ideas to entertain you with!

D. E. White

facebook.com/DaisyWhiteAuthor

x.com/DEWhiteAuthor

instagram.com/d.e._white_author

tiktok.com/@d.e.whiteauthor